P
BEAVE
THE N

"I came ove
after yesterday's fire, and to show you
something. This was in yesterday's
paper." Colleen handed Lucia a clipping
she had pulled from her purse.

Lucia read the large ad. "'Let fire come down from Heaven and consume you, for our God is a consuming fire.'"

"I checked, and nobody knows who paid for this. But I think this is related to the fire at the hospital." Colleen raised a hand. "And I knew this was a Bible verse even if I couldn't figure out which one, so I called Pastor Dawson and found out it's actually two verses. So, whoever bought the ad was sending someone a message, don't you think?"

* * *

FAITH AT THE CROSSROADS: Can faith and love sustain two families against a diabolical enemy?

PROPERTY OF
BEAVERTON CHURCH OF
THE NAZARENE LIBRARY

Books by Sharon Mignerey

Love Inspired Suspense

Through the Fire #17

SHARON MIGNEREY

lives in Colorado with her husband, a couple of dogs and a cat. From the time she figured out that spelling words could be turned into stories, she knew being a writer was what she wanted. Her first novel garnered several awards, first as an unpublished manuscript when she won RWA's Golden Heart Award in 1995, and later as a published work in 1997 when she won the National Reader's Choice Award and The Heart of Romance Reader's Choice Award. With each new book out, she's as thrilled as she was with that first one.

When she's not writing, she loves enjoying the Colorado sunshine, whether along the South Platte River near her home or at the family cabin in the Four Corners region. Even more, she loves spending time with her daughters and granddaughter.

She loves hearing from readers, and you can write to her in care of Steeple Hill Books, 233 Broadway, Suite 1001, New York, NY 10279.

Through the Fire

Sharon Mignerey

**Steeple
Hill®**

Published by Steeple Hill Books™

If you purchased this book without a cover you should be aware that this book is stolen property. It was reported as "unsold and destroyed" to the publisher, and neither the author nor the publisher has received any payment for this "stripped book."

Special thanks and acknowledgment are given to Sharon Mignerey for her contribution to the FAITH AT THE CROSSROADS series.

STEEPLE HILL BOOKS

Steeple Hill®

ISBN 0-373-87353-0

THROUGH THE FIRE

Copyright © 2006 by Harlequin Books S.A.

All rights reserved. Except for use in any review, the reproduction or utilization of this work in whole or in part in any form by any electronic, mechanical or other means, now known or hereafter invented, including xerography, photocopying and recording, or in any information storage or retrieval system, is forbidden without the written permission of the editorial office, Steeple Hill Books, 233 Broadway, New York, NY 10279 U.S.A.

All characters in this book have no existence outside the imagination of the author and have no relation whatsoever to anyone bearing the same name or names. They are not even distantly inspired by any individual known or unknown to the author, and all incidents are pure invention.

This edition published by arrangement with Steeple Hill Books.

® and TM are trademarks of Steeple Hill Books, used under license. Trademarks indicated with ® are registered in the United States Patent and Trademark Office, the Canadian Trade Marks Office and in other countries.

www.SteepleHill.com

Printed in U.S.A.

As thou hast believed, so be it done unto thee.
—*Matthew* 8:13

To Susan Litman, editor extraordinaire

My thanks to:

Carol Steward for answering dozens of questions about Sam Vance (*Finding Amy,* LI#263 8/04). I hope I did justice to Lucia's big brother. For those thousand and one things I didn't know about firefighting and firefighters, Sue Richardson, Fire Fighter Paramedic (Colorado Springs), and Joe Whitensand, Retired Fire Chief, were generous beyond call. The good stuff is all theirs and the mistakes are all mine. Celeste Mignerey and Paul N. Black, Ph.D. filled in all those little details about safety and precautionary systems in large buildings and hospital settings. As always, you two are an awesome resource, and I couldn't have done this without you. Robin, Steve, Denée, Karen G., Amy, Daniele, Danica—my amazing first readers and critique partners. You guys are the best.

My fellow authors in this series, Lois Richer, Valerie Hansen, Marta Perry, Terri Reed and Margaret Daley. You each made this wonderful journey one to be remembered. Blessings to each of you.

CAST OF CHARACTERS

Rafael "Rafe" Wright—He saved Lucia's life once by being in the right place at the right time. Was the gorgeous smoke jumper also the "right" man for her?

Lucia Vance—The female firefighter was tired of being coddled and protected by her family. She felt secure with Rafe, but his nearness also stirred feelings for love she'd thought long buried....

Neil O'Brien—Was there more to the battalion chief's animosity toward Lucia beyond his accusations that her father the mayor got her her job?

*El Jéfe/*The Chief—His name kept coming up in investigations. Was he somehow connected to Baltasar Escalante, the drug lord whose body was never recovered following his plane crash?

PROLOGUE

"It's really quite simple, Neil. I own you." She held the condemning papers up for him to see as though he somehow wouldn't have recognized his own signature on copies of the promissory notes. "You borrowed money, and I bought the loan from that rather unscrupulous man you've been doing business with in Cripple Creek." Turning the papers around, she glanced through them, then folded them back into neat thirds. "Such a lot of money."

Despite the cold breeze that swept off Pikes Peak on this cold March day, Neil O'Brien felt a bead of sweat slide down his back as he contemplated taking the papers away before choking her to death. Wondering where the originals were, he stared at the woman standing under the pavilion with him, her words echoing through his head.

When he had agreed to meet her at this remote corner of Bear Creek Park, a well-known lovers' lane for teenagers, he'd had a visceral sense of anticipation. Foolish thought that she might be interested in a man like him—they didn't run in the same circles. The extra thirty pounds he carried and his thinning hair made him look ten years older than he was. He wished he didn't mind quite so much.

He looked away from her to the snow beginning to fall.

The flakes left little white splatters on the sidewalk. Farther away, the parking lot was empty except for their two cars.

Quite literally, she held the power to ruin him in that sheaf of papers.

"You have nothing," he said, deciding on a bluff and making a point to look at the documents in her hand. "O'Brien is a common name."

"Then why did you agree to meet me?" She waved toward the remote expanse of the park to the west, the sleeve of her wool coat riding up her arm enough to expose a diamond bracelet that probably cost more than he earned in half a year. "Here?" She smiled. "Away from work and home and your pretty, pregnant wife?"

Neil stared at her. The antacid he had swallowed just before getting out of the car turned sour in his mouth. Another foolish hope. That he could keep his gambling—and his mountain of debt—from Mary.

"I wonder…does she know about this, Neil?" She tapped a finger against her lips. "A phone call to her—"

"Get to the point. What do you want?"

She opened her purple leather handbag, the designer name discreetly embossed onto the surface, and put the folded papers inside. "Cooperation, Neil, that's all."

"What kind of cooperation?" Whatever it took to keep his wife from finding out that he had accumulated gambling debts greater than the mortgage on their brand-new home was worth considering in the short run. In the long run, there was only one way to be rid of a blackmailer—a remedy he would take just as soon as he had the originals of the promissory notes in his possession.

"You want all this to go away?" She pressed the flat of her hand against the purse. "All of it?"

"The debt would go away?"

She tapped her finger against her lip again. "Neil, my dear, Neil. You do understand, don't you?"

What he understood was that he was being played, and he didn't like it. And without a big win, he didn't see a way out, either. She held the winning hand.

"What do you want?" he repeated, shivering as the wind shifted and fine, cold snowflakes blew across his face.

"There's a certain firefighter in your department who will have a tragic accident that will end her life."

Another cold bead of sweat trickled down Neil's back. What she was suggesting was impossible. Murder, like he was contemplating just now, was easy. Murder by fire and made to look like an accident…nearly impossible.

"The poor thing went against the wishes of her family to take on such a dangerous job, alienated herself from her father, worried her mother to death and all those protective older brothers… Why, they were opposed down to the last man."

The woman was talking about Lucia Vance, Neil realized. Personally, Neil thought she represented nepotism at its finest. Her daddy was the mayor, and her brother Sam was a detective on the Colorado Springs police force. It had been Neil's goal for the last year to get her kicked out of the department. But deliberately setting her up to be injured—killed—he couldn't do it.

He shook his head. "That's not an easy thing to do. If you want her dead, why not simply shoot her?"

Her mouth tightened. "Easier, yes. But then her parents and her brothers wouldn't understand."

"What?"

"That for every choice there is a consequence." She patted her purse again. "Think about it, Neil. All this goes away. Your sweet little pregnant wife doesn't find out. You're not ruined."

"What you're asking—"

She pressed a shockingly hot finger against his lips, her eyes wide and luminous, making her look like a girlfriend instead of a blackmailer. "I'm not asking."

When she took her finger away, he shuddered inside his heavy parka.

"A perfect place would be Vance Memorial Hospital, where her mother keeps a vigil over her poor injured father."

"You can't be serious." Mayor Maxwell Vance had been shot in an assassination attempt last November. He was still in critical condition, and Neil knew the investigation had drawn in the FBI. Security in the hospital was tight.

"Oh, but I am."

Neil shook his head. "It can't be done. Hospitals have sprinklers and preactionary systems, all designed to prevent even the smallest fire."

She stared at him as though what he had just told her didn't make any sense.

"I can see the headline now," she said. "Assistant Fire Chief Neil O'Brien Ruined." She smiled again, but her expression was as warm as the icy snow falling around them. "Only you will have died tragically, maybe suicide in your despondence over your gambling. And your wife will be left to raise your child in poverty and shame, all because you wouldn't do a simple thing." She paused and shifted the purse on her arm. "A simple thing, Neil, that would make all your troubles go away."

Wishing he'd had the guts to simply kill her, he watched with his hands in his pockets as she walked away. As she got into her silver luxury coupe, she blew him a kiss. A second later, the car purred to life.

A simple thing. As if there was anything simple about planning a murder that was supposed to look like an accident.

ONE

Last night, Rafael Wright had been too consumed with guilt to pay attention to the hospital room numbers, so he paused at the doorway to make sure he was at the correct one. He knocked lightly on the door before pushing it open. The bed closest to the door was empty, and his good friend Malik Williams lay in the other, raised to a reclining position. The television mounted near the ceiling was tuned to a police drama.

"Hey, you came," Malik said as Rafe moved toward him.

A bandage at one corner of his forehead covered a gash that had bled like crazy yesterday when he was knocked over by a fifteen-foot ladder when it fell. Last night, Malik had been asleep when Rafe checked on him.

"Of course I came." His fault that Malik was here—an accident, but one that should not have happened. Malik wouldn't have been hurt if Rafe had been focused on the training exercise they were doing instead of the news that his younger sister Lisa was separating from her husband.

His dark eyes gleaming, Malik craned his head as Rafe came farther into the room. "If you don't have a big vanilla malt hidden behind your back, you can leave right now."

Rafe clicked his tongue. "That concussion must not be too bad since you're cranky." He pulled his hand from behind his back and set the tall paper cup containing his friend's favorite dessert on the table pulled next to the bed.

Malik grinned, pressing the volume control to turn the television down. "Figured I should play on your sympathy—"

"Which won't last long if you keep this up." Rafe shrugged out of his leather bomber jacket, which he set on the chair in the corner.

"That's you, all right. All bark. No bite."

"I wouldn't count on that." Since Rafe was the foreman for a Type 1 hotshot crew of forest-fire fighters, part of the territory was making sure he came across as a major tough guy. Since Malik was both his roommate and his friend, just now he seemed more like a kid brother than simply one of the guys on the crew. Not that many years separated them, but a lifetime of experience did. Malik worked full-time during the summer, then went to school and skied in the winter while continuing to work part-time for the Forest Service. "I thought I'd been properly sympathetic—"

"If you don't count yelling."

Inwardly, Rafe winced. He *had* yelled. At the time he had been furious, a hundred percent of it directed at himself for not seeing the accident coming.

At his discomfiture, Malik grinned. "Speaking of biting and the screams of pain that come after…" He waited a beat while Rafe raised an eyebrow. "I bet you didn't know they don't sound alarms in hospitals. They want things to be calm," he added, raising his hands to punctuate quotation marks around the last word. "About an hour ago, I'm lying here talking to a real pretty nurse, and there was this page for Dr. Firestone. She tore out of here like she was on her way to a fire." He tore the paper off the straw and plunged it through the plastic top of the cup, then took a long sip of the malt.

"About a half hour later she came back—I'm irresistible, you know—and told me that 'Dr. Firestone' is the code for a fire. She said they've had about a dozen false alarms over the last couple of days."

"That's got to be annoying."

"That's what she said. She told me that 'Dr. Quick' is for combative patients and 'Dr. Avery' is for a bomb threat." Malik grinned. "And I've been thinking—"

"Always a bad sign."

"I need something to get that nurse back in here to see me."

"A page from Dr. Valentine?"

Malik laughed. "Yeah. Something like that."

"Sounds to me like you're going to live," Rafe said.

"The doc told me I can go home in the morning. They just want to keep an eye on me overnight." Another of his easy grins came, his teeth flashing white against his African-American complexion. "If you ask me, I think it's because a certain nurse thinks I'm—"

"A klutz," Rafe filled in.

"Man, don't insult me like that." Malik took another sip of the malt. "That's real good. Thanks."

"Least I can do."

Malik grinned again. "You mean, since you tried to kill me."

"Anything to get rid of a pest," Rafe said deadpan.

"This mean you won't be giving me a ride home? That'd actually be okay because that good-looking nurse—"

"Like she'd give you the time of day."

"Like," Malik returned in their good-natured banter.

Rafe studied his friend. Clearly, the obvious question didn't have to be asked if the guy was going to be okay. Since he was thinking about girls and malts, he'd undoubtedly be his old self in a day or two. Rafe, though, was feeling old. As he had driven to the hospital, he had counted the fires he had fought since he was eighteen years old. One hundred and twelve, and he felt every single one. Those fires had taken him from the Everglades to inside the Arctic Circle in Alaska.

The nomadic life was the one he had wanted…once… which brought him full circle back to his sister. Her husband was walking away from everything Rafe had recently decided his life was missing. A woman to come home to. A child barely two years old. Now that Rafe was nearly finished with his master's degree in fire science, he had choices. He could settle down and work on finding the right woman.

"You get much more quiet and I'm going to think I'm sitting here alone," Malik said.

"Then turn up the TV."

"You're not thinking stupid things like blaming yourself for what happened to me, are you?"

Rafe met his friend's gaze. "You know the drill about accountability."

"Yeah, I do. It's what makes you the best."

There was nothing Rafe could say about that, so he remained quiet, folding his arms over his chest as he leaned against the wide ledge in front of the window. At his back, the glass felt cold. "Think it will snow?"

Malik laughed. "Hope so. Since I have a few days off, maybe I'll head up to Breckenridge or Keystone for a little skiing—"

"Not the best plan for a man with a concussion." If Rafe had the time, he'd head for Wolf Creek, which boasted the deepest snow in the state. The only drawback was the six-and-a-half-hour drive to get there.

Malik took another sip of his malt. "You're sounding more like my grandpa every day."

"Now who's being insulting?"

Just then, the lights flickered, and the television went off.

"It's definitely going to snow," Malik announced, clicking

on the remote for the television, which remained off. "You'd think a brand-new hospital would have built-in surge protectors."

"You'd think," Rafe agreed, glancing toward the hallway as the lights flickered again. The TV suddenly blared, and Malik turned it down.

The hospital had undergone extensive renovations over the last couple of years, the most recent being the addition of a new pediatric wing. According to a recent article in the *Colorado Springs Sentinel,* it had attracted the necessary grants and research money to become the premier orthopedic center for children in the western United States. The part of the article Rafe remembered best was a picture of a chapel at the end of the wing, which boasted a great view of Pikes Peak. That was something to check out before he left. He didn't like hospitals much, but he always made a point to visit the chapels.

Once again, his thoughts returned to his sister and her little girl. He wished they lived closer, wished he could ease their heartache. He needed to do something more for them than simply including them in his daily prayers.

"Are you going to be okay?" he asked.

"Fine." Malik leaned his head against the pillow. "Might as well take a little snooze, especially since you're so talkative."

"Then I'll head out." Rafe grabbed his jacket off the back of the chair and headed toward the door.

"Hey."

He turned around.

Malik grinned. "If you see that pretty nurse—the petite one with black hair all done up in a bun on the top of her head—send her in to see me." He clapped a hand over his heart. "I think I'm in pain."

Rafe shook his head and waved at his friend. "There's a

difference between being *in* pain and being *a* pain, you know."

"Get out of here. Send back a real friend."

He waved again and headed down the hall, where it widened into a big rotunda and a set of wide stairs that led to the main lobby of the hospital. From the balcony, he looked down to the first floor, where the gift shop and information desk flanked the exterior door. Directly opposite from where he stood was the entrance to the new pediatric wing. Rafe headed in that direction, drawn by the cheerful pale-yellow walls that had flying birds painted on them as if leading the way into the area. He stopped in front of a big marble plaque and read the dedication of the wing, which had a list of major donors. The familiar names of Colorado Springs society were there, topped by the Montgomery and Vance families.

Everything about the addition seemed to be of the highest quality, Rafe thought as he wandered farther into the wing. The smoke doors that would close during an emergency were painted to look like arched gates entering a brilliantly colored park.

Wondering where the chapel was, Rafe followed a set of animal tracks painted on the floor, which took him past the X-ray lab. A quick peek through the door showed an X-ray machine painted to look like an elephant. He didn't see many people, and even here, where he expected the noise level would be higher because of the children, there was instead the overall hush that seemed to permeate hospitals.

Ahead he saw the sign for the chapel, and when he peeked through the window in the door he saw that it too was designed with children in mind. Instead of formal pews, there were a couple of comfortable-looking sofas and several beanbag chairs covered in plush fabric. A couple of children were sitting together on one of the giant beanbags.

Rafe watched them a moment, knowing too well how

they felt if they were waiting for news of a sick family member. Not wanting to intrude, he made his way to the end of the hallway, where a large window looked down on a park. In the distance, he could see the spire of the Good Shepherd Church.

Hands in the pockets of his jacket, Rafe made his way back down the hallway, which continued to be mostly deserted, a thought that made him smile since the parking lot had been packed when he arrived. About halfway back to the chapel door, he suddenly smelled smoke.

Between the chapel and the nurse's station he saw a door discreetly labeled Janitor's Closet. From beneath the door, smoke curled across the spotless tiled floor. He ran those last few feet to the door.

He pressed a hand against the door, which felt warm. Too warm.

His thoughts raced as he hurried on to the nurse's station. Was this the reason the lights had flickered a few minutes ago? How could the door be that warm? And in a brand-new facility, why hadn't the sprinklers come on? Why hadn't some computer-generated warning notified someone?

Only one nurse was at the station. She raised her head when she saw him coming, gave him an automatic smile, then bent her head down once again.

"Miss," Rafe said, "there's smoke coming from under a door down the hall."

She gave him another smile, the sort that indicated he was about to be dismissed even before she spoke. "I'll check on that in just a minute. Thanks for letting me know."

"I'm not just letting you know," Rafe said, coming around the tall counter and reaching for the phone. "I'm calling for help."

"Sir, you can't be back here."

Rafe thrust the receiver into her hand. "You have a fire. Call 9-1-1."

"Sir, if you'll just calm down—"

"I'm calm." He stepped back into the hallway and reached into the pocket of his jacket for his cell phone. "Take a look for yourself."

"Your child couldn't be safer here, even though we've had quite a few false alarms over the last few days," she said, finally standing. "We have all the latest monitors." She waved toward a computer monitor. "I'd know if there was a problem." She came around the counter toward the hallway. "But I will look…" Her gaze lit on the smoke. "Oh, no!"

By then, Rafe had dialed 9-1-1, and the instant the dispatcher answered, he said, "There's a fire in the children's wing of Vance Memorial Hospital." He looked up and down the hallway for the ever-present fire extinguisher that should have been somewhere close by.

The nurse was back inside the nurse's station, finally calling for help.

Over the cell phone, the dispatcher said, "We should have received an automatic call if there was a problem—"

"The fire started in the janitor's closet," Rafe interrupted, running up the hallway, searching for an extinguisher. "The sprinklers haven't come on and—"

"What's your location, sir?"

Rafe relayed that information as best he could, noticing that the nurse had called whomever she needed to because he heard a summons over the intercom. "Dr. Firestone to the pediatric wing."

Just then, he saw another nurse notice the smoke coming from beneath the door. She punched a code on the keypad next to the door.

Rafe raced back toward her. "Don't open the door!"

But he was too late. The latch clicked and she pushed the door open. Acrid black smoke billowed out of the room, accompanied by the unmistakable whish of air being sucked into the room. Rafe pulled the nurse from her frozen position in front of the door. In the next instant, flames licked into the hallway, flicking like a snake's tongue.

"Are you okay?" he asked her, urging her away from the open door.

Her eyes wide and frightened, she nodded, then ran toward the nurse's station. Suddenly, there were people everywhere, while someone shouted orders.

Rafe ran back toward the entrance to the wing, wishing he remembered where he had seen the fire extinguisher. Finally, he found it near the entrance where the doors were now closed. He grabbed the canister and rushed back to the fire, where black smoke continued to pour out of the closet.

He lost track of time after that, something that always happened when he was fighting a fire. Prayer and intense concentration on the task at hand occupied his mind. The only things he knew for sure were that the sprinklers weren't coming on and the canister didn't contain nearly enough volume to put out the fire. The best he could hope for was to contain it until the fire department arrived.

Lucia Vance arrived at the hospital with her fellow firefighters a scant six minutes later. Since their station was the closest, they arrived before the four other engines that had also been called out, just as they had when they had responded to a false alarm an hour earlier. During her last shift, they had answered four false alarms here, and this was the second call today. Just as she had the previous times they had responded, she carried a roll of hose over one shoulder and an ax in her hand. She and the other four firefighters followed the incident commander,

Neil O'Brien, into the building. Each time they had responded to a call, the alarm had come from somewhere in the remodeled section of the hospital. This time, the emergency panel indicated the fire was on the second floor of the brand-new pediatric wing. Each time, the panel had showed a suspected fire in different areas—no two calls had been the same.

"It's gotta be another false alarm," said Lucia's partner, Luke Donovan. "No way would there be a fire there. Not with all the sprinklers and sensors."

"You're probably right," O'Brien said, leading the way. "Meyers and Jackson, secure the elevators. The rest of you come with me."

They entered the stairwell and made their way to the second floor. As soon as they came through the door, Lucia smelled smoke.

This was no false alarm.

The floor was bustling with activity, and a nurse rushed toward them, pointing toward one of the adjoining hallways. "Down there."

"Vance and Donovan, make an assessment and report back," O'Brien ordered.

Lucia followed her partner down the hall, the smell of smoke stronger with each step they took. They turned a corner, and the smoke hung from the ceiling like an ugly black blanket billowing in a breeze.

The silhouette of a man kneeling on one knee suddenly became visible. He was clearly a civilian since he wasn't in turnout gear, but he expertly wielded the extinguisher.

He violently started when Lucia touched his back. "We've got it, sir," she said through her mask. He looked up, his face streaked with smoke, his eyes the most vivid green she ever remembered seeing.

"The stairwell is that way," she said when he stared blankly at her. "You can go."

He nodded, his eyes somehow boring right through her, then handed her the canister, the athletic grace of his stride catching her attention while she and Luke briefly assessed the fire. All around them, hospital personnel were busy evacuating patients, but despite the fire, everything seemed calm. Eerily so, Lucia thought as the assistant fire chief joined them.

"At least it's confined," O'Brien said. "Donovan, they need extra help with a couple of critical patients that they have to get away from this smoke right now. Since you've got the back for the job, you're the man."

Luke shook his head. "Can't leave my partner—"

"This isn't a discussion. Get going. I'll stay here with Vance."

Lucia looked over her shoulder at O'Brien, who stood there with his radio to his mouth as he talked to one of the lieutenants on an engine that had just arrived. Since he had been gunning for her for months, she thought it odd that he had dismissed her partner. It would have made more sense if he'd had three other people around to do the job of putting out this confined fire.

"Be safe," Donovan said as he headed back in the direction they had come.

"Get going, Vance," O'Brien ordered.

Refocusing her thoughts on the task at hand, she found the valve halfway toward the end of the hall. She hooked up the hose and switched on the valve. As she aimed the nozzle toward the open door, she thought she smelled the distinct aroma of lacquer vapors. One more odd thing, almost as odd as O'Brien sending her partner away.

In the next instant, an explosion knocked her off her feet, the force of the blast throwing her against the opposite wall.

A monstrous blossom of fire unfurled through the space where the closet door had been, pinning her in place and reaching for her.

TWO

Giving the firefighters a backward glance, Rafe headed for the stairwell. All around him, there was a buzz of controlled activity, the kind that came when a crew had trained for this kind of disaster and knew exactly what to do. It was clear that an evacuation was being prepared for.

He looked back at the firefighters one last time, wondering if there was something more to the fire that he hadn't noticed. Figuring he was an extra set of hands for whatever might be needed, he headed toward the nurse's station.

Within a few steps, his heart lurched when he remembered the kids in the chapel. Surely they were gone already. But what if they were still there? Since they weren't patients, they might have been overlooked. He reversed his direction and headed for the chapel across the hall from the janitor's closet. How could he have forgotten about them while he was searching for the extinguisher? Rescue was always the first order of the day with fire—a fact as basic as breathing.

"Get out of here," one of the firefighters said, a stocky man, the insignia on his helmet identifying him as a battalion chief.

The man rushed past him, speaking into his radio before Rafe could answer.

Relieved to see another firefighter hooking a hose up to the valve, Rafe opened the chapel door.

He stepped inside, the door automatically closing behind him. The two kids were nowhere to be seen, the beanbag where they had been sitting empty. Since kids often hid from fire, he couldn't assume they were gone simply because he didn't see them.

"Anyone here?" he called. Through the big window, Pikes Peak was beautifully framed, just as advertised in the news article that had made him look for the chapel in the first place. Snow gleamed on the mountain, pristine and surreal compared to the smoke-filled hallway. Whispering a quick prayer for the safety of everyone around him, Rafe looked around for the kids once more.

Just then an explosion in the hallway rattled the windows, the concussion of it dropping Rafe to his knees. A brilliant flash of orange flared through the hallway window.

Behind him, a child cried out.

He whirled around and found the two children huddled behind the heavy drape that framed the window. Relieved they were safe, at least for the moment, he went to the door to check on what had happened.

"It'll be okay," he said reassuringly to the kids as he peered through the window. The smoke was thicker, obscuring the view of anything in the hallway, then shifting and revealing a reflective stripe on a bundle on the floor next to the door. Not a bundle. A person. The firefighter he had last seen hooking up the hose to the valve.

Without a second thought, Rafe knelt, flung open the door, grabbed on to the coat and pulled. The firefighter moaned.

"I've got you." Through the smoke, Rafe could see the closet was fully engulfed, and, oddly, there was a wall of flames between them and their route to safety. There shouldn't be that much fire. Once again he wondered why the sprinklers weren't coming on.

The instant he had the two of them back inside the chapel, he closed the door. During those scant seconds, the small room had filled with smoke, which rose to the ceiling.

Next to the window, the two children watched him with wide eyes, neither of them speaking.

"Why don't you two sit down on the floor there next to the window? Breathing will be easier," Rafe said, eyeing the smoke that was seeping beneath the doorway. He went to the window and pulled down the drape. Rolling up the fabric, he laid it on the floor next to the door, covering the crack as best he could.

Rafe pulled the helmet and mask off the firefighter, doing his best not to jar him—her! he realized as a long, black braid tumbled out of the hat. Her eyelashes were as dark as her hair, making her skin look all the more pale.

"¿Está muerta?" one of the children asked, a little boy who looked as though he could be no more than four or five.

"No," Rafe answered, reassured by the pulse beating strongly beneath his fingertips. She wasn't dead. *"La señorita no está muerta. ¿Hablas inglés?"*

The boy shook his head.

To the woman, he said, "Can you hear me?"

She moaned again.

Rafe took off his jacket, folded it, and slipped it beneath her head as she lay on her side, her canister of air still strapped to her back.

"Are you visiting a brother or sister?" he asked the children in Spanish.

"Mi hermana," the other child said, creeping closer to hold the boy's hand. "Ana."

"Ah. This is your brother—*tu hermano?*"

She nodded. "Ramón."

"And what's your name?" Rafe asked, continuing to speak in Spanish while keeping a close eye on the firefighter. Thankfully, color was beginning to seep back into her cheeks. She didn't seem to be unconscious, but she wasn't with it, either.

"Teresa."

Pulling his cell phone from his jeans pocket, Rafe dialed 9-1-1, reminded of when he had done so a little earlier. This time the line was busy, and it remained that way for the next several times he dialed the number.

Next to him on the floor, the woman opened her eyes. When her gaze lit on him, she immediately struggled to sit up.

Rafe pressed a hand against her shoulder. "Just take a breath first."

Her eyes were huge in her face, her skin too pale. "I'm okay," she said around a cough. "The explosion just knocked me down."

"All the more reason to take a minute." Rafe figured she was lucky. Her lungs could have been seared by the heat from the explosion.

"I've got to get back—"

"There's fire clear across the hall."

"We're trapped?"

There was still a way out of the chapel, though not his first choice. Rafe glanced toward the big, west-facing window, and her gaze followed his.

"That's a last resort," she said, evidently coming to the same conclusion he had. Sitting up, she put the small radio strapped to the outside of her turnout coat to her mouth. "Donovan, are you there?"

There was a moment of static, then a voice said, "Lucia, where are you?"

When she met Rafe's gaze, he said, "The chapel across the hall from the janitor's closet that's on fire."

She nodded and repeated the information, adding, "I'm in here with a civilian and two kids."

"Stay put," Donovan said. "We'll have water on the fire in the hallway in a minute."

Her gaze lit on the two children, then came back to Rafe. "You were the one fighting the fire when we got here." After he nodded, she added, "Your children?"

"No. Just met them." He motioned toward them. "This is Ramón and Teresa, and they've been visiting their sister, Ana. I'm Rafael Wright. Are you okay?"

"Not bad for having the breath knocked out of me." She pulled off her gloves, then ran a slim hand over her forehead. "I'd just hooked up the hose to the valve. I hadn't gotten a drop of water on the fire before the explosion." With an easy motion that came only with practiced repetition, she slipped the air tank off her shoulders and set it with her helmet and mask.

"I didn't see your partner."

She looked at Rafe. "Chief O'Brien sent him away. Said he'd stay with me."

"A heavyset guy?" When she nodded, Rafe added, "He was headed back toward the stairwell right before the explosion."

"Well, that figures." The inflection in her voice gave Rafe the idea that she didn't like or respect O'Brien. Still, she spoke into the radio once more. "Vance reporting in."

"Are you hurt?" came a gruff voice, clearly not Donovan's, over the speaker.

"Your chief?" Rafe asked.

She nodded, and into the radio said, "I'm okay, sir."

"Donovan said you're trapped in the chapel. When we get this baby put out, you've got some explaining to do."

Rafe bristled at the man's tone. As a hotshot superintendent who had often been the commander on a fire, he knew
there was a time to hold your people accountable and a time
to put their well-being and safety first. A fleeting look of irritation chased across her face, confirming to Rafe that he
hadn't imagined the man's imperious tone.

"Strange the sprinklers in this brand-new building haven't
come on," Rafe said.

She nodded. "As strange as all the false alarms we've had
the last few days. We expected this to be another one."

The smoke at the ceiling grew thicker, and Rafe motioned
to the kids. *"Ven acá,"* Rafe said, motioning for them to come
sit beside him and the firefighter. *"Sentémonos aquí."*

"They don't speak English?" Lucia asked as the kids approached.

Rafe shook his head, and again spoke to the children, repeating the same words, then adding in English, "Come sit
next to me."

She held her arms out to the little girl, who somehow
recognized the gesture of comfort and came toward her.
Settling the child in her lap, the woman touched the child's
chest. "Teresa." Then she repeated the gesture against her own
chest. "Lucia."

Lucia, Rafe mentally echoed. The name fit her. As exotic
as her dark brown eyes and her creamy complexion.

"My partner is out there," she said, "and he's going to have
us out of here *muy pronto.*"

Her fractured Spanish made the kids smile, just as Rafe
suspected she had intended. She looked from the child to him
and the little boy, who had sat down between them.

"If these kids are like my nieces and nephews, they don't
care what you're saying—they just need to hear the sound of
a calm voice."

Rafe nodded.

"What brought you to the hospital?" she asked.

"A friend."

She grinned when he didn't add anything more, the expression transforming her face from pretty to vibrant. "Ah, the old visiting-a-friend routine. Personally, I thought this was the place to meet strangers."

Rafe smiled back, recognizing that she was deliberately trying to turn their attention away from the fire on the other side of the door. "So far, that strategy is working."

She glanced at the children. "Ask them about their sister."

In Spanish, Rafe asked about Ana's illness but was only able to find out that she was a couple of years older—seven to their three and four—and that she was very sick.

"I know what that's like," Lucia said, her gaze going from one child to the other. "My father is in this very hospital in intensive care." Rafe watched her as she looked around the small chapel. "As soon as we get out of here, I'll need to go see my mother and call my brothers. They'll all be worried." She glanced at Rafe. "Do your parents worry?"

"About what?" He was still caught on the part of her statement that her father was in the hospital.

"You."

He shrugged. "Some, I suppose. More about my sisters."

She smiled down at the little girl in her lap, who automatically smiled back. "See? A man can go off to be a policeman or a spy or a mountain climber and that's okay. But a girl is supposed to play it safe—"

"Don't be including me in your generalities. I never said that." Some of the best firefighters on his hotshot crew were women. "I don't believe that."

"Do you worry about your sisters?"

"Of course. One is a homemaker and has a little girl. My

other sister teaches school." He gave Lucia a grin. "Now there's a dangerous occupation."

Lucia gazed down at the two children. "That wasn't a very nice thing for him to say, especially since he doesn't think you can understand him." She brushed a hand over Teresa's hair. "Children are gifts from God—everyone knows that. I wish that I could make you understand that I'll be praying for your sister."

The gesture was so nurturing that Rafe was entranced. Movies painted the heroic picture of a big firefighter tenderly caring for those smaller, weaker. This more feminine version of that same image made Lucia more appealing than she could know—especially since the gesture was not even a conscious one on her part.

Teresa leaned her head against the sleeve of Lucia's turnout coat.

"Rezebo mi oraciónes por vuestra hermana," Rafe said. When Lucia looked at him, he repeated in English, "I'll say prayers for your sister."

She smiled and looked from one child to the other, repeating the words, words that made both of the children smile.

Rafe knew too well what it was like to have a parent in intensive care. Even though that had been a whole lifetime ago, the feelings suddenly at the surface were as sharp as they had been when he was no older than Ramón. He hadn't understood the significance of his mother being moved from intensive care into hospice. For a while, he had even hoped the change meant she was getting better. Since he was again allowed to sit next to her on her bed and put his arms around her, that had to have meant she was getting better—or, at least, so he had reasoned as a four-year-old boy.

Too vivid was the memory of that last day when she had taken him to the chapel and cradled him in her lap. He had sensed something was terribly wrong, and the ache in his chest that day had been suffocating.

"God is always with you," his mother had whispered, her hand warm against his chest. "Always. No matter where you are or what you are doing, just look inside. God is right there." She'd had tears in her eyes when he had looked up at her. "He loves you, just as I love you." She gathered him closer, and to this day, he could still feel her cheek against the top of his head. "All you have to do is close your eyes and pray. You'll feel God, and you'll feel me. Both of us loving you."

He had hung on to the promise his entire life, and he had always found it to be true. Especially in tense situations like this one, with a fire in the hallway and a two-story drop to safety through the window.

Lucia's radio crackled to life, and Donovan said, "A little break at last, partner. The sprinklers finally came on. You should be seeing water seep under the door."

Glad to have an activity that brought his mind back to the present, Rafe scooted across the floor toward the door and, sure enough, the drape he had taken off the window was wet. "That's exactly what's happening."

Lucia relayed the information.

"It won't be long now," came the answer.

While they waited, Lucia continued to talk to the children, and as she had predicted, they responded simply to the sound of her voice.

"You're good with kids. Do you have children? I know you mentioned nieces and nephews," Rafe asked, wanting to ask her instead if she was married.

"No children," she said. "Three nieces and two nephews so far, plus some honorary ones. What about you?"

"Never been married," he said.

"Me neither," she said.

"So no children," he continued, as though finding out she was single hadn't meant anything. *She was single.*

He looked down at the two children sitting between him and Lucia. Men weren't supposed to have the ticking biological clock, but he did. He didn't like the sudden realization that even if he found a woman today that he'd like to marry, he was still several years away from having children.

"You mentioned a sister—"

"With a little girl," Rafe said. "Yeah. She'll be two soon. They live in Atlanta."

"A long way from here."

"Yeah." For the ninety-ninth time over the last day, Rafe thought maybe he could talk his sister into moving closer if her marriage ended. *If,* he reminded himself. Better that things work out in her marriage instead of his selfish wish to have her closer.

"What do you do, Rafael Wright?" Lucia asked with a smile, "when you're not putting out fires and rescuing small children and damsels in distress?"

"Put out fires," he said, looking steadily at her and thinking a man could lose himself in her dark eyes. "Don't rescue many damsels, though." When she raised an eyebrow in question, he added, "I'm the superintendent for the Sangre de Cristo hotshot crew."

"You're a firefighter?"

"Big difference between structure fires and wildfires," he said.

"But you're a firefighter?"

He nodded. "I'm also a volunteer for the city wildfire volunteer squad." In the year he had been here, the volunteers had been called upon only once, since the city had a well-trained wildfire unit. He liked being involved, though, and feeling as though he was part of the community.

"Well, that at least explains why you're so calm," she

said, glancing toward the smoke clinging to the upper part of the room. "Most civilians would have been climbing the walls by now."

The radio crackled to life once more. "We're coming in," came her partner's voice at the same moment as the door was pushed open, shoving the wet drape out of the way.

The big firefighter who came through the door had removed his mask. He grinned when his gaze lit on Lucia. "Way to go, partner. Sit in here where you can hug the kiddies while Jackson and I do the hard work. You slacker," he said without a bit of heat in his voice.

"I love you, too, Donovan," Lucia said from where she sat on the floor with little Teresa in her lap.

"Everybody in here okay?" asked another firefighter who came through the door.

Rafe stood. "She needs to be checked out," he said, nodding to Lucia. "The explosion knocked her out."

"That would be down, not out," she said tartly. "There's a big difference."

Donovan's attention sharpened and he pinned Lucia with a laser-sharp stare. "I knew I shouldn't have left you—"

"I'm fine." As if to prove it, Lucia handed him the little girl, then stood in a fluid movement. "Say hello to Teresa." Smiling reassuringly at the little girl, she patted Donovan's turnout coat and said, "Teddy Bear."

"Teddy Bear?" Teresa repeated.

"That's right." Lucia grinned at the big firefighter. "Be nicer to her than you are to your own little girls."

"Don't you start," Donovan said to Lucia before smiling at the child. "Everything is going to be just fine, little one."

Lucia grinned at Rafe while waving toward the big fire-fighter. "This lug is Luke Donovan." She nodded toward the other firefighter. "Gideon Jackson."

"Rafe," he said, extending his hand first to Jackson, then to Donovan. "Rafael Wright."

"Wright. I remember you," Jackson said. "I was in one of your classes last spring when I was getting recertified to fight wildfires."

"Nice to meet you again." Rafe drew Teresa's brother forward. "This is Ramón. These two have a sister here somewhere and I bet parents looking for them, too. They don't speak any English."

"No problem," Jackson said, offering a hand to the little boy and heading for the door. "We'll go find them. *¿Cómo se llaman su mamá y su papá?*"

Rafe smiled as Ramón told Jackson his father's name as they went into the hallway.

"Where's Vance?" a gruff voice demanded from the hallway.

"In there," came Jackson's answer through the open door.

The stocky fireman Rafe had seen earlier came into the chapel, an angry scowl on his face. "This is the final straw," he said, waving toward the blackened hallway. "Do you have any idea how much damage was done out there because you left your post? You're on notice, Lucia Vance, and when I'm done with you, you'll be finished as a firefighter."

THREE

"**Y**ou don't know what you're talking about." Rafe took a step toward the man. "She didn't abandon her post."

"No?" The battalion chief gave Rafe a scathing once-over. "Here's some advice for you. Keep your nose out of things you don't know a thing about." He looked over at Lucia. "Get out there on the mop-up crew. Since you sat out the fire, it's the least you can do."

Obeying the order the way Rafe would have expected of his own people, she left without a word while he folded his arms over his chest. The difference was, *he* was reasonable. Lucia's chief wasn't. "That explosion threw her against the wall. She could have died out there if—"

"That would be just like her," O'Brien said. "Find a pretty boy to tell pretty lies for her."

Feeling his temper rise, Rafe pointed a finger at the man. "She was nothing but professional, which is more than I can say for you." He headed for the door, then turned around. "Your name is O'Brien, right?"

The battalion chief nodded. "What's it to you?"

Rafe shrugged. "Personally, I like to have my facts straight when I file a report." He gave the other man a smile that was all teeth, adding, "Battalion Chief O'Brien."

Rafe strode out of the chapel, then came to a dead stop in the hallway. Ceiling tiles were curled and melted, and the Sheetrock was charred. Here and there, the metal framing beneath the Sheetrock was visible, the metal studs twisted into grotesque shapes. Not just surface smoke damage, but real structural damage, Rafe thought. That said a lot about how hot the fire had been and how close it had been to getting out of control. He shuddered as he imagined what might have happened to Lucia if he hadn't been there to pull her out of harm's way. That thought brought him back to square one with Chief O'Brien. No wonder Lucia didn't respect the man. In Rafe's book the man was an idiot.

Lucia Vance, he thought. Vance. Vance, as in Mayor Vance, who had been shot several months ago and who was still in the hospital? Rafe figured he had to be right. How many other Vances were likely to be in this hospital in intensive care? What made no sense was why the daughter of a wealthy and powerful family was a firefighter.

He looked around, hoping for a glimpse of her. He'd have to ask her about that the next time he saw her. And he knew he would be seeing her. For the first time in his life, he had envisioned his children's faces within a woman he was attracted to.

"Are you really okay?" Lucia's mother asked a couple of hours later in the hallway outside the intensive-care room where her father was still in a coma.

"Fine." Lucia didn't dare hug her mother, much as she wanted to, since she was still in her filthy turnout gear and her mom was dressed in chic black linen pants and a turquoise jacket. "I can't stay. We're headed back to the station in a few minutes." She looked toward the room where her father was. "No change today?"

"I think his color is better," her mother said. She always had something positive to say about any sliver of improvement in his condition. Lucia studied her father through the window between the hallway and his room. He looked the same to Lucia, but she hoped the change her mother saw was indeed there. When her dad woke up, they had a lot to talk about. First on the list was the apology she owed him for an argument they'd had the day before he was shot.

"What's with the coat?" Her mother pointed to the jacket in Lucia's arms.

Lucia glanced down at the well-worn leather bomber jacket she had found in the chapel after she had checked on it the last time. Rafael Wright's name was neatly printed on a label on the lining. She didn't dare blurt out that the least she could do was return the man's jacket since he had saved her life—at least not to her mother, who didn't need to know how close a call it had been. "It belongs to a guy who rescued a couple of little kids in the chapel," she said, striving for a nonchalant tone. "He was so kind that…"

"One of the staff can take care of getting it returned," her mother filled in after Lucia's voice trailed away.

"Yes, I'm sure they could."

"But you're taking it back to him." A statement of fact.

Lucia nodded.

"He must have made an impression."

He had and, though Lucia knew her mother would have figured that out anyway, she wasn't ready to say so aloud. Her mother would say something to her brothers, and with their police and FBI connections, they'd probably run a criminal history on Rafe before allowing her to get close enough to return the man's coat. It wasn't like she was planning on marrying the man, or even dating him, for that matter. She just wanted to return his coat.

"Lucia?"

She jerked her gaze to her mother's. "Don't mind me. I'm just a little muddled, that's all. Reverend Dawson has another prayer service scheduled for Dad tomorrow night."

"I know."

"Since I'll be off work then, I'll be there, too. And I'll be back tomorrow afternoon to spend a couple of hours with Dad. Emily said she'd come after me so you can have most of the day to yourself."

Her mother glanced through the window to the bed where her father lay, and Lucia's gaze followed. For all her life, her dad had been the strongest man she knew—invincible. Logically, she knew he was in a coma, but emotionally—where she still felt like a six-year-old where her father was concerned—she wanted to believe he was merely taking a nap. Each day he remained in the coma added to her worry that he might never recover.

These long months since he had been shot by an unknown would-be assassin had taken on a grotesque normalcy, where her mother kept a vigil while the rest of them took turns spelling her and pretended to live life as though it wasn't in limbo. Lucia wondered if she would recognize normal if it ever came again. She could only hope.

The one thing that had remained constant through these months of waiting for her dad to wake up was their sustaining faith. As her mother had often said, whether her dad awoke or not, he was in God's hands. Though Lucia knew that, she longed for her dad to simply open his eyes.

"You better get going," her mother said, ignoring Lucia's filthy gear and planting a kiss on her cheek. "And I'll see you tomorrow."

Once more, Lucia resisted the urge to sink into her mother's arms and managed a smile that, she hoped, hid how needy she felt. She moved toward the stairwell. "Tomorrow."

When she came out of the hospital toward the pumper, she'd hoped to make it back to her crew without any further comment from Battalion Chief O'Brien. No such luck, though. He watched her approach with narrowed eyes.

"Any time you're ready to go, Vance." He had taken off his turnout gear and his slacks and shirt were crisply pressed, as though he hadn't just been through a fire.

Gideon Jackson mildly said to him, "We just got the hose rolled back up, Chief. She's not late."

"She wasn't *here,* which is more to the point," O'Brien said. "You want to go on report, Jackson?"

"If you think you've got something that should be brought to my attention," Gideon replied in that same calm tone.

Without saying anything more, O'Brien got in his red SUV, the insignia on the door identifying his rank.

After he was gone, the rest of the crew took off their turnout gear and finished stowing the equipment. Once they were underway, Gideon Jackson said to Lucia, "Don't let him get to you. He doesn't have a leg to stand on, and the rest of us know it."

Donovan grinned at her over his shoulder from the front seat. "That happens when you walk around with your foot in your mouth all the time."

"Did you guys find those two little kids' parents?" Lucia asked instead of telling the two she appreciated their support. Donovan wouldn't respond to anything mushy, and Gideon would be embarrassed.

"Yep," Gideon said. "It was a happy reunion all around. You never did say how you found them."

"I didn't," Lucia said. "I didn't have any idea anyone was in the chapel. The explosion threw me across the hall and I must have landed near the chapel door. Next thing I knew, this guy pulled me into the room, and there were the kids."

"All I can say is it's a good thing Wright was there," Gideon said, "and a good thing the door to the chapel was steel with reinforced glass. We were afraid for a few minutes that fire was going to get away from us and take the entire floor."

Lucia shuddered, remembering the burn marks on the ceiling and wall in the hallway. She didn't know what had led Rafe to be on the floor, but she was thankful. If not for him, today's call could have turned out very differently. It was definitely something to include in her evening prayers later.

The rest of the shift went without incident, and though she was able to sleep during part of the night that finished her twenty-four-hour shift, Lucia was exhausted when she got home the following morning. She knew her emotional upheaval was the cause, not the lack of sleep. As usual, her big orange tabby, Michelangelo—nicknamed Gelo—greeted her at the door.

"Hey, you." She picked up the cat, enjoying their ritual of being mutually needed. Emotion clogged her throat, and she pressed her cheek against the cat's soft fur, a purr rumbling against her face. Gelo kneaded her arm and continued to purr loudly as Lucia headed for the kitchen to brew a pot of green tea. "Anything exciting happen while I was gone?"

The cat gave her a soft meow.

"Good." She sniffed, then squared her shoulders, mentally going through the list of why she shouldn't be so weepy. Setting Gelo on the floor, she brewed the pot of tea, choosing a favorite pot that she had purchased during a visit to Italy with her mother.

Lucia knew she was a good firefighter who had done her job well, no matter what Neil O'Brien thought. She hadn't been seriously hurt. Her fellow firefighters had rallied around her. Compared to her father's injuries and the worry that that was causing her mother, Lucia's problems with Chief O'Brien were small potatoes.

The front doorbell rang, and the cat ran toward the door. Lucia followed, peeked through the security peephole, then held open the door for her good friend Colleen Montgomery. As the two youngest children of their respective large families and the only daughters as well, they had become allies early on.

Colleen breezed into the living room with her usual boundless energy. "I heard about the hospital fire. Just came by to make sure that you're okay."

"Why wouldn't I be?"

"According to Gideon Jackson—who would cut off an arm before lying, I might add—you were trapped in the chapel on the pediatric wing and had been hurt—" She took a breath to give Lucia the once-over. "You don't look hurt."

"I'm fine."

"And you rescued a good-looking guy and his two kids."

"I didn't rescue him. And they weren't his kids." Lucia headed toward the kitchen, where she pulled a couple of mugs out of the cupboard.

Colleen grinned. "And he's not ugly."

Feeling her cheeks heat, Lucia shook her head. "No, he's not ugly."

"That, my friend, is a topic we're going to pursue later." Colleen raised her eyebrows while patting the outside pocket of her purse, which was large enough to hold a notebook and other things she needed as an investigative reporter for the *Colorado Springs Sentinel*.

"There's nothing to talk about."

"The lady doth protest too much." She handed Lucia a

clipping she had pulled from her purse. "This was in yesterday's paper."

Lucia read the large print of text put into a black-framed, two-column-wide box like an ad. "'Let fire come down from heaven and consume you, for our God is a consuming fire.'"

"Pretty strange, don't you think?" Colleen lifted the lid of the teapot to peek at the brew. "I checked, and nobody knows who paid for this. But I think this is related to the fire at the hospital." She raised a hand. "And I knew this was a Bible verse, even though I couldn't figure out which one, so I called Pastor Dawson and he says it's actually two verses, one from Kings and one from Hebrews." Pointing at the clipping, she added, "So whoever bought the ad was sending someone a message, don't you think?"

"I don't know." Lucia handed back the clipping, then poured tea into the two mugs. "But if you think so, then you should turn this over to my brother Sam." Since he was a detective on the Colorado Springs police force, he'd know how to track things down if this was as suspicious as Colleen thought. "Or maybe you should talk to Brendan." He was Colleen's cousin and a special agent with the FBI.

Colleen smiled brilliantly. "Now that I know you don't think I'm crazy, I will." She took a sip of tea, then added, "Too creepy and too much of a coincidence not to be related."

Lucia hoped Colleen was wrong.

"Nice jacket," Colleen said, fingering the collar of Rafe's leather jacket, which Lucia had brought into the house and hung across the back of a kitchen chair. "Doesn't look like anything I've seen your brothers wearing, though."

"It's not," Lucia admitted, remembering that she had caressed the soft leather in the same way her friend was doing now. "It belongs to Rafe—Rafael—Wright." When her friend raised her eyebrows in question, she tacked on, "The guy from the hospital."

"Ah…the one you didn't rescue. The one who's not ugly." Sipping her tea, Colleen gazed at Lucia over the top of her mug. "You're finally ready to move on?"

"Maybe," Lucia admitted.

The expression in Colleen's eyes softened. "Not every guy is the kind of lowlife Stan was." Then she smiled. "This Rafe…Rafael guy…he might be the answer to my prayers for you. Tall, dark, handsome, gainfully employed." She paused a beat while she took another sip of tea, smile lines crinkling at her eyes. "And somebody who wants you just as you are."

Lucia grinned at her friend. "Sounds like the guy you should be praying for—not for me, but for yourself."

"Hey. Maybe your guy has a brother."

"Two sisters," Lucia said.

"I'm going to be good and not even say a word that you would know about the man's family."

They talked a while longer, their comfortable conversation turning to family matters, the plans Lucia had for her day off before going back to work for another twenty-four-hour shift and the research Colleen was doing for a new story—a series of articles about how drug traffic had changed in Colorado Springs since the demise of the drug cartel taken down the previous year. Since both of them had brothers who had been very involved in the case, the story was personal for Colleen.

After she left, Lucia worked around her house for a while, starting a load of laundry and taking care of other chores before heading for the hospital, where she would spend a few hours so her mother could get a break. That was a routine she would be happy to give up, Lucia thought as she drove to the hospital, her automatic prayer for her father's quick recovery at her lips. Quick, though, hadn't happened.

"Whatever Your greater plan, Lord," she quietly prayed, *"help us to understand."* Though she believed the potential for good flowed from every situation, she was hard-pressed to imagine what greater good was to come from her dad's lingering coma.

She arrived a half hour early as she had planned so she could check on Ramón and Teresa, or at least their sister. With that in mind, she made her way to the makeshift children's ward. She found the children with their parents, who spoke no more English than the children did. Immediately frustrated with the limited communication available with her own poor Spanish and vague hand gestures, Lucia cut her visit short, wishing she spoke the language well enough to communicate and wishing Rafe had been with her to translate.

Leaving the ward, she went through the main rotunda of the hospital and was drawn to the security tape that cordoned off the damaged pediatric wing. The fire doors at the entrance to the wing were closed. They didn't keep the pungent scent of smoke, water and charred debris inside, however, the odors oozing into the rotunda.

"It sure smells awful, doesn't it?" came a voice from the other side of the rotunda.

Lucia turned around to see Chloe Tanner, an intensive-care nurse who had thwarted a second attempt on her father's life, coming toward her. That alone would have made her an honorary family member. She had also been a great nurse, taking good care of Lucia's dad during those first harrowing days after he was shot.

That had been the beginning of a romance between Chloe and Colleen's cousin Brendan, and they had recently announced their engagement.

Smiling, Lucia said, "It does, but it's about the usual."

"I saw the trucks for your station here."

Lucia nodded. "We were the first to arrive."

"I just don't understand how a fire of that magnitude happened," Chloe said. "After all those false alarms kept happening, one of the chiefs was out here several times doing inspections. You would have thought he might have noticed the problem with the sprinklers."

"Do you remember which one?" Lucia asked.

Chloe grinned. "I won't be forgetting about a man who talked to me like I had the IQ of a gnat. Battalion Chief Neil O'Brien. He's in charge of your station house, isn't he?"

Again Lucia nodded, knowing just how Chloe felt. "A gnat, huh?"

Chloe's smile widened. "We might be insulting gnats."

Lucia laughed, reminded of how much she had appreciated Chloe's wry humor during those first tense days her dad was in intensive care. "I just had to come see—even though I knew I wouldn't be able to get in. It was a strange fire." That was an understatement. From the explosion to the two kids in the chapel to Rafael Wright, there wasn't a single ordinary thing about it.

"I'm so thankful no one was seriously injured," Chloe said. "Only some smoke inhalation, though that can be very serious, too." She walked with Lucia toward the wide staircase that led to the first floor.

"Let's keep an eye on the weather," Lucia said as they parted ways. "I'd be more than happy to take your kids skiing some weekend."

Chloe laughed. "My kids, but not me."

"You, too." Lucia grinned at her. "I suppose I could even put up with Brendan, too, if he can get away."

"He'd like that." Chloe waved goodbye.

With that, Lucia headed for the intensive-care wing where

her father was. Though at least one FBI agent was always in the hallway outside her dad's room, Lucia still wasn't used to their presence. The man on duty today said hello as she walked past him and headed for her mother, who was sitting next to the bed.

"Hi, Mom," Lucia said from the doorway.

"You're early," her mother said.

"Not that much." Lucia moved into the room, taking off her coat. "I've been reading to him, and to be honest, now I'm wanting to know how the story turns out."

They talked a few minutes longer, and after her mother left, Lucia sat down next to the bed and began reading to her dad, a novel from his collection of Zane Grey Westerns. He loved those stories, and she understood why. In the end, justice prevailed and evil was vanquished. That thought took root, along with the newspaper ad that Colleen had shown her.

What if Colleen was right and it was a message? Lucia looked up from the book to her father's sleeping face. She thought about that some more, trying to analyze the problem the way her brother Sam would. As a detective, he was good at sifting through the puzzle pieces and putting the right ones together.

If the message was a warning, she wondered if it was somehow connected to her dad's shooting. Or was she simply giving too much importance to her own family? And if the ad was connected to her father somehow, surely one of the FBI agents who had been assigned to the case would see how everything fit together. Deciding others were far better equipped to figure out the puzzle, if there even was one, Lucia returned to reading to her father.

She spent the rest of the afternoon with her dad, not leaving until one of her sisters-in-law arrived, a continuation of the family agreement that Mayor Vance would always have a family member by his side.

Lucia left the hospital, her attention drawn to the leather

jacket on the front seat of her car. Since she had looked up Rafe's address before she left home and discovered he lived only a couple of miles from the hospital, returning his jacket seemed the neighborly thing to do. Except that she hadn't called, mostly because she hadn't been able to figure out what she would say after the initial hello. Her internal argument continued while she drove. Since it wasn't yet five o'clock, maybe he wouldn't even be home. So she'd be off the hook, a thought that brought a pang of disappointment.

Her stomach clenched with unaccustomed butterflies as she pulled into the parking lot. The apartment complex where he lived was large, but she easily found his building. The jacket firmly wrapped in her arms, she climbed the two flights of exterior stairs to his floor, found the apartment number and knocked on the door.

She could hear music from inside, so clearly someone was home.

A second later, the door opened and a tall, good-looking man with coffee-colored skin and dark eyes smiled at her.

"I was looking for Rafe," she said.

His smile widened. "I wish I could say that you found him."

"Is this the right apartment?"

He nodded. "Right apartment, wrong guy." He extended his hand. "I'm his roommate, Malik Williams. And you are?"

"Lucia Vance," Rafe said, appearing behind Malik.

The butterflies in her stomach fluttered at the sound of Rafe's deep voice. Her gaze latched on to his, and she lost herself within his green eyes that were so at odds with his dark brown hair and olive skin. The outside of the iris was a pure, dark jade. As she realized he was studying her just as intently, her own gaze shifted to Malik's openly curious and teasing one. She noticed a bandage above one eyebrow.

Malik's smile grew into a wide grin that flustered her even

more. He took her hand. "He wouldn't tell me a single thing about the lovely firefighter, except for your name." He clucked his tongue. "I knew you'd be pretty."

They had talked about her, Lucia thought, the butterflies beating against her chest, her attention still on Rafe's smiling face. His hair was longer than she had remembered, the color a warm, dark brown.

"And I'm pretty sure you have something else to do," he said, taking Lucia's hand out of Malik's and drawing her into the apartment. "Like now."

Malik laughed. "I do?" At Rafe's glower, he repeated, "I do. Something very, very important back here that I'm sure I'll remember real soon." He slapped Rafe on the back. "She's *fine,* so you be extra nice."

Completely bemused, Lucia watched Malik amble toward a hallway. Rafe's hand around her own was warm and solid, which made sense since the man had proven to be both yesterday.

Rafe led her through a living room that was dominated by a huge black leather couch, a matching loveseat and an equally masculine recliner. An enormous black television was surrounded by various high-tech components, smooth jazz emanating from the speakers. The kitchen was small, the stainless-steel appliances gleamed, and the counters were neatly lined with various gadgets, from a cappuccino machine that looked too complicated to use to an electric ice-cream maker. Something savory-smelling bubbled in a glass-lid-covered pot on the stove.

Letting go of her hand, Rafe said, "I'm glad to see you. Would you like something to drink?" Without waiting for an answer, he opened the refrigerator. "A soda or a lemonade, or the ever-popular iced tea?"

I'm glad to see you. Those simple words warmed her

beyond anything reasonable—maybe because it was an echo of how she felt. She realized he was looking at her expectantly, and her attention shifted to the open refrigerator door.

"Iced tea." At the breathless tone in her voice, she silently marshaled her thoughts into some coherent order. "That sounds good."

Rafael Wright wasn't the first man she had ever found alluring. But he was the most potent.

FOUR

"**I**'ve got to warn you," Rafe said, taking the jug of tea out of the refrigerator. "It's sweet tea—a taste I acquired when I was living in North Carolina a few years ago."

"That's fine," Lucia said. "Were you fighting wildfires there?"

Filling the glasses with ice, he nodded. "They were having a drought, and I spent most of the season there."

"Fires have a season?"

He grinned, that killer dimple flashing. "They do. Brush fires as early as February or March, sometimes, in Florida and southern California. Or late. There was a big fire in the Everglades in November the same year I worked in North Carolina." He filled the glasses from a pitcher in the refrigerator. "I see you brought my jacket back."

She glanced down at the coat still clutched in her arms. "Yes."

He handed her the glass. "I was hoping it would turn up."

She extended her arm so he could take the jacket. "It looks like you've had it a long time."

"I have." He set it over the back of a chair and motioned her toward the living room. "It was a gift from my sisters one Christmas."

"The schoolteacher and the homemaker," she said, heading

for one end of the monstrous black leather couch, where she sat down. Setting the iced tea on the chrome-and-glass coffee table, she slipped off her lightweight coat.

"You remembered," he said.

She didn't respond to that, especially since everything from yesterday was vividly etched in her mind. "Your friend that you were visiting when the fire started, how is she—"

"He," Rafe corrected, cocking his head toward the hallway. "Malik. He was released this morning." Rafe sat down on the other end of the couch, extending one arm across the back and balancing the iced tea glass on his thigh. "A ladder fell on him during a training exercise, and since he had a concussion to go with the gash over his eye, they wanted to keep him overnight for observation."

His gaze on her was so thorough that she looked away, noticing details about the room beyond the high-tech, masculine toys. The mostly barren glass and chrome shelves didn't have a speck of dust—unlike her own oak furniture. There was a picture of Rafe with a couple of pretty women, the kind of photo she would have thought was a posed family picture, except they didn't look anything like him.

"My sisters," he said.

She looked back at him.

"I was adopted when I was nine," he added, as if understanding her unasked question of why there wasn't a family resemblance, and smoothly moved on to a new subject. "I went by the children's ward this afternoon to find out how Ramón and Teresa—and their sister—were doing."

"I did, too," she said.

"They told me I had just missed you." His gaze roved over her face.

She smiled. "I was wishing you were with me…or that I spoke Spanish. I couldn't understand them."

"They were happy you came to see them," he said. "Their sister has some rare kind of bone cancer, and she's going to be in the hospital for a while, so you'll have other chances to see them."

"I'm sorry for that. Not that I'll have a chance to see them, but because their sister is sick. That's hard—the long wait and not knowing…"

"You're talking about your father?"

"Yes." She met his gaze, reassured when she saw only curiosity and compassion in his expression. Speculation about the extent of her father's injuries and whether he would be able to return to work had dominated the news. Lucia hated the spotlight that her family had been thrust into.

He moved his arm from the back of the couch to take her hand. "Your family has had a rough several months, if the reports on the news are to be believed."

His touch was warm, offering support that she didn't quite know what to make of. When she pulled her hand away to once again pick up the glass of iced tea, she had the fleeting thought that a hug from this man would be just as warm, just as supportive. Those were the kinds of thoughts she couldn't afford, even though she had told Colleen that…maybe…she was ready to move on. The all-too-familiar knot in her stomach reminded her that she was no longer as confident as she once had been or as certain of her own judgment of others. She reminded herself that she had come to return his jacket—that was all. The sooner she drank her tea and left, the better.

Taking a sip of the tea and focusing on the last thing he had mentioned, she said, "You know the news—you have to make it exciting somehow. And the truth is, we're just waiting for him to wake up, just as we've been doing since those first days."

"Waiting and praying," he said.

"Yes," she breathed, her silent admonishment to hurry lost beneath the feeling that Rafe somehow understood. "Exactly that."

"Then you're doing all you can."

"It doesn't feel like enough," she said, setting the glass back on the coffee table.

"Prayers are heard."

She met his kind gaze once more, feeling as though the ground had subtly shifted beneath her. He had confirmed what she had been taught all her life, what she believed to the depths of her soul. Prayers *were* heard. One more thing that added to her awareness of him.

"Now then." He winked at her. "I have a mondo huge favor to ask."

The butterflies returned as she realized he was flirting with her. "I'm not sure I know you well enough for 'mondo huge' favors."

"I figure being trapped together by a fire means you know me very well," he said. "My niece's birthday is coming up, and my sister tells me she's not old enough for Barbie dolls, which were always my fallback gift for my sisters."

"A safe choice." Personally, she hadn't been that interested in playing with dolls when she was a girl, nor had she had the endless fascination of dressing them that she had seen in her friends.

"And since I'm her only uncle and her godfather—"

"You take your responsibilities seriously."

His grin widened. "You get the picture. So you'll go shopping with me?"

"When?" That was a far cry from the "I can't" she had intended to say.

He glanced at his watch. "No time like the present."

"But your dinner—"

"It will keep."

"I'm not sure that I know that much about two-year-olds. Plus…" *Plus what?* she wondered.

Evidently, he had the same thought because he asked, "Plus?" He stood, picking up the glasses from the coffee table, and headed for the kitchen. Lucia trailed after him, watching as he set the glasses in the sink and turned off the stove.

"I don't have a lot of time," she said. "There's a prayer service for my dad at seven thirty."

"We have plenty of time. If it runs tight, I'll go with you. Do you want to take your car or mine?" he asked, coming back toward her, snagging her coat off the end of the couch and holding it up so she could put it on.

She remained fixed on his matter-of-fact announcement that he'd go to the prayer service. The idea of sitting in church with him was one thing, but the idea of him being around her mother and brothers—she'd be setting herself up for questions she wasn't prepared to think about, much less answer.

So tell the man you can't go with him, she crossly said to herself. *Or tell him that you have to hurry.* Instead, she slipped her arms through the sleeves of her jacket. Her silent reminder that she had only wanted to return his coat now seemed hollow…and increasingly like a fib to herself.

"Well?"

Refocusing her thoughts once more and remembering that he'd asked whose car they should take, she admitted to herself that she was way out of her depth.

"If we take my car, are you one of those guys who will want to drive?"

Putting on his own jacket, he said, "Only if you have a BMW Z4."

Deciding that she probably lived under a rock, at least in the car department, because she had no idea what kind of car that was—she said, "I left it in the garage."

"Hey, Malik, you can come out now," Rafe called toward the back of the apartment. "The sloppy joes are done, so help yourself. We're leaving."

"Catch you later," Malik called back.

"It would fit in a normal-size garage, wouldn't it?" Lucia asked as they went out the door, her initial idea of the vehicle changing from a sports car to some oversize SUV.

Rafe laughed, following her down the stairs. "You're not into sports cars, hmm?"

She shook her head, walking toward her small SUV.

"A Honda CR-V," Rafe said, identifying the model of her vehicle and going around to the passenger door. "Sweet. And I can see that you're a skier," he added, patting the ski rack on the roof of the vehicle.

"You're now privy to my weakness," she said, opening the door and flicking the switch to unlock the passenger door.

"You like to ski?" Rafe's smile was even wider as he got into the car. When she nodded, he asked, "What's your favorite run in the state?"

"Timberwolf," she instantly said, "and then that nice, long, fast ride down Coyote Caper."

"You ski Keystone," he said. "Speed *and* altitude."

She smiled at him. "In Summit County, altitude is the only thing you've got. Where's your favorite run?"

While she backed out of the parking spot, he said, "I couldn't name one favorite. Iron Horse Trail over at Winter Park is a good one. I like to get up to the top of Alberta Peak a couple of times a year."

"I'm not familiar with that one."

"Wolf Creek Ski Area," he said. "And the prettiest run

through timber in the state is there, too. Simpatico—and let me tell you, the name fits." As he had done with the couch, he stretched his arm across the back of the seat. "Sounds like we need to make a ski date."

"I don't date," she answered, the words so automatic they were out before she gave them any thought.

Without missing a beat, he said, "Good. If it was a date, you'd expect me to pay for the lift tickets—"

"I have my own Colorado Pass."

"And rent you skis—"

"I have a new pair of Völkl skis."

He whistled in appreciation. "It's a good thing you don't date, Lucia Vance. You'd be high maintenance." The teasing quality in his voice took away any possible sting.

"You'd be surprised."

Actually, Rafe was. She clearly skied a lot since she had a season pass that gave her access to all the ski areas in Summit County. And since she had named a couple of runs that came close to the kind of extreme skiing he preferred, she was clearly a good skier—make that an expert skier— something that increased her appeal a thousandfold. As for being high maintenance, she clearly wasn't. Not from her modest SUV to her shiny, nearly black hair that she wore in a no-fuss ponytail. Her nails were cut short, and given her choice in careers—plus her interest in skiing—he figured she was a tomboy, not a high-maintenance, frilly woman.

This woman, he thought, would be easy to fall in love with. Even though she didn't date. Maybe *especially* because she didn't date.

She pulled the vehicle to a stop at the traffic light a couple of blocks from the apartment. "You need to provide some direction for this shopping expedition," she told him.

"I'm thinking we should head for Citadel Mall," he said.

"I think my niece would like one of those made-while-you-watch teddy bears."

Lucia smiled. "And here you wanted me to think you didn't know what you wanted to get."

"It got you to agree to come with me." He waited a beat until she took her gaze off the traffic and looked at him. "Now tell me why it is that you don't date."

She looked away, worrying her lower lip with her teeth. Her focus on the traffic kept her from looking at him, but she didn't answer right away. Figuring her answer would be more interesting and hopefully closer to the real reason if he didn't push, he waited, fascinated by the way her fingers tapped the edge of the steering wheel.

"Three older, overprotective brothers," she finally said.

"And their names, just in case they come looking for me—"

"Which they won't because we aren't dating."

"Humor me," he encouraged, wishing she'd look at him again.

"Travis, Peter and Sam," she said. "In that order."

"Why else?"

She shrugged. "Nothing. Just big brothers who like to think they know what's best for me."

He figured there had to be more to her not dating but let it go, returning to the safe topic of skiing and the merits of various ski slopes throughout the state. In the process, he learned her family had a condo in Breckenridge. By the time they had reached the teddy bear store, she had also revealed that she had a soft spot for stuffed animals. He paid attention to the ones she picked up before handing him a soft brown traditional-looking bear, tucking that information away for use at some future time.

They spent the next half hour going through the ritual of

placing a satin heart in the bear's chest before stuffing it and picking out accessories.

By the time they were finished making the purchase, it was after seven and time to head for the prayer service.

"I don't expect you to come with me," Lucia told him. "I can't impose on you."

"Why not?" Rafe asked from the passenger seat of her SUV. "I imposed on you to go shopping."

"That's different."

"I don't see how," Rafe said, figuring this was a chance to meet at least a couple of her brothers. If they were as overprotective of her as Lucia indicated, the sooner he crossed that hurdle, the better. That he was even thinking so was an indication he was getting in deep already. He had known her slightly more than twenty-four hours but already knew they had shared values and shared interests. If she thought he'd be turned off by going to church with her, he also needed to put that to rest. "Let's put it this way, I *want* to come with you."

"You're sure?"

"Yes." As she put the car in gear and eased slowly through the parking lot, he watched her, absorbing everything he could about her in the dim light. Her skin was fair, a sharp contrast to her dark hair and eyes. Tendrils of hair had come loose from her ponytail. One day, he'd wrap one of those around his finger to see if her hair was as soft and as silky as it looked.

"You're staring," she said, a flush staining her cheeks.

"There's a lot to stare at," he said without any apology. "If I made you uncomfortable—"

"We're not going to date."

"I heard you." Much as he suspected she needed a more solid agreement than that from him, he wouldn't lie to her. If she was so dead set against dating, he'd find another way to spend time with her.

"So you can stop looking at me like that."

"I'll do my best," he promised, sure that he had heard a tremor of underlying fear in her voice. What happened to you, Lucia Vance? he wondered.

The service had just started when they came through the door to the church. To Rafe's surprise, the church was nearly full, so they sat down in one of the rear pews. Even though he was extremely aware of Lucia next to him, the lifelong habit of being in church during good times and bad brought that awareness to the forefront. Familiar comfort seeped into him.

His own silent prayer for Mayor Vance's healing joined Reverend Dawson's. Along with that prayer were others. For Lucia to find a sense of peace within this challenging time for her and her family. For a chance to know her better. For Rafe's actions to be guided by what was ultimately good for Lucia, not simply by his own selfish desires.

When the service ended, they remained in the pew as people made their way out of the church, many of them stopping to speak with Lucia. Some he recognized. Battalion Chief Neil O'Brien with a petite woman who was several months pregnant—the woman smiled at Lucia while the chief pointedly ignored her. Several other firefighters, including the two men he had met the previous day. Gideon Jackson stopped to say hello to Rafe and introduce his son, a little boy who was his spitting image and who quietly held tight to his hand. Luke Donovan held a toddler who had fallen asleep on his shoulder. Two other little girls with his blond hair and blue eyes skipped alongside of him and his wife, a pretty redhead who looked to be several months pregnant.

The little girls clearly knew Lucia well because they immediately launched themselves into her arms. She responded affectionately with them, chatting with their mother. A second later, they were joined by a blonde who caught Rafe's eye and immediately stuck out her hand, saying, "Hi, I'm Colleen Montgomery."

"This is Rafael Wright," Lucia said.

Colleen lightly touched the front of his jacket. "Ah, the mysterious owner of the leather jacket." Her inspection of him was frankly speculative before she said to Lucia, "I'll see you tomorrow, girlfriend."

When a trio of men came down the aisle toward them, Rafe figured these had to be Lucia's brothers. All dark-haired and as tall as himself, they surrounded Lucia as though she needed protection. From him. That thought made him inwardly grin, since he recognized the posture—he had used it a time or two to intimidate guys hitting on his sisters, though they had both been older.

"I'm Rafael Wright," Rafe said to the man who came to a stop at Lucia's left, deliberately smiling in the face of the man's glower and offering his hand.

"Samuel Vance." He had Lucia's dark brown eyes.

Rafe turned his attention to the other two, both of them with black hair and blue eyes. Of the three, Sam looked most like Lucia, though her hair was the near black of these two.

"I'm Travis," one said, shaking Rafe's hand. "And this is Peter."

"How do you know Lucia?" Peter asked.

"Stop the third degree," came the soft command from a striking petite woman who came to a stop next to them. She had the same velvety-looking skin and nearly black hair as Lucia. She extended her hand to Rafe. "I'm Lidia Vance. Thanks for saving my daughter's life yesterday."

When he took her hand, she stood on tiptoe and kissed his

cheek. And for one of the rare times in his life, Rafe had no idea what to say.

"What's this?" Travis demanded at the same time Lucia turned and asked her mother, "How did you know?"

"You, my daughter," Lidia said, "were just a little too casual yesterday, so I called Gideon." Without releasing Rafe's hand, she faced Lucia's brothers. "There was an explosion during yesterday's fire—"

"My partner, Becca, told me about that," Sam said.

"—that knocked Lucia out—"

"I was not unconscious, Mom," Lucia interrupted.

"—and put up a wall of fire between her and her escape route," Lidia continued. "Rafe, here, happened to be in the chapel—and if that wasn't a Godsend, I don't know what could have been—and he pulled her to safety." Lucia's mother looked at Rafe. "According to Gideon, our Lucia would have been in serious trouble if you hadn't been there." She tipped her head toward him. "I thank you. We all do."

"It was nothing. Just at the right place at the right time," Rafe said.

Sam took Lucia by the shoulders and looked her up and down as though assuring himself she had no injuries. "You're sure you're okay, sis?"

Her "I'm fine" was nearly lost beneath Travis's annoyed "Everything else going on around here and you don't say a word?"

"Because I knew it would be like this," Lucia said, her voice surprisingly even. She smiled at Travis. "When have I ever kept something big from you?"

"Only once," he said, his gaze turning to Rafe. "And it was one time too many."

FIVE

"Could you please tell us step-by-step what happened after you arrived at the hospital?" Chief O'Brien said to Lucia two days later.

She had been summoned to the downtown station shortly after her arrival to work that same morning. The wide expanse of the polished oak table stretched like a brown lake between Lucia on one side and O'Brien and two other battalion chiefs on the other. As intimidation went, it was highly effective, just as it was supposed to be. She wasn't intimidated so much as annoyed.

This inquiry seemed a continuation of O'Brien's belief that she had become a firefighter because of her father's influence rather than on her own merits. O'Brien had repeatedly ignored the fact that she had become a firefighter long before her father was elected and that she had consistently scored well on her exams and performance reviews.

Furthermore, since O'Brien had been the commander on the fire and had been with her until shortly before the explosion, he knew very well what had happened.

Even so, she repeated the events as she remembered them, doing her best to conceal her irritation and to relate the facts only.

When she was finished, one of the other chiefs, Alex

Jones, said, "That was unusual, wasn't it, to split up you and your partner?"

"It was." Lucia looked steadily at O'Brien.

"And entirely within the scope of the fire. Her partner was needed elsewhere," he interjected. "She was assigned a simple task that she failed to complete."

"Because of the explosion," Lucia said.

"Which shouldn't have happened if you had gotten water on the fire more quickly."

"Can you tell us how many minutes elapsed from the time you hooked up the water until the explosion?" Chief Jones asked.

"Less than a minute," Lucia said. "I had just connected the hose when it happened. I hadn't gotten a drop of water on the fire."

O'Brien shook his head. "That's because you spent a good five minutes horsing around before you hooked up the hose."

A lie, Lucia thought, her annoyance growing. Challenging him in this setting, though, would be a mistake, starting a fight she had no hope of winning. Her attention shifted to the other two battalion chiefs.

"I don't remember the elapse of time being that long," she said evenly. "You should probably check with the other firefighters assigned to the floor." Still, the accusation that she had been slow nagged at her. Had her memory failed her about that? *Had* she been slow? Enough so that the explosion and subsequent expansion of the fire was a result of her neglect? "At the time, I thought I was doing all that I could as fast as I could."

The other battalion chief, Michelle Simpson, said, "Do you have anything else to add, Ms. Vance?"

"No," Lucia said.

Chief Simpson glanced around the room. "I still have

questions that I think should be asked of the other firefighters who responded. But until we talk to them, I'm willing to go along with your recommendation, Chief O'Brien, that Ms. Vance be placed on light duty."

"I agree," Chief Jones said.

Lucia watched the three of them, her heart sinking. She'd been down this road before, and she actively disliked light duty. Generally O'Brien found the most menial tasks possible to occupy the nine-to-five schedule that was far more difficult to adjust to than twenty-four-hour shifts of full duty. Though she worked no more hours during the course of a week, the light-duty hours wore on her. Not only did she feel as though she had less time at home, she knew for certain that she was letting down her fellow firefighters because someone else would have to be called in to fill in for her.

"Report to my office after lunch," O'Brien told her, "and I'll have your work assignment for you."

"Yes, sir," she responded, deliberately reverting to the formal manners that her parents had instilled in her. Manners that reminded her to keep her temper in check.

She left the building, which was across the street from the county courthouse. The day was a cold, blustery March one, the sort that made her wish she could be at home working on the latest stained glass she was making, this one a planned wedding gift for Brendan Montgomery and Chloe Tanner. Instead, the best she could hope for was a day that would creep by at a snail's pace, where she was denied the opportunity to do the job she loved.

Since she was only a few blocks away from the police station her brother Sam worked from, she called him from her cell phone, and they made plans to meet for lunch at the Stagecoach Café, a favorite hangout for the family. Sam and his partner, Becca Hilliard, were already there when Lucia arrived.

"You're looking a little blue," Sam said as she slid into the booth next to Becca.

Lucia glanced at her brother's partner. "He does know how to flatter a girl, doesn't he?"

"You know Sam," Becca said.

"I just call it like I see it," Sam said. "Plus, the only reason you'd be downtown instead of at your station house is because O'Brien called you in. Tell her I'm right, Becky."

"I'm not telling her anything," Becca responded.

"You're right," Lucia said. "He called a review board first thing this morning and I'm on light duty until the investigation is complete."

"What investigation?" Sam demanded.

Lucia shrugged. "The one where the scope of the fire is my fault for abandoning my post." Now that she'd said the words aloud, they sounded awful, and she swallowed back tears that she hadn't allowed earlier.

"That is a bunch of horseradish," Sam said, his voice low and fierce. "This vendetta O'Brien has had against you for the last year has gone too far this time."

"Sooner or later, he'll hang himself with his groundless accusations," Becca said.

Lucia managed a smile. "Sooner or later."

"It will be a lot sooner if I have anything to say about it."

"Don't you dare go talk to him! That will only make him more convinced than he already is that the only reason I have this job is because—"

"You're a good firefighter," Becca interrupted. "This will be like the other times he's gone after you. You'll come out just fine, and he'll have another notation on his record to that effect."

The waitress arrived to take their orders, and the next few minutes were focused on that. While they waited for their food to be delivered, Becca complained about how expensive it was going to be to replace the leaky roof on her big, old Victorian house.

"You should just sell it," Sam advised in what Lucia knew to be an ongoing exchange between the two. "Your brother and sister are finally all grown up, and you could be free." He grinned as he spoke, and as always, Becca scowled at him when he urged her to sell her family home.

Lucia smiled at the interplay between the two. Becca had a love-hate relationship with the house. It was special to her because it had been in the family for so many generations and a burden to her because she had put aside her own dreams to finish raising her brother and sister after both of her parents had died.

She nudged Becca. "Tell my brother to give away his dog—"

"Like that will happen," Sam said. "My kids would have a fit."

Becca grinned. "And I'll be getting rid of my house about the same time."

A couple of minutes later, their lunches arrived, salads for Lucia and Becca and a huge hamburger and fries for Sam.

He was quiet for a moment while he took a couple of healthy bites of his burger. "I went to see your new friend, Rafael Wright." He wiped the corner of his mouth.

"You didn't." Her heart sinking, Lucia looked up from her salad.

"Did you know he's lived all over the United States?" Sam continued as though he hadn't heard her exclamation. "He's only been here a little over a year, and the way he talks, he might be transferred."

"So?"

"So why risk getting involved with a guy who has no roots?"

"He has roots," Lucia said. "In addition to his job, he's one of the volunteers for the wildland fire unit."

"Not that he'd be around if there was a fire, since those happen while he's running all over the United States being a hotshot."

"You say that like it's an insult." Lucia glared at her brother. "Being a hotshot firefighter puts him in an elite group and you know it."

Sam grinned at his partner. "She's way too easy to bait." His gaze turned on Lucia. "Look at the way you defend the guy, sis. You wouldn't do that if you weren't involved."

"We're not—"

"You brought him to church the other night."

She couldn't deny that. She had. And Sam, and probably her other two brothers as well, had jumped to all the wrong conclusions she had been afraid they would. Explaining that they had been shopping and had run out of time would only strengthen the perception.

"Plus," Sam bulldozed on, "I've seen how he looks at you."

"You're imagining things," Lucia said. She wasn't planning on getting involved with Rafe, but her brother's attitude rankled. She set down her fork and glared across the table at him. "And you keep acting like I'm about twelve and don't know how to take care of myself."

He met her glare with one of his own, his dark brown eyes filled with concern. "I just don't want to see you get hurt again, that's all."

The idea of feeling as emotionally vulnerable as she had when Stan Felini had broken their engagement had Lucia in agreement with her brother. She didn't want to be hurt again, either. Equally, she didn't want her three older brothers running interference for her.

"It's my choice to make," Lucia said. "And you might inform Travis and Peter of that, too." Taking a deep breath, she picked her fork back up and glanced at Becca. "Be glad you don't have any big brothers. They are a royal pain."

Becca smiled. "I've been told big sisters are, too."

They finished eating, paid the bill and made their way toward the door. Waiting to be seated was Alessandro Donato, Lucia and Sam's cousin, who smiled when he saw them.

"How are you?" he said, his dark eyes warm. He took both of Lucia's hands and kissed her on one cheek, then the other, his usual greeting left over from his Italian upbringing. "I heard about your close call with the fire the other day."

"Does everyone watch the evening news?" Lucia asked. "I'll be just as happy when my fifteen minutes of fame are over."

"Your mother told me," he said, offering his hand to Sam. "Cousin, I haven't seen you for a while."

"I'm not the jet-setter continually off to mysterious places unknown," Sam said, his tone far less warm than Alessandro's.

Seemingly unfazed, Alessandro said, "That sounds far more exotic than my life is." He shrugged negligently. "Unfortunately, I spend so much time poring over computer printouts and studying financials that I don't have much time to enjoy the scenery."

"Paperwork, huh?" Sam asked the question as though he didn't believe Alessandro.

"Alas, yes." He smiled at Lucia. "Though if you came to Italy with me, I would take the time to give you that tour of Tuscany I promised you."

Lucia remembered. He'd made the offer shortly after her engagement had ended. "Is that where you're off to? Italy?"

He nodded. "I leave on the red-eye tomorrow night." He glanced at Sam, then looked back at Becca and Lucia. "It's not too late to add two additional tickets if I could interest you ladies in a trip."

He had that Italian flirting thing down pat, Lucia thought, shaking her head and laughing with Becca, who was also making a similar denial.

"You have no idea how good that sounds right now," Lucia said, thinking about the boring days ahead when she'd be tied to paperwork, as well. "Unfortunately, I have no vacation time."

"Too bad."

"But there *is* something you could do for me."

"Name it."

"I'd like pictures of the stained glass window from the chapel—"

"The one near your grandparents' home?"

"That's the one," she said. "Big pictures of the whole window and lots of detail shots." She had been planning a gift for her mother for a while—a reproduction of some small part of the gorgeous window from the church where her mother had worshipped as a child.

"Consider it already done," Alessandro said. "I'll use my digital camera and put it on disk."

"That would be perfect," Lucia said.

The hostess approached them, carrying a menu. "I can seat you now, sir."

He touched Lucia's sleeve. "Be safe, *cugina*." Following the hostess to his table, he called, *"Addio."*

"Be safe," Sam muttered as they went outside. "Cousin or not, he's as smooth as olive oil."

"I know he was teasing," Becca said. "But a trip to Italy? Very tempting."

"It sure was." Lucia grinned, lightly punching her brother. "Smooth as olive oil? Some insult. I don't know why you don't like him."

"Because he's smooth. Too smooth. Plus, you can never quite pin down exactly what he does."

"Hmm. You mean, like the times I've asked you about what you do? Like that?"

Sam shook his head. "Not the same thing at all."

"Well, at the risk of sounding smooth, be safe, big brother. You, too, Becca," Lucia said with a wave, heading toward the downtown station, where her undoubtedly boring work assignment awaited her. In that, she had a lot of sympathy for her cousin.

"¿Caridad?"

Her gaze jerked up to the whipcord-lean man leaning negligently against the doorway of her office. Today, he was well dressed, the wool-and-silk sports coat casually elegant. He watched her with the dark intensity he always had. Though a good twelve feet separated her Louis XVI rosewood writing table from him, she had the sensation of him touching her.

Thrusting her thoughts about the deadly game of double cross she played to the back of her mind, where they could not be reflected in her eyes, she stood, smiled in welcome and crossed the room to him. "An unexpected surprise. What are you doing here?"

When she lifted her face to kiss him, he turned his head slightly so her lips brushed his cheek instead. A sign he was displeased.

She stepped back and moved to the breakfront, where she kept refreshments for her clients. He closed the door to her office, then came toward her with the smooth, silent grace of a cat.

"Can I get you something?" She pulled an imported water from the small concealed refrigerator, twisted off the cap and poured it into a crystal tumbler.

"Results." He brushed a single finger across her nape, twisting a tendril of hair that had escaped her chignon. Though he frequently caressed her in this way, she understood there was a fine line between the touch of a lover and the touch of a man who would kill her if he knew her true agenda.

Taking a sip from the glass, she ignored the shiver that slid like a single drop of icy water down her spine. She knew exactly what he was talking about. There had been a fire at the hospital, to be sure, but it had done nothing more than cause extensive smoke damage to the new pediatric wing of the hospital and displace patients. In the end, the fire had created a nuisance—nothing more.

"I've already called Neil O'Brien," she said, moving away from him toward the window that overlooked the street below. A couple of workmen stood on a scaffold, adding the finishing touches to an ornate sign above a restaurant scheduled to open in a few days. It was one more indication of the revitalization of this once run-down area of town.

"The man failed," he said, coming to stand beside her. "Perhaps he needs a bit more persuasion. What does he fear most?"

She thought a moment about that question, hoping it was one that he would never ask about her. "Being discovered," she said, giving voice to her own fear as well as O'Brien's, "since he was willing to commit a murder to keep his wife from finding out."

"Then see that she does," he instructed. "Send her a copy of one of the promissory notes."

That was, she conceded, a good idea. "As you wish."

He moved toward the doorway, stopped midstride and turned back to look at her. "You do know to use ordinary paper and an inexpensive envelope. Nothing is to tie this back to us."

She smiled at him. "I am not entirely stupid, *El Jefe*." A subtle way of showing her own displeasure.

He inclined his head. "The next time you talk to our friend, let him know that he has one more chance to succeed." Without waiting for an answer, he left, moving as silently as he had arrived.

She waited next to the window, the tumbler clasped in her cool hands. At last, she heard the chime of the exterior door, and a moment later, she watched him cross the street below, skirting the workmen on the scaffold, then continue on his way around the corner, where she lost sight of him.

Only then did she return to her writing table. She took the copies of the notes from her purse, selected the top one and placed it on the glass of the compact printer-copier that sat on the credenza along the cream-colored wall. Going to her sleek laptop computer, she typed in Mary O'Brien's name and address and sent it to print. Then she closed the file without saving it.

The envelope she selected was the inexpensive type Baltasar had instructed she use. The cotton gloves she pulled on might leave fibers behind, she conceded, but nothing that could be connected to her, and since she used them in her work, a far less suspicious item to have in her desk than vinyl gloves. Only then did she pick up the copy, fold it and put it into the envelope.

With the copy, she placed one of the hairs she had collected from *El Jefe*'s brush. She smiled, thinking about that name. *El Jefe*—a bold name for a man who would soon be the chief of nothing. As clues went, this one was nearly invisible—perhaps too subtle. But it would lead back to Baltasar Escalante should anyone decide to look. Still wearing the gloves, she put a stamp on the envelope, then set it with some other correspondence that the postman would pick up when he delivered the mail.

SIX

"Hi, Lucia."

Since she had been dreaming about that deep voice over the last few days, Lucia didn't really expect to find Rafael Wright standing outside of her cubicle when she looked up. But there he was. She couldn't deny it to herself. She was unreasonably happy to see him. Maybe especially because she hadn't expected to.

"Hi."

His smile reached his eyes, that dimple creasing his cheek. He nodded toward the stack of papers piled precariously on the end of the desk. "This doesn't look like any fun."

"It's a blast if you like paper cuts." She held up her Band-Aid-covered index finger.

"Ouch," he said sympathetically. "So O'Brien followed through and put you on light duty."

"Just like he said he would."

Rafe looked down the hallway, then back at her. "Do you have time for a cup of coffee?"

"Sure." She stood, stretching a kink out of her back. "I haven't taken a break yet this afternoon."

He stepped aside so she could slip out of the cubicle, then followed her through the maze of offices and cubicles to the front of the building. "If you'd like real coffee, we could go across the street," he said.

"That sounds fine, but I should have grabbed my jacket."

"No problem." He took off his and held it up for her to slip her arms through.

Liking his concern—and a little thrilled by it, too—she glanced back at him. The jacket was warm as the weight of it settled over her shoulders. Warm and way too big, a vague surprise since she wasn't a small woman. Who would have thought? Beneath the jacket, he was wearing a green-and-gray plaid wool shirt that brought out the color of his amazing eyes. When they reached the exterior door, he held it open for the woman coming inside—Mary O'Brien, Lucia realized.

"Thanks," Mary said to Rafe, then added, "Hi, Lucia. I saw you the other night at the prayer service but didn't have a chance to say hello."

That was because her husband had ushered her out of the church without stopping to talk to anyone. "It was nice of you to come," Lucia said. "Thank you."

"It's such a sad thing that your dad is still in a coma."

"It is," she responded, managing to keep her voice even though emotion threatened to clog her throat just as it did each time anyone expressed sympathy for her dad. "But the doctors continue to be encouraged."

"That's good news." Mary glanced away, a pervasive sadness enveloping her when she stopped smiling. "I need to go find Neil. Have you talked to him this morning?"

Lucia shook her head, thankful that she hadn't. "But I think he's been in his office."

"Good." There was a minuscule crack in her voice. "I need to talk with him and it simply can't wait."

"Are you okay?" Lucia asked, watching the smaller woman closely. She seemed near tears.

Mary looked up at her, her eyes luminous. "No, I'm not, but there's no help for it. Thank you for asking." With that, she made her way down the hallway toward the windowed offices used by the battalion chiefs when they weren't at their assigned firehouses.

"That's one worried lady," Rafe said as Lucia came out of the building and they went down the steps toward the street.

"I hope it's not bad news about her pregnancy," Lucia said. "She told me a while back that they've been trying to have children for years."

"Isn't that the way it goes," Rafe said as they stopped at the edge of the street and waited for a few cars to pass so they could cross to the coffee shop on the other side. "People who really want kids can't seem to have them."

"It's certainly a gift when it happens," Lucia said.

"I think so, too." They stepped off the curb and crossed the street.

She shot him a sideways look, wondering if he had thought about having children and deciding the question was way too personal. Especially since they weren't dating. Especially since her brothers would undoubtedly chase him off if he got too close. That thought made her throat clog with unexpected emotion. Then she remembered Sam had already been to see him.

Inside the coffee shop, Lucia ordered her usual green tea and Rafe ordered a coffee—a plain coffee that he brought to the table without even sugar.

"I was real sorry to see that you were placed on light duty," Rafe said as they sat down next to the window. "That shouldn't have happened."

"This isn't the first time," she said. "And for as long as Chief O'Brien is my battalion chief, it probably won't be the last."

"That sounds a little pessimistic. Why?"

"Simple. He thinks I got the job because my dad is the mayor."

"Ah." Rafe took a sip of his coffee and then looked at her. "I have to admit, I wondered why you chose being a firefighter."

"I wanted to help people," she said. "In a meaningful way, you know?" When he nodded, she added, "It's still a very ordinary job compared to what my brothers and my dad have done."

"I don't think there's a single ordinary thing about being a firefighter," he returned.

"Takes one to know one," she teased, making him smile. "My brothers have all done amazing things. And they're all terrific at what they do."

"I've heard you are, too, so it must be a family trait."

She shook her head. "Compared to my brothers and my parents, I'm the most ordinary person imaginable."

Rafe opened his mouth to say "Not to me." Since she had warned him off, that kind of comment was only likely to put roadblocks in his way. Instead, he said, "I doubt that. So Sam is a detective on the CSPD. What do Travis and Peter do?"

"They run AdVance, a private investigation firm."

Rafe shook his head. "I'll take being a firefighter." To keep from reaching for her hand the way he wanted to, he took another sip of his coffee.

Holding her cup in front of her and looking at him through the vapor of steam rising from the tea, she said, "Speaking of Sam…"

"Were we?" He met her gaze, carefully keeping his tone light and teasing. Her brother had all but threatened him if he pursued Lucia.

"He told me that he'd been to see you." She averted her gaze.

"He said you two were very close."

She nodded. "He's closest to my age." She sighed, then looked at Rafe, a spark of humor lighting her eyes. "I took great delight in torturing him when I was a kid."

"He must have forgiven you, because he's got a protective streak a mile wide." The one thing Rafe wanted her to know was that she could count on him to tell her the truth. She would only be offended if she knew that he had taken her brother's warning like a schoolboy would take a double dog dare. No way was he staying away from her simply because he'd been warned off by her brother. "I feel the same way about my sisters."

"You told me that the day of the fire."

"So the way I figure it, your brothers and I have something in common." Deftly changing the subject, he asked, "What do you like to do when you're not working? Besides ski?"

"Hobbies, you mean?"

"Sure."

"I make stained glass pieces," she said. "When I was a little girl, I used to look at the windows in church and watch the way the light made the colors glow. Then, a couple of years ago, I took a class, and I was hooked."

"Maybe you'll show me your work sometime?"

She met his gaze, her own filled with a warning look.

He raised his hands in surrender. "I wasn't asking you on a date, I swear."

To his relief, she grinned. "In that case, I'd be happy to show you." She glanced at her watch. "I've got to get back to work."

Rafe drained the rest of his coffee, then stood when she did. "How much longer will you be on light duty?"

"I'm not sure. The only good part is that I have weekends free."

"I was hoping you'd say that." She shot him another of her suspicious looks. "I promised Ramón and Teresa that I'd take them to the zoo Saturday morning, and I thought you might want to come." When she continued to look at him without answering, he tacked on, "This isn't a date. This is chasing up and down the hills at the zoo, keeping track of two little kids who've been cooped up too much at the hospital. That sounds like work, not a date."

"Work that you want to rope me in for," she pointed out, a smile twitching at the corner of her mouth.

"Well," he drawled, "I need a woman along for all that girl stuff that goes on."

Lucia's eyes lit up. "You're laying all this on pretty thick."

When they reached the door of the coffee house, he pushed it open, the outside air cool and carrying a hint of snow.

"What if it snows?" she asked.

"Then we'll bundle up and it will be a short visit."

They came to a stop at the curb, waiting for a car to pass before they crossed the street back to the fire department headquarters.

"Okay," she said when they stepped onto the sidewalk.

"Okay?"

"Don't look so surprised. You knew very well that I wanted to see those two kids again."

He'd been hoping that was the case, though he hadn't known for sure.

"Good. I'll call you on Friday and finalize the details."

"Okay." She handed him back his jacket and took a step toward the front door of the building. "Thanks for the tea."

"You're welcome." He put on the jacket and watched her go, completely pleased that she had agreed to the outing. For not dating, this was going far better than he had had any right to hope. Heading down the street toward his SUV, he turned his face into the collar of his jacket. There it was. Lucia's scent. Something floral with a hint of something tangy.

Whistling under his breath, he got into his truck and headed for work. There was a cross-training class to plan and recruits to contact for the upcoming fire season. Normally those jobs had his complete focus. Just now, though, all he could think about was Lucia.

Later that same afternoon, Rafe met with the CSFD chief arson investigator and the two detectives assigned to the case, Samuel Vance and his partner, Becca Hilliard. Rafe had taken classes from the arson investigator, Ben Johnson, a crusty old-timer who knew more about fire than anyone Rafe had ever met. He was looking forward to seeing Ben again as much as he was dreading seeing Lucia's brother again. Since the man had come to his office and warned him to stay away from Lucia, Rafe knew he was putting her in a tough position. Since he liked her, that bothered him—it bothered him a lot.

"Glad you could make it," Ben said to Rafe as he came down the blackened hallway of the cordoned-off pediatric wing. "I sorta figured you might be out of town on one of your recruiting junkets."

"I just got back," Rafe said. "I heard on the news this was arson."

"Nobody could have been surprised about that. I'm not telling you any secrets, but nothing about this adds up. Sprinklers that don't come on, false positives on the alarm system. Only time will tell if it was all coincidental or if something else was going on." Ben led the way down the hall toward the janitor's closet—or at least what was left of it.

"Personally, I never went much for coincidence."

"Finally, something we agree on," said Sam Vance, coming up behind Rafe and Ben.

"Probably more than one thing," Rafe said, his gaze moving from Sam to the woman with him.

"This is my partner, Becky Hilliard," Sam said. "Rafe Wright."

"Becca," she corrected, smiling at Rafe. "Nice to meet you. I've heard good things."

Sam shot her a glance, which made Rafe inwardly grin. "It's all true."

She laughed, turning her attention to Ben Johnson. "What's the verdict?"

Ben scratched his gray hair. "No verdict yet. I just wanted to get Rafe's take on things since he was closest to the fire and manned the fire extinguishers when the fire first broke out."

He told the story as best he remembered it, trying to include the pertinent details to the moment when the explosion knocked him off his feet and he found Lucia on the other side of the door.

"What do you mean she was by herself?" Sam said, latching on to the one part of the whole incident that kept bothering Rafe. "Firefighters work in teams. Where was her partner?"

"I don't know, but he wasn't with her." Rafe met Sam's angry gaze. "I remember thinking it was a pretty strange thing at the time. And in light of O'Brien being so mad at her, the whole thing didn't make any sense. So that makes me wonder if O'Brien was somehow involved—"

"No way," Becca said. "He's a battalion fire chief responsible for the safety of his people."

"You might have a point," Sam said, "except that he's been riding Lucia ever since he was assigned to her fire station. His vendetta against her isn't new."

"Maybe not," Rafe said, "but this still makes no sense."

Ben waved to his assistant. "Track down her partner—"

"That would be Luke Donovan," Sam interrupted.

The assistant made a note in his notebook, then followed

Ben down toward the blackened remains of the janitor's closet, where the two of them gathered additional evidence.

"I don't know why you've taken such a personal interest in my sister," Sam said, the statement bland enough to not be a challenge. Rafe recognized it as such, however.

"Hard not to take an interest," Rafe said. "She's a special woman." He waved at the space between the two of them. "This dislike you have for me, is it your usual way of dealing with men interested in your sister or is it more personal?"

Sam took a step toward him. "It's personal. If you can't handle that, it's real simple. You can back off."

Rafe stared at Lucia's brother, whose dark eyes were so like hers. Despite Sam's assertion that his dislike was personal, Rafe had the feeling any man interested in Lucia would be equally suspect. Rafe's strong suspicion was that someone—probably a boyfriend—had badly hurt her somewhere along the way. Given her assertion that she didn't date and Sam's warning to keep his distance, that was the only thing that made sense to Rafe.

"I won't be backing off," he said to Sam. "Not until she makes it clear that's what she wants."

SEVEN

When the doorbell rang on Saturday morning, Lucia answered it with a smile on her face, expecting to find Rafe on the other side. Instead, there stood her ex-fiancé, Stan Felini, leaning against the door in that negligent I-own-the-world stance that she'd once found alluring and intriguing. Blond and blue-eyed, dressed as usual in jeans and a tweed sports coat, he was good-looking and knew it.

He must have taken her smile as welcoming because he leaned forward to kiss her, a kiss that landed on her cheek when she turned her head. "Hey, Lucia," he said, unfazed. "Great to see you." Straightening, he slipped past her into the house without waiting for an invitation.

"What do you want?" she asked, closing the door only because it was freezing outside, not because she wanted him in her house.

He was looking around the room, assessing it the way he always did. Once, she had thought it was because he was a real estate agent. Later, she had figured out he did it because he had a cash register where his heart should have been.

"I heard about the fire at the hospital and came to see if you were okay," he said, his gaze sliding over her to a painting she had bought last year when she and her mother had traveled to Italy. "I've missed you."

"You have a funny way of showing it." His picture was regularly featured in the society pages of the *Colorado Springs Sentinel* and he always had a glamorous woman on his arm. "You could have called."

He smiled. "I tried that, but you didn't return my phone calls."

"That was more than a year ago."

He came toward her, his fingertips lightly riding the edge of his jean pockets. "You've done a lot with the place. New couch, or did you reupholster the old one?" Without waiting for a reply, he added, "I can't believe you still have that same old stereo system."

"It works," she returned with barely restrained patience, remembering how he had taken the new one they had bought together—and with *her* money—when they had broken up. How like him to say that he'd come to see if she was okay and then focus on other things.

"I hear the FBI still isn't any closer to knowing who shot your dad."

"That's what the news says." She made a point of looking at her watch.

At last, his gaze lit on her, and for all the world he looked sincere. Except she recognized this particular expression when he was either going to ask her for something or going to try to explain away something.

"We had a good thing going," he said.

"At one time I would have agreed with you."

He took a step closer. "And you would have been right."

"Before you took money from me." She was positive it wasn't the reason, but the fact that he still owed her several thousand dollars rankled. "Maybe you'd like to set up that payment schedule we talked about last year?"

Instead of answering her question, he said, "I saw you at

the Valentine Gala at the Broadmoor last month and realized that I really screwed things up."

"Finally, something we agree about." Lucia was surprised he had seen her there. At the time, he'd had all his attention on one of the Pencrest heiresses, a family who had been one of the founders of the city when railroads were king. She remembered watching him and feeling relieved that she hadn't felt an ounce of jealousy over his attention to another woman. It had been a banner moment.

"Sarcasm, Lucia?" He shook his head. "I was being sincere."

"So was I."

"You could have been seriously injured this week. I worry about you, you know."

That was the way it always started. Her actions worried him, and she was too spoiled or too insensitive to take his feelings into consideration. She'd heard it a hundred times, and boy, she didn't want to go there today.

He reached for her hand, and she stepped beyond his reach. "I'd like to have another chance."

"Same condition as before?" she asked, not because she cared or was the least interested in getting back together, but simply to see if the old argument between them would still play out in the same way it always did. "That I give up being a firefighter?"

"Sooner or later, this is a stage you're going to outgrow," he said.

Yep, she thought. The same old argument.

"It's not a stage." She shook her head, keeping a tight rein on the anger that suddenly swamped her. Somehow she managed to keep her voice even when she asked, "How hard would it be for you to simply accept me just as I am?"

"I do."

"But you want me to give up a job that I love—"

"Because I'm concerned for your safety." He pressed a hand against his chest. "Give me a little credit, Lucia. I want to be with you again."

"With me? Or the wealth you thought I had? Or with my 'family connections,' as you once put it?"

"That's not fair."

The doorbell rang, and Lucia felt as though she was literally being saved by the bell since she was a hair's breadth away from blowing up. No way did she want him to know that he had the power to move her to anger or anything beyond indifference.

She went to the door, and this time there stood Rafe with Teresa and Ramón in front of him. She was ridiculously glad to see him.

"Hi," she said, her welcoming smile including the two children. She gave each of them a hug, urging them to come into the house. As Rafe came in, she realized she had the opportunity to let Felini know things were completely, irrevocably over. And so, before she could change her mind, she put her arms around Rafe—the leather of his jacket cool and buttery soft beneath her fingertips—and kissed him.

Her intent—merely for show—instantly vanished when he kissed her back and put his arms around her and lifted her to her tiptoes, the scent and feel of him surrounding her and making her feel alive and cherished.

"Hi," he whispered against her mouth, then kissed her again.

"You didn't tell me you were expecting company," Felini said from behind her.

Sanity returned with the crash of her conscience.

Rafe raised his head and looked at the man standing in the middle of the room, a man he distrusted—disliked, if he were honest with himself—on sight.

Lucia stepped out of his arms and turned around, crimson pulsing from her neck to her forehead. Motioning toward the kids, she said, "This is Ramón and Teresa." She took Rafe's hand, her own clammy, which made him clasp his own reassuringly around hers. "This is Rafael Wright."

"I'm Stan Felini," the guy said, easing a card out of his sports coat pocket with the dexterity of someone who did so all the time. "Felini Real Estate Investments. You've probably seen my television spots." When Rafe shook his head, he added, "Lucia's ex-fiancé."

Pieces of a puzzle clicked into place. The reason she had just kissed him after professing that she didn't date.

"So you're the new guy," Stan said, making it sound like Lucia had men lined up on her doorstep.

"Yeah," Rafe drawled, ignoring the card. "I'm the new guy." He looked at Lucia, who was looking more uncomfortable by the moment. Though he was certain he was being used and equally certain that sweet kiss had everything to do with this guy, Rafe couldn't—wouldn't—let her down. "Are you ready to go?"

Relief crept into her eyes, and she squeezed his hand before letting it go. "Give me just a minute to gather up my things." Making a not-so-subtle detour around her ex-fiancé, she headed toward the kitchen, where a coat was folded over the back of a chair. Ramón and Teresa followed her.

"Well." Stan clapped his hands together and eased toward the doorway. "I've got to be going." He opened the door and stepped outside, then turned around. "Are you serious about Lucia?"

"Very," Rafe said instantly.

Stan's gaze fell to the two children who had followed Lucia into the kitchen. "Cute kids."

"I think so."

"You'll always be second fiddle," Stan said. "No matter how cute your kids, her nosy, busybody family will always come first." Evidently satisfied he'd had the last word, he pulled the door closed behind him. On the other side of the room, the children were chattering with Lucia, who was engaged with them despite the language barrier. They had taken off their coats and put them on the chair with Lucia's.

Not quite certain what to do next, Rafe looked around the living room, which couldn't have been more different than his own. Where his sofa was black leather, hers was cream and loaded with the pillows that women seemed to like. The walls were painted a soft peach, and a big tapestry hung on the wall, its scene a set of stone steps overlooking a European-style garden. Instead of military neatness—his only way of keeping ahead of clutter—books and magazines were scatted across the coffee table, along with a basket of materials that looked like some sort of in-progress craft project.

The big difference, he decided, was this was a real home rather than someplace she simply slept and watched television.

With a surge of jealousy, he wondered if the ex-fiancé had lived here with her. Refocusing his thoughts, he realized that Lucia was talking about making hot chocolate, which had Teresa clasping her hands with an eager *"Sí,"* and the claim that hot chocolate was her favorite.

"Do we have time?" Lucia asked, her gaze colliding with Rafe's.

As usual, he felt a jolt when she looked at him, all the more potent because he now knew that he liked kissing her. A lot.

"Sure, I'm in no hurry." He took off his coat and set it with the others.

An orange tabby wandered into the kitchen, its tail held high in the air. Ramón bent to pet the cat.

"This is Michelangelo," Lucia said.

"That's a mouthful."

"It is." She took a saucepan from the cupboard next to the stove. Her kitchen had all those womanly touches missing in his own. No high-tech gadgets, but instead big, hand-painted pottery canisters. A plate of cookies sat on the counter in front of a row of stools. "That's why I call him Gelo."

"Yellow Gelo?" Rafe teased.

She laughed. "No, but it fits."

They were, he realized with appreciation, about to have homemade hot chocolate, rather than the variety from a premixed package dumped in a cup of hot water.

"What can I do to help?" he asked while she measured out the milk.

"The cocoa is in there," she said, pointing to one of the cabinets. "And the sugar is in that canister. How is their sister doing?"

"About the same." Figuring all this chatter was to cover up the fact that she was nervous and as conscious of that kiss as he was, he pulled out the requested items and glanced back at the two children who were sitting on the floor and petting the cat. "Their parents said to tell you thanks."

Lucia shook her head, efficiently putting the ingredients together in a pot on the stove. "I haven't done a thing."

"Except for going to see them every time you visit your dad," he said. "And finding some Spanish storybooks for Ana. And getting Teresa and Ramón enrolled at the church's day care center at no charge, along with someone to pick them up and deliver them back to their parents."

"You're assuming a lot," she told him.

"And I don't see you denying it, either."

"I don't want to talk about it." She added milk to the mixture in the saucepan.

Rafe grinned, figuring there was at least one more thing she didn't want to talk about, either. "I know we're not dating, but if we were…" He waited until she looked up from the stove and across the countertop separating them. He somehow managed to refrain from leaning toward her and kissing her again. "The kind of woman who is most appealing is one who spreads around those random acts of kindness like you have with Teresa and Ramón's family."

Once again, a blush spread across her face. She didn't say anything as her gaze dropped back to the stove. A moment later, while she continued to stir the mixture, she said, "If you want to be helpful, the mugs are over there." She pointed in the direction of another cabinet.

The mugs inside the cabinet were all different, but again, all had the same vibrant colors he'd seen in the living room and kitchen. In no time, the hot chocolate was made and the two kids climbed onto the stools at the counter, both of them polite and on their best behavior. Lucia kept Rafe busy translating while they drank the hot chocolate, inquiring about their favorite animals at the zoo, what they had been doing in day care and what they thought of her cat—all, Rafe suspected, to keep the conversation away from what had happened earlier.

After they finished the hot chocolate, Lucia had the kids wash their hands and visit the bathroom. Since neither tasks were ones he would have remembered, he admitted that his ruse of needing Lucia's help was off the mark. He really did need her help. Granted, talking about that kiss in front of the kids wasn't the thing to do, but he kept remembering it.

Within a half hour of being at the zoo, Rafe was doubly glad Lucia was with him since Teresa wanted to visit the giraffes first and Ramón was set on seeing the tigers, which were, of course, on opposite sides of the park. Lucia persuaded Teresa they should see the tigers first and plan to be at the giraffe exhibit at their feeding time.

"You'll want to see their purple tongues," she told Ramón, which Rafe translated.

"That is a strange thing to know," Rafe told her.

"Not when you visit regularly with nieces and nephews."

At the big-cat exhibit, the kids spotted two tigers resting in the shadows. Teresa wanted to know where the babies were, and Ramón asked out-of-the blue if Lucia was Rafe's girlfriend, adding that since they kissed they must be.

Since the question was posed in Spanish, Rafe was pretty sure that Lucia hadn't understood, especially when she said, "What's he asking about? *Novia* and *beso*—is he asking the names of the tigers?"

Rafe shook his head. "He wants to know if you're my girl-friend—*novia*." Lucia's blush came back, then deepened when he added, "He thinks you must be since I gave you a kiss—*beso*."

While they walked toward the next exhibit featuring leopards, Rafe said, "That whole not-dating thing. Your ex-fiancé is the reason?"

She nodded without saying anything more until after he had read the sign about the leopards to the kids, translating it into Spanish. "My mother always told me that I should keep my mouth shut if I didn't have something nice to say about a person."

Rafe looked at her. "That bad, huh?"

"Toward the end, yes."

"Did he live with you?" Rafe figured asking was stupid but wanted to know anyway.

"No." She turned a shocked gaze on him. "Are you kidding? I could never do that, because I believe there should be a wedding first. Besides, my dad would kill me, then the guy. No marriage, no living together."

"That's always been my thought, too. If I liked a woman enough to move in with her, I ought to like her enough to marry her first." He wondered if she knew just how unusual that attitude was, even though it was one he shared.

"You've never lived with anyone?"

He chuckled. "Just Malik. It's a good arrangement. Saves him money while he goes to school and keeps me from having to eat alone."

It was Lucia's turn to chuckle. "I don't like that very much, either."

The kids had run ahead to the reptile and bird house, so Rafe used that as an excuse to take Lucia's hand to run and catch up with the kids. She didn't immediately pull her hand away, not until Teresa demanded her company to investigate the colobus monkeys. Over the next hour, they looked at families of monkeys, tortoises and owls, prairie dogs and black-footed ferrets before going into the chimpanzee exhibit, where a group of youngsters played on a big tire swing.

"If you were dating…" Rafe said, earning a sideways look from her before she returned her attention to the kids.

"You are persistent, aren't you?"

"A fault," he agreed, then added, "What kind of man would you be looking for?"

She was so long in not answering that he had decided she was going to ignore the question when she finally said, "Someone who accepts me just as I am. Someone who tells the truth. Someone who keeps his word."

Rafe listened without comment, thinking all her requests were ones he'd want for himself and, again, told him much about the relationship she'd had with Stan-Felini-the-ex-fiancé. Much as Rafe practiced not judging others, he found himself disliking the man, mostly because he had hurt Lucia.

Despite speaking very little Spanish, Lucia made sure a healthy amount of play at the playground and tot train was intermixed with looking at the animals and making sure they were at the giraffe exhibit at their feeding time. And, sure enough, they had long purple tongues that had both of the kids giggling when one of the zoo staff showed them how to feed the animals from the elevated platform that brought them to eye level with the tall animals.

It was a nearly perfect day, Rafe decided, despite the cold temperatures and a pace set by the kids that equaled a training day designed to separate hotshots from the wanna-bes. Once again, the memory of her in his arms had him wondering why her ex had been at her house this morning. Rafe hated the idea she might still be hung up on the guy.

At different times, he was so struck by Lucia's expression that his heart squeezed around the surprising thought that she might be the woman he had been searching for all these years. Her face lit as much as the child's when she climbed onto one of the carousel horses with Teresa and when she tenderly wiped mustard off Ramón's face after they'd stopped for hot dogs. She smiled when she caught Rafe's glance over the children's delight with a baby elephant.

After a full day, they delivered the kids back to the hospital where their parents sat with the older sister, Ana. A huge grin erased her pallor when her brother and sister presented her with the huge stuffed giraffe they had picked out. After chatting for a few minutes, Rafe and Lucia said their goodbyes.

"Do you want to go see your dad?" Rafe asked as they walked away from the temporary children's wing.

"I can come back later."

Since he was hoping for dinner later, something he had already promised her before they left the zoo, he said, "Since we're here—"

"I can't impose on you like that."

"It's not an imposition."

"There will be someone from my family there," she warned. "You could find yourself on the end of another inquisition."

Doing his best to reassure her, even though he didn't want to have another confrontation with her brothers, he grinned. "There could be worse things. Besides, I have a black belt in repartee."

She laughed, just as he had hoped she would.

"I don't remember whose turn it is this afternoon," Lucia said, "but there's a good chance it's one of my brothers." She touched his arm, the first time she had done so all day. "You can wait down in the lobby if you want."

Rafe took her hand, lacing her fingers through his. "I'm not afraid of your brothers, Lucia. What kind of man would I be if I spent the day with you, then left you to do this by yourself?"

She didn't say anything, but the fact that she didn't pull her hand away until they reached the hospital room encouraged him that maybe, just maybe, she was beginning to let down her guard. Maybe, just maybe, he'd find out what had been going on between her and her ex this morning. And finally, if her family's disapproval was going to be a problem, the sooner he knew that for sure, the better.

Through the window to the room, he could see a couple of women sitting on chairs next to the bed, both of them about Lucia's age. No brothers, he thought with relief.

"Hi, guys," Lucia said from the doorway.

"Lucia, I wasn't expecting to see you today," one of the women said, standing to give her a hug. She was taller than Lucia by an inch or two, with short auburn hair and warm brown eyes that were shades lighter than Lucia's.

The other woman, fragile-looking with shoulder-length hair curled softly around her face, met Rafe's gaze. Despite the half smile that curved her lips, her own gaze immediately became speculative, giving him the feeling she knew who he was without any introduction.

Lucia pulled Rafe into the room. "This is my friend Rafael

Wright. These are two of my sisters-in-law. Tricia," she said, nodding toward the redhead, "and Jessica."

Tricia gave him a firm handshake, her gaze direct. Jessica merely nodded in his direction.

"Tricia is married to my oldest brother, Travis," Lucia was explaining, "and Jessica is married to Sam."

Ah, Rafe thought. That explained why Jessica seemed to recognize him.

To his surprise, Tricia grinned. "Don't hold that against us. Jessica told me about the grilling Sam gave you."

Jessica stood, her smile wider. "We'll at least wait until after we know you before deciding we don't like you."

"Uh, thanks?" Rafe said, earning a chuckle from the two women.

"I did warn you," Lucia told him.

"You did," he agreed, "and I'm man enough to live with my choice." Silently, he wondered if that was so. The deep suspicion her family members all seemed to have about him brought back feelings of insecurity that had been a constant in his life when he had been shuffled from foster home to foster home after his mother died. He'd worked hard to get past that need to please. Yet here he was once again, hoping that he would be liked for himself and not at all sure he was worthy enough to be liked.

EIGHT

"And we've just come from the zoo," Lucia continued. "You remember me telling you about the two kids, Teresa and Ramón. They wore us out." She glanced back at Rafe. "Or, at least, they did me." While she talked, she slipped out of her coat and went to her father's bedside, where she kissed his clean-shaven cheek. "Hi, Dad," she said, as though he would actually hear her. "I have a friend with me today. His name is Rafael Wright."

Rafe swallowed, wondering if he was supposed to say something to the man. Knowing someone in a coma might be aware of his surroundings and acting natural in the situation were two very different things.

She turned her attention to Jessica. "I should have asked you if Amy wanted to come along. Since she and Ramón are about the same age, they would have had a good time."

"That wouldn't have been such a great idea," Jessica said, her attention still mostly on Rafe. "She's just getting over a cold. So Rafe, what do you think of the zoo?"

"It's great," he responded. "Gives me a workout every time I go there, so going in winter has some advantages."

Tricia asked, "You're a hotshot, right?" When he nodded, she added, "I know you guys—"

"Gals, too," Rafe said. "Some of the best firefighters on my crew are women."

Tricia nodded. "Point taken. So I've heard you're the best. But the name. I never could figure out what it refers to."

"Other than attitude?" Rafe said with a grin. "It's simple. We go into the hottest, most dangerous part of the fire."

"Like smoke jumpers," Jessica said.

"Same idea, and sometimes we work side by side with them. The difference is, they are trained to jump from airplanes, usually into an area remote enough that you can't easily get there any other way."

While they talked, Lucia sat next to her father, holding his hand as if encouraging him to be part of the exchange. Since the man looked as though he was sleeping, sitting here talking in a normal tone of voice as though everything was ordinary seemed strange to Rafe. He kept wondering if Lucia's father was aware of any of the conversation. And with that thought came the idea that, in a coma or not, this man was entitled to Rafe's consideration since he was interested in Lucia.

As he answered Jessica's and Tricia's thoughtful questions and told them about his job, he was struck by another realization. This routine was somehow normal for the members of Lucia's family, caught in the limbo of waiting for her father to wake up and having faith that he would. Rafe had no doubt he was seeing prayer in action, which brought a surge of admiration, not only for Lucia, but for her sisters-in-law who were bound by nothing except loyalty.

"It's clear you have a lot of pride in your work," Tricia said.

"Yes, ma'am."

"And you've lived all over the United States," Jessica said.

"Well, all over the west," Rafe told her. "And when the fire season gets underway, I could be sent anywhere the crew is needed."

"That sounds like it would be hard on a family," Jessica said.

"It can be," Rafe admitted, his attention drawn to Lucia. Though he had just met her, he didn't like the idea of being away from her for months at a time. For the first time since becoming a hotshot, he didn't look forward to the upcoming fire season. But it was what he was trained for, what he was good at. And he had lots of other people counting on him, since he was a supervisor responsible for a crew. Now that he was nearly finished with his master's degree in fire science, he'd begun thinking about other jobs he could do.

"It couldn't be worse than a lot of other work," Lucia said, glancing at her father, then looking at Rafe. "When I was growing up, my dad was sometimes gone for months at a time." She squeezed his hand, and sudden tears shimmered in her eyes. "And just like now, he was in our thoughts, and we prayed for him. Mom used to say he was with us in spirit, just not in body."

"I didn't mean that to sound like a criticism," Jessica said. "Really."

"No offense taken," Rafe said.

"Since you were there when the fire happened, what's your take on this investigation of Lucia?" Jessica asked. "Sam thinks it's a witch hunt."

"He could be right. Personally, I don't see any merit in it," Rafe said. "And I don't understand the politics of the situation, allowing him to get away with it."

"Thank you," Tricia said, her voice dry. "Another voice of reason."

"I met with the arson investigator the other day," he added, "and he's sharp. When he reports on the evidence he's gathered, it's going to show that Lucia was not responsible for the acceleration of the fire in any way."

"You sound so sure," Lucia said from her seat next to the hospital bed.

Rafe met her glance, remembering that instant of fear he'd had when he'd seen her on the floor after the explosion. Now that he knew her, his fear for her well-being in that moment was even stronger. The silence stretched between them, and when she looked away, Rafe noticed that both Jessica and Tricia were staring at him.

"Did you get to feed the giraffes?" Tricia asked, breaking the sudden tension in the room.

"Rafe did the honors," Lucia said, "and then Ramón jumped right in. Teresa seemed a little worried about getting that close."

"Do you like living in Colorado Springs?" Jessica asked Rafe.

Questions again. Since Lucia's family had closed ranks around her and since he'd met her ex-fiancé, at some level he understood it, even though he didn't like it.

"Stop," Lucia said, setting her father's hand on his chest. She was smiling, but there was no mistaking the command in her voice. "No more grilling."

Tricia grinned. "Oh, boy. We weren't exactly subtle, were we?"

Returning her smile, Rafe said, "No, ma'am."

"Enough of calling me *ma'am*," she returned. "You'll make me think I'm back in the air force."

"We've got to go," Lucia said, picking up her coat. She bent over her father and kissed his cheek as she had done when they arrived. "I'll see you tomorrow, Dad." Then she ushered Rafe toward the door.

"Have fun," Tricia said, while Jessica added, "Nice to meet you."

"You, too." His gaze went to Lucia's father. "I hope I see you all again," he added before following Lucia through the door.

"I shouldn't have made you come with me," Lucia said

when they were outside. "Man, you'd think Jessica has been taking interrogation lessons from my brother. And Tricia! I'd forgotten how intense she can be. She was a major before she retired from the air force. Now she helps out at AdVance, so she's got that casual getting-acquainted-while-grilling-you thing down pat."

Rafe reached for Lucia's hand. "It's okay. Don't worry about it. Actually, I like your sisters-in-law."

"Are you sure?" She pulled her hand away and buried it in the deep pockets of her coat. "My family can be pretty overwhelming."

"Your family is fine." She was right—they were overwhelming, even in ones and twos. Since he was interested in her, the sooner he figured out how difficult that would be, the better, so he took her by the arm and stopped walking. "What I really want to know about is your ex-fiancé."

Instantly, crimson suffused her cheeks, and she looked away, worrying her lip between her teeth.

"I'm sorry I kissed you," she whispered.

"I'm not." He took her hand. "But I would like to know what—"

"I was using you, okay?" She met his gaze then, her eyes filled with unshed tears. "I'm sorry for that. Especially after you've been so kind—terrific, really—all day." She waved her free hand. "He makes me crazy and instead of telling him to get lost like I should have done, I took the easy way out—"

"By kissing me and making him think we're—"

"Yes," she said miserably. "He definitely came under the heading of 'beware of what you ask for.'" She took a deep breath, her head dropped, and her shoulders slumped. "You already know my dad was gone a lot when I was a kid. He and my brothers all had these dangerous jobs, and while I admired it, I decided I wanted somebody who would be around, who didn't carry a gun and who had a more ordinary life. You know?"

"I can understand that." Carry a gun? Besides her brother Sam, who was a detective on the Colorado Springs police force, Rafe hadn't thought about what her other brothers did or what kind of work her father had done before he was elected mayor.

"What I should have been asking for was a guy with character. Instead, I got a guy who was always looking for an angle. Family get-togethers were okay if he could schmooze, but if we were just hanging out, he didn't like them. He liked being out so he could be seen—he was always on, you know?" Without waiting for an answer, she added, "Always looking for the big deal that would make him rich. And he would never have offered to come see my dad like you did today. Not once did he ever go to church with me."

She looked up suddenly as though she'd had some startling revelation, and he remembered the night he'd gone to the prayer vigil with her.

After another shuddering breath, she said, "I was so mad at myself that I let him get under my skin this morning. And so I kissed you, used you."

He ducked his head, coming into her line of vision. "I was there, remember?"

She looked suddenly at him.

"You didn't hear me complaining. It's okay."

Her gaze fell to the ground. "It's not."

"I only have one question." He waited until she looked back at him, then asked, "Are you still in love with him?"

Lucia felt as though she had been punched in the stomach, matching the intensity in Rafe's expression.

"No." She caught his other hand and faced him straight on, then repeated, "No. I haven't been for a long time. In fact…"

After a moment, he encouraged. "In fact?"

"I'm not sure I ever really was."

Some unnamed thing eased in his eyes, and after half an eternity, he smiled, his dimple creasing his cheek. "Want some dinner?"

"Yes."

"I'm starving for a big Chicago-style pizza. I might even be persuaded to eat a salad with it if you want to pretend this is a healthy meal."

"That sounds good," Lucia said as they began walking again. "You're not mad at me?"

His smile grew wider. "The most beautiful woman I know kissed me this morning. How could I be mad?" They reached his SUV, where he unlocked and opened the door for her. When she climbed in, he leaned toward her. "Next time, though, it will be only about us." He pointed at her, then himself. "Agreed?"

Her mouth dry, she nodded.

He closed the door and walked around the front of the vehicle. He thought she was beautiful? Though she knew how untrue that was, the thought thrilled her.

At the pizza place, they had the good fortune of being seated in a booth far enough away from the television, where a hockey game blared, that they could talk to each other.

"Any word yet on when you'll get to go back to full duty?" Rafe asked her after they were settled and their soft drinks had been delivered.

"No. It can't come soon enough, though. The only good part is having weekends off so we can have days like today."

"It was a good one, wasn't it?"

She grinned. "Exhausting, if you want to know. I'm not this tired after skiing."

"The snow is still good," Rafe said. "How about next weekend?"

"Breckenridge?" she asked.

"Sure."

"Because I already have a trip planned for next weekend. I'm leaving Friday night, and if you'd like to come along—"

"I would."

"I'm not…it's not…" She could feel her face growing unbearably hot. Telling the man it wasn't a date after kissing him this morning seemed stupid. But still. "A date."

He grinned at her. "I remember. You don't date, so an invitation to go skiing couldn't be a date."

"We have a condo—"

"I can get a hotel room."

She shook her head. "Don't be silly. There's plenty of room. It's not like we'll be alone because Brendan Montgomery, his fiancée and her kids are going to be there, too."

"Brendan Montgomery, the FBI agent?" he asked.

"Yes. How did you know?"

"He lives in my building. How do you know him?"

"I've known him all my life," Lucia said. "His grandfather and my grandfather were friends and our two families have been close ever since. His cousin Jake married my cousin Holly last year, and Jake's sister Colleen is one of my best friends."

"You don't actually expect me to keep this straight, do you? Next thing I know, you'll be telling me that his uncle's brother is your grandfather's son."

Lucia laughed. "Not quite that bad, but close."

The pizza came then, smelling wonderful and tasting just as good.

"How did your niece like her teddy bear?" Lucia asked. At Rafe's blank look, she added, "You remember…the birthday present we bought the other night?"

"Her birthday isn't for a couple more days yet, so I don't know. Got it all shipped off to her, though."

"In Atlanta."

He nodded.

"Is that where the rest of your family is?"

"No. My other sister lives in Spokane, and my parents are still in Missoula, Montana. That's where I grew up—at least, from the time I was nine."

While they finished their pizza, they shared childhood stories, Rafe's growing up in a college town and how it compared with Lucia's experiences growing up in a military town. Their shared love of nature and skiing came from his growing up next door to the Rattlesnake Wilderness Area and her growing up in the shadow of Pikes Peak. He had paid for college by working as a wildland firefighter during the summer before becoming a hotshot, and confessed to being hooked by the time he had graduated and become a full-time employee. She'd had it far easier, she told him, since she'd had a scholarship and her parents had paid for what the scholarship hadn't covered, leaving her with only spending money to earn.

By the time he told her about how he was nearly finished with his master's degree in fire science, she wasn't surprised—everything he had shared about himself conveyed a man who strove to do his best. She related growing up as the youngest of four—and the only girl—with her father gone sometimes for months at a time on mysterious trips and how she hadn't known her father was a CIA agent until after he retired. And Rafe told her that he had spent four years being shuffled from one foster home to another after his mother died until the Wrights adopted him when he was nine.

"I was five when my mother died," Rafe said in response to her asking about the first years of his life. "I never knew who my dad was, and my mother's parents were dead by the time she got sick, so there wasn't any other family, either. I remember staying with a neighbor lady while she was in the hospital." A wistful smile crossed his face. "I don't remember much about her, except that she had white hair and baked me oatmeal cookies."

"That sounds like a good memory."

"Yeah." He cleared his throat. "Then I ended up being shuffled from one foster home to another until I landed with the Wrights. My dad used to say, 'Wright place, Wright time.' And it was. I got the family I had prayed for since the day my mother died—two big sisters, plus a mom and dad."

Lucia squeezed his hand, which was sitting on the table between them. "Did you really pray?"

"Sure," he said, lacing her fingers through his, then looking up at her. "The last clear memory I have of my mom was sitting on her lap in the hospital chapel. She told me that she was going to go live with God and that I wouldn't be able to come with her. At the time, I didn't know what that meant. But she put her hand right here." He pressed a hand against his heart. "And she told me that she'd always be right here and that I'd be able to feel her when I thought about her. And that feeling would mean that she was watching over me." He took a deep breath, then continued. "She told me that feeling was my reminder that God would always love me and be with me, no matter where I was or what I was doing. All I had to do was pray." He looked back up at Lucia, his eyes bright. "So, yeah, I really prayed and I really believed that my prayers would be answered."

NINE

"**I** wondered why you were in the hospital chapel that day," Lucia said.

"I'd seen a picture of it in the paper and was curious."

"And chapels hold a special place in your heart."

Rafe nodded at her insight. "I know that my prayers are heard no matter where I pray, but—" he paused, then grinned "—I always seem to have a better connection in a hospital chapel."

"I can understand why."

They talked a while longer before leaving the pizza house and driving back to Lucia's townhome. When they got out of his SUV and he walked her to the door, she was all too conscious of her mandate that she didn't date. And that she had kissed him this morning. And that he'd promised the next time—*the next time*—a kiss would be only about them.

"It's been a really lovely day," she told him as she unlocked the door.

"It has," he agreed, his hands stuffed in the pockets of his jacket.

"I'll call you on Thursday and we'll set up going to Breckenridge on Friday."

"That sounds good," he said.

She stared at him, feeling more awkward by the second. "Maybe I'll see you at church in the morning," he said.

"You go to the Good Shepherd?"

He nodded. "The eight-thirty service."

Her brothers always went to that service, but she usually went to the ten o'clock service. She decided that she must have been blind to have never noticed him there before. "In the morning, then."

He leaned forward, and she had that heady, breathless anticipation of his kiss…which landed high on her cheek. "Good night, Lucia." And he turned and trotted down the steps to his car.

"'Night." Leave it to him to be a gentleman. That knowledge didn't keep her from being disappointed.

The following morning, Lucia sat down on the church pew next to her brother Peter, who was in silent prayer. His wife, Emily, sat on his other side, their small son on her lap. Lucia closed her eyes and took a breath, seeking the Presence she usually found in church. Though she didn't immediately feel it, she knew it was because of the chatter in her mind that came with worry. Still the chatter, and she would feel the Presence, just as she always did. Taking a deep breath, she began her own silent prayer. A prayer for her father's recovery was first, and the well-being of her family was next, as always. Then a prayer for the quick resolution of Chief O'Brien's investigation so she could return to full duty. And patience to let things unfold in their own time, she tacked on. And finally, she asked for guidance to know how to handle her attraction to Rafael Wright.

Everything about him suggested that he was a good man, but she no longer trusted her own ability to assess that. The doubting what-ifs had kept her from sleeping well and were driving her crazy. She wished she could trust that Rafe truly was the man he appeared to be. Knowing that he prayed and that he shared her faith reassured her, but not quite enough for her to let go of her fears.

"Give me guidance," she silently prayed, *"to recognize the truth."*

As if realizing she was finished, Peter squeezed her hand and she leaned into him. Of her three brothers, he reminded her most of their father—maybe because like their father, he had been a CIA agent and had developed some of those same strengths and sensibilities. She wasn't about to pour her heart out to him, but she longed for some of his ability to instinctively know what was true and what wasn't.

Shortly after sitting down, her brother Travis slid into the pew on her other side with Tricia next to him. After bowing his head in prayer for a few moments, Travis bent his head toward Lucia's and whispered, "Nice dress. What's the occasion?"

She instantly took offense, much as she had been doing with her brothers' comments all her life, and nudged him with her elbow, whispering, "No occasion. Can't I put on something new without you saying something?"

He put his hands up in surrender. "Sorry."

She folded her hands in her lap and took a breath. The truth was that she had spent a lot of time deciding what to wear. Knowing that she was going to see Rafe, she wanted to look nice. To be as beautiful as he had told her she was. Normally, she threw on a pair of dress slacks, a sweater and a blazer. This morning, though, she had pulled from the closet the dress her mother had given her for Christmas, which she hadn't worn yet. Lucia had stared at herself in the mirror for a long time after putting on the deep burgundy dress that had tone-on-tone embroidery across the bodice. Her usual ponytail looked juvenile with the dress, so she left her hair down.

Instead of feeling pretty, like she wanted, she felt like a stranger in her own skin. During that final confrontation with Felini when she had given back the engagement ring, he had been scathing of her as a woman, criticizing her choice in profession and her tomboy ways, including how she dressed.

Colleen had insisted his criticism said more about his insecurity as a man than about her as a woman. In her head, Lucia agreed. In her heart, though, she wasn't so sure.

"God forgive me for my vanity," she silently prayed.

Moments later, the choir took its place, along with her brother Sam, who was playing the keyboard this morning. They stood to sing the first hymn, which was followed by the bible reading and the sermon.

"Our reading this morning is from Job 22, verse 12," Reverend Dawson said from the pulpit. "'Does not God live high in the heavens, does He not see the zenith of the stars?' You may recall this question to Job comes at a time when he is seeking answers to his multitude of problems, just as you may be. I tell you, friends, that God can help you with every decision, large and small, where you work and in your home."

As always, Lucia found that Reverend Dawson was somehow speaking directly to her when he advised that she couldn't depend on her own mind alone, primarily because that thinking is what created the problem. "You have to go to a Higher mind," he said, "and a Higher thinking. Conventional wisdom says you must begin at the bottom. Instead, I tell you, begin at the top, where God is. By beginning at the top, full of awareness of Divine direction and instruction, you'll be above the toil, the stress and the strain." He went on to remind her that Divine direction would help her find the work she was meant to do, even if she seemed on a detour at any given moment.

"Let us pray," he said at the end of the sermon. *"We ask You, God, to help with every decision. For each of us today,*

I ask. Help me wisely use my time. Help us work together to make a difference. Guide me to the people where I can be Your blessing and make a difference. Lord, guide and direct my life so I make a positive difference." He went on to include prayers for healing for many church members, including her father, then had the congregation join in the Lord's Prayer.

After the final hymn, Lucia walked out of the church with her brothers and their families. Happy as she was to be with them, she watched for Rafe. She hung around with her brothers until the crowd thinned and the people waiting to go into the ten o'clock service had entered the church.

Much to her disappointment, Rafe was nowhere to be seen. Unfair as the comparison was, she found herself thinking about all the times that her ex-fiancé had promised to come to church with her and never shown up. Long after the ten o'clock service had begun and it was clear that anyone coming to church would already be there, she drove home.

Disgruntled and annoyed with herself that she was, she took off her shoes the minute she got into her house. Gelo greeted her as usual, but the routine didn't comfort her as it usually did.

She was on her way upstairs to change her clothes when the doorbell rang. Remembering that Felini had been on the other side of the door yesterday morning, she peered through the peephole. Rafe stood on the stoop. Her heart clinched, which left her wondering if it would always be like this with him.

"Hi," he said after she opened the door. He was wearing the leather jacket and jeans. His glance slid away from hers as he encompassed the dress. "You look great."

"Want to come in?" The compliment simultaneously warmed her and annoyed her. She liked knowing he thought she was pretty and hated that she wished he had told her so when she was dressed in her usual clothes.

He slipped past her into the house. "Did you just come from church?"

"Yes," she said, deciding not to add that she had chosen to go to the earlier service in the hope of seeing him.

"I wanted to be there," he said. "But my sister Julie called—the one who lives in Atlanta."

"Is she okay?" Lucia asked.

"Hanging in there. Her husband moved out and she's having some problems. And I've been her sounding board. She doesn't want the marriage to end, but she's also fed up."

"And you drove over here to tell me that?"

He shook his head, his grin a little sheepish. "No. I came to tell you I'm going to be out of town for a few days. I'm going to Bozeman to teach a class. I'm filling in for a friend who broke his leg yesterday." Jamming his hands in his pockets, he met her gaze full on and added, "And I worried about that."

"Why?"

He took a single step closer. "Because of yesterday and what you told me about wanting someone you could count on, someone who kept his word." One more step closer. "And that's the kind of guy I want to be for you."

"Oh." *The kind of guy he wanted to be for her.* That echoed through her head and lodged in her heart. Oh, how she wanted to believe him.

He grinned. "Even though we're not dating."

She had no idea what to say to that. Last night had felt like a date.

"I felt like I was breaking my word to you when I missed church this morning."

"You were there for your sister—that was important," she replied, meaning it. "When will you be back?"

The grin widened. "In time to go to Breckenridge with you on Friday."

The dread that had momentarily constricted her chest eased, and she sighed.

"And I wanted to give you my cell phone number."

She liked that he wanted her to have it. "When are you leaving?" she asked, heading for the kitchen drawer next to the phone where she kept her address book.

"In a couple of hours."

She opened it to the correct page and wrote down his name, then his phone number when he gave it to her.

"You came over here just to give me your number?"

He shook his head. "I came because I wanted to see you."

He had followed her across the room and was close enough to touch if she had been brave enough to reach out.

He took that final step toward her, so close she could see the deep jade circle around the edges of his irises. So close she could smell his shaving cream. So close…

"I came for this," he whispered, then lowered his head slowly as though giving her all the time in the world to step away.

She didn't but instead waited. The moment of waiting stretched tautly. At last, his lips touched hers.

She sighed. This was exactly where she wanted to be, and she put her arms around him.

Like yesterday morning, the leather of his jacket was smooth and soft beneath her fingertips, and the skin of his cheek smooth-shaven next to her own. His arms came around her, renewing that sense of being cherished. Too soon, he lifted his head.

"See you Friday," he said.

"Yes." She wasn't ready to step out of his hug. Not quite yet.

He kissed her again, then hurried out the door.

She followed him to the door and watched him back out of the parking space, then wave at her when he looked toward her.

He'd been right about the kiss, she thought. This one had been only about them. And it reawakened dreams she had long ago put away.

For reasons she didn't understand, that made her cry.

"Here you are," Colleen said to Lucia a couple of days later, coming to a stop at the entrance of her cubicle. "This place is more confusing than the offices of the *Colorado Springs Sentinel*."

Happy for the interruption, Lucia looked up from her mountain of paperwork to see her friend. With a grin, she said, "Investigative journalism at its finest—a quest of find your way through the gray cubes."

"Something like that." Grinning, Colleen moved one of the stacks of paper to the side and propped a hip on the corner of the desk. "I came down to get a statement from Chief O'Brien about the latest in the investigation on the hospital fire."

"Nobody was really surprised that it was arson," Lucia said, repeating what she had heard on the news last night.

"Yeah, but what I can't figure out is why anybody would want to set fire to a hospital. That just doesn't add up."

"I take it that you talked with my brother."

Colleen nodded. "He and Becca seem to think that if there was a real threat, something more direct would have been done to get close to your father. And since that wasn't the case, they don't think it was related to your dad at all." She took a breath, then smiled at Lucia. "Actually, that's very good news. Leaves me without a story, but hey! I can live with that."

"I'm sure you'll dig up another one," Lucia said drily.

"You mean like the new guy in your life?"

The feelings Lucia had about that were too fresh to be shared, so she shook her head. "There's no new guy."

"This is me you're talking to," Colleen said, "your good, good friend. The one who covers for you sometimes, I might add." When Lucia met her gaze, she added, "Brendan told me that you had invited Rafe to Breckenridge this weekend."

"He likes to ski," Lucia said, knowing full well how lame that sounded.

Colleen laughed. "Oh, girl! I'm liking this better by the minute. You're going down hard."

"I'm not falling in love," Lucia insisted. Silently, her mind tacked on "yet." "I'm just…" Just what, she wondered? There was no fooling Colleen, especially since they had been sharing their deepest longings with each other for more than a decade.

"I think you're just looking the man over," Colleen said, "and it's about time." She touched the end of Lucia's ponytail. "You might think about a new do. Or at least getting these split ends trimmed."

"Maybe. But no manicures. No pedicures."

"And no more visiting," came Chief Neil O'Brien's voice from next to the cubicle. He frowned at them both. "See your friends on your own time, Vance."

Colleen slid off the end of the desk. "Actually, Chief O'Brien, I was on my way to see you, and since you weren't in your office, I came by to ask Lucia what she thought about the investigation into the hospital fire so far."

O'Brien glared at Lucia but answered Colleen, "As you know, the only comments that carry any weight are those that come through the public information officer. I suggest you contact him."

Colleen smiled, the professional one that didn't hide the steel in her tone. "I did, and he told me that I should talk to you about whether there are any suspects."

"For what?"

"Setting the fire. Do you have any leads on who the arsonist might be?"

Chief O'Brien looked her up and down. "I don't have any intention of answering that question." He pointed a finger at Lucia. "And if there's one scrap of news that can be traced back to you, Vance, I'm going to recommend you be dismissed."

"I—"

"Don't even bother to deny anything," he interrupted. "I know exactly what kind of person you are."

"And I know what kind of person *you* are," Colleen interrupted, her earlier effervescence dissolving. "Rumor on the street, Chief O'Brien, is that you're up to your ears in gambling debts."

"You print that and I'll be suing you for slander."

"Only if it's not true," she said with a shrug.

"Get out before I have you thrown out," O'Brien ordered, his face turning red.

Colleen winked at Lucia and sauntered down the aisleway between the gray cubicles as though she owned the place.

Lucia wasn't even aware she had stood up until Chief O'Brien turned around to face her.

"Just what did she say about the arson investigation?" he demanded, loud enough that Lucia could see a couple of people peeking over the top of the gray cubicles.

"Only what she told you," Lucia said.

"Reporters," he muttered, then added, "Get back to work, Vance."

Get back to work, Lucia silently echoed, eyeing the mountain of busywork he had piled onto her desk. More than ever, she longed to be back at the firehouse, where her real work was.

TEN

"Welcome to mayhem," a slender redhead said as Rafe and Lucia came through the door of the condo in Breckenridge. She hugged Lucia and stuck her hand out to him, her smile welcoming. "I'm Chloe. You must be Rafe. Brendan said you two live in the same building."

"Just down the hall," Rafe confirmed, returning her smile and taking in the chaos around them, a stark contrast to the night outside, where lazy snowflakes were falling out of a black sky.

When Lucia had told him that Brendan and his fiancée would also be here, he'd known there would be kids. He simply hadn't considered how many there might be. The living room was burgeoning with them, along with the accompanying activity and noise.

A couple of little girls were engaged in a board game of some kind, squealing and laughing. A pair of toddlers were throwing big LEGO blocks at each other and ignoring the television that blared a basketball game at a bored-looking teenage boy sprawled on the couch.

"Sam and Jessica are here, too?" Lucia asked as the twins noticed her and crawled toward her at warp speed.

"I thought you knew," Chloe said.

Sam? Rafe thought. Lucia's brother Sam? The one so determined to make sure Rafe knew his place as an outsider? Great.

"No." Lucia knelt and kissed one child, then the other. She glanced back at Rafe. "These two darlings are Dario and Isabella—they belong to Sam and Jessica. Over there, you have Madison—"

"She's mine," Chloe interrupted.

"And Amy, who is also Sam and Jessica's."

"And that's Kyle," Chloe inserted. "Also mine. You and I are sharing the north bedroom. The bachelors are taking the bunks in the loft."

"And we get to sleep on an airbed right here next to the fireplace," said one of the little girls with a giggle.

"Where is everybody else?" Lucia asked.

"Brendan and Sam are picking up Chinese food, and Jessica went to the grocery store to get milk and makings for breakfast."

"We'll have plenty, then." Lucia extracted herself from the twins, who bounced along behind her with all the enthusiasm and grace of puppies, taking the bag of groceries that had been in her arms toward the kitchen. "We brought juice and bagels."

Still wrapping his head around the fact that he had Lucia's brother to deal with on top of all the kids, Rafe followed with his own bag of groceries.

"That's the first load," Lucia said.

"Kyle," Chloe called, "put on your coat and give Rafe a hand."

Instead of the protest typical of teenage boys, the kid got up, gave Rafe a rueful smile and retrieved his jacket from a peg next to the door.

As Rafe headed in that direction, Lucia called to him. "I know you weren't expecting Sam, but don't you dare leave me here alone with him," she said with a grin.

"Alone?" Deliberately, he glanced around the room, then back at her. "You've got a strange definition of *alone*." Outside, snow was still drifting from the sky, which made him smile. If this kept up for the night, by morning there'd be a nice layer of powder, which meant the skiing would be great. A day like that was one to look forward to, and since he'd get to ski with Lucia, it was doubly so.

"Ah, peace and quiet," Kyle said with such fervor that Rafe laughed.

"Is it always that noisy?"

The teenager shrugged his shoulders. "Don't know. This is our first time here."

He and Kyle went down a shoveled walkway toward the parking lot, toward Lucia's SUV. "Did you ski today?"

"Nah, we just got here," Kyle said. "Tomorrow will be my first time."

"No kidding." Rafe unlocked the door and reached inside for Lucia's small suitcase and his duffel bag. "I remember my first time. I was ten and I loved it."

"Brendan said I need lessons, so he signed me up for a half day in the morning." Kyle hoisted the duffel bag over his shoulder. "Just what I wanted—to spend the morning on a bunny slope with a bunch of little kids like my sister."

"You might be surprised," Rafe said, reaching for the skis strapped to the top of the vehicle. "You might find yourself taking lessons with a pretty girl."

"A guy can hope."

Rafe laughed. "I bet you get the hang of it in no time and become a master of the greenies by the end of the day."

"Greenies?"

"The easy slopes. You'll have a good time."

Kyle managed a grin. "And you're sure about that girl?"

"More sure about the powder, but chances are good." The

statement left Rafe thinking about the girl he'd hoped to spend time with, nice quality alone time where they could talk, get to know each other better, hold hands and maybe sneak in a few kisses.

As they brought in bags and equipment, Rafe learned that Brendan and Chloe were only recently engaged and planning to marry soon, though Kyle didn't know when. They talked more about skiing and Kyle's scheduled snowboarding lesson the following day.

Sam, Jessica and Brendan returned minutes later, and the decibel level in the condo went up as well. Brendan slapped Rafe on the back with a "Great to see you, bud" before Chloe's daughter snagged him and dragged him off to join the board game she and Amy were playing. From across the room, Sam held up a soft drink in a salute—at least, Rafe hoped it was that and not a challenge to survive the utter chaos surrounding them all.

So much for hoping for a romantic evening with Lucia, who had the two toddlers hanging on to her. No wonder she had been so good with Ramón and Teresa at the zoo. Unlike him, she'd had practice with more than one child at a time.

Sam and Jessica set out the cartons of Chinese food in the middle of the coffee table, along with paper plates, and they all gathered around, sitting mostly on the floor.

"Want some applesauce?" Lucia asked Dario, pulling him onto her lap.

"We're going to watch *The Little Mermaid* after dinner," Madison said, earning a groan from Kyle, while Sam said to Brendan, "We've been processing the evidence collected from Harry Redding's apartment."

"The guy who committed suicide?" Brendan questioned while Jessica said, "No business tonight, Sam."

"The guy who ran me off the road," Chloe added. "I'm also

sure he's the man who attacked me and your dad that night at the hospital."

"And that's why we had a crime-scene investigation unit comb through his apartment," Sam explained. "They turned up a couple of interesting and strange things. You know that missing foreman from Michael's ranch? His name was found on a sheet of paper in Redding's apartment."

"Sam," Jessica said, "you promised."

He squeezed Jessica's hand, his attention still on Brendan. "Along with Alastair Barclay's."

That name was familiar, but Rafe couldn't remember where he'd heard it. The connection was clearly important because Brendan's head came up. Since Brendan was an FBI agent and the news reporters had repeatedly emphasized that the FBI was investigating Mayor Vance's shooting, Rafe figured this was somehow related.

"Up," Isabella said, patting Rafe's knee, then holding her arms out to him. Dutifully, he picked her up while Brendan asked, "Any fingerprint matches come back from IAFIS yet?"

"Nope," Sam said, "but Redding had a couple of bogus driver's licenses with other names, so chances are good that we don't know his real name yet."

Isabella patted Rafe's cheek and gave him a beguiling smile when he looked at her. "Play ball?"

"Later," he promised, "after we've eaten."

"I'm going for a walk," Kyle grumbled. "A guy can't even hear himself think around here."

Isabella reached a grubby hand for Rafe's plate, and Jessica grabbed the child out of his arms with a "How about some applesauce, like your brother?"

"Don't go too far," Chloe said to her son, then asked, "Wasn't Alastair Barclay the guy running that drug cartel that you busted last year?"

Brendan nodded. "He was killed in prison a few weeks ago."

"Is it okay, Mom, if we watch a movie?" Amy was asking as Kyle went through the door.

"No movies tonight," Jessica said to her older daughter while settling the younger one on her lap. "Kyle's right. It's pretty noisy right now."

"Mom," Amy whined.

When Madison opened her mouth, Chloe shook her head and said, "Tomorrow evening."

Across the table, Lucia caught Rafe's eye, her nephew held in her arms. The child's face—and Lucia's sweater—were smeared with the applesauce he was busy feeding himself.

"Welcome to my world," she said with a smile. Her expression was warm and content as she leaned a cheek against Dario's shiny dark brown hair.

Teasing as the comment was, Rafe realized she spoke the truth. In her world, dinner conversations included both ongoing investigations and the mundane stuff of family life. In her world, her family would always be an integral part of her life.

In his mind's eye, he looked forward a couple of years. The quiet romantic nights he'd imagined with her would be rare, he decided. Often as not, there'd likely be family and friends around, the climate noisy and boisterous, just like now. He tested that thought and didn't find it quite as terrifying as he thought he would. Anticipation curled through him, along with that feeling in his gut that he trusted.

He was in the right place, and this was the right woman. In his head, he heard the echo of his dad's voice all those years ago when he was first adopted. *Wright place, Wright time, Wright family.*

"Noisy, huh?" Chloe said.

He nodded. "Do you ever get used to it?"

From the other side of Chloe, Brendan laughed, though his eyes remained speculative as though he was still thinking about what Sam had told him. "Nope. You just learn to tune it out."

"And this is only a tiny portion of the clan," Chloe said. "I was pretty overwhelmed the first time."

Brendan put a companionable arm around his fiancée. "Don't let her fool you. She's still overwhelmed."

"What about you, Wright? Overwhelmed yet?" Sam asked with a grin that almost took the sting out of his question from the other side of the coffee table.

"No." Rafe met the man's gaze, recognizing the challenge. "I've been in hotter fires."

Brendan laughed. "You tell him, Rafe."

Sam's glower melted as Dario clambered out of Lucia's lap and into his. "What he's trying to say is you get to choose your friends but not your relatives."

"And now he's family," Brendan said. "All because his cousin Holly married my cousin—"

"Jake?" Rafe asked, grinning at the surprised expression on Sam's face. "I heard about that."

"And you remembered," Jessica filled in. "I'm impressed."

Brendan chuckled. "Family or not, my badge is bigger than Sam's."

Chloe rolled her eyes. "Not that again."

"Personally," Lucia piped in, "if you're looking for real help, you need a firefighter, not a guy carrying a badge."

"Or a nurse," Chloe added.

"Fi fighter," Dario said from Sam's lap.

"You're hired, kid," Rafe promptly said, raising his soft drink to Sam in an echo of his earlier salute and finding himself surprisingly relaxed in the midst of the chaos. This wasn't so different from the testing period new recruits went through when they joined his hotshot crew. He could do this.

Even so, Sam's question about being overwhelmed echoed through his head. Rafe admitted to himself that he was, but no way was he going to let Sam know that. He caught Lucia's smile. No way at all. Not when her smile lit up all the dark places in his lonely heart.

Getting the kids to bed was a huge undertaking that Rafe decided was a reality check for his ticking biological clock. He never would have imagined there were so many last-minute drinks of water, searches for favorite stuffed animals and bedtime stories before things quieted down. Kyle returned from his walk with the news that it was still snowing before heading for his bunk, headphones over his ears. While Sam and Jessica settled the twins, Rafe helped Brendan blow up the air mattress and make up the bed where Madison and Amy would sleep. When the little girls returned from one of the bedrooms with Chloe and Lucia, all scrubbed and ready for bed in their fuzzy slippers and pajamas, Rafe developed an unexpected lump in his throat. No doubt about it—they looked like little dolls. All too easily, he imagined what Lucia's daughter would look like.

"I'm making a cup of tea," Lucia said after the girls had said their prayers and were snuggled into bed. "Anyone else want anything?"

"A cup of your green tea?" Jessica asked, coming down the stairs. "That sounds good."

Following her, Sam made an exaggerated shudder. "Coffee, anyone?"

"I knew you'd say that," Lucia returned. "It's already made."

After the beverages were served, they gathered around the kitchen table, the only illumination from the light above the stove in deference to getting the two little girls to sleep in the adjoining room.

"Peace and quiet at last," Chloe said after taking a sip of her tea.

"Tomorrow night they'll be tired," Brendan said.

Sam chuckled. "We can only hope."

"Okay if we talk business for a minute, big brother?" Lucia asked, her glance sliding to his wife. "Even though you promised?"

"Sure, sis," he returned. "What's on your mind?"

"I've been talking to Ben Johnson."

Rafe looked at her more closely at the mention of the chief arson investigator's name.

"According to him, the fire at the hospital could have been a lot more serious. Right before the explosion, I smelled lacquer." She glanced at Brendan. "At the time, I remember thinking it was odd, and I couldn't quite put my finger on what it was until I was in the finishing room at your brother's carpentry shop the other day."

"Ben told me lacquer was the accelerant for the fire," Rafe said. "Whoever chose it had to have known it had highly flammable vapors."

"That's sort of an odd thing to use," Sam said.

"Unless the arsonist was working on a construction crew," Brendan said.

"Or trying to make it look that way," Rafe interjected. "Ben told me the same thing, so I asked around. Because of all the fumes, the millwork was finished before it was brought on site."

"Maybe it was used for touch-ups," Sam said.

"Doubtful." Rafe picked up his coffee cup. "I think the arsonist put an open container in the storage closet with the lid cracked open so it would seep vapors. I also think he miscalculated. A pint of the stuff giving off vapors would have been plenty to give you a hot, out-of-control fire. Ben said there was a gallon, which was what caused the explosion."

Sam said, "That sounds—"

"Sinister?" Chloe interrupted.

Rafe looked around the table. "What else would a deliberate fire in a hospital be?" He looked at Lucia. "If I was investigating this fire, I'd want to know why Lucia was sent into this without her partner and why her chief is so determined to place the responsibility at her door."

"Are you drawing the line I think you are?" Brendan asked. "That there's a connection between O'Brien and the fire?"

Rafe looked from Brendan to Sam. "It's worth checking out, don't you think?"

"Somebody should take a look at the security tapes around the entrance to the hospital," Jessica suggested.

Sam nodded. "First thing Monday morning."

Lucia's expression became so pensive that Rafe wished he had brought this up with Sam alone. If his hunch was right, she had been deliberately placed in harm's way. And she now knew it, too.

The following morning, Lucia was looking forward to a day of skiing even more than she usually did. She loved the sport far more than her brothers, and it was the one thing she did better than they, which gave her an ongoing sense of satisfaction. Competitive as she was about skiing with her brothers, she didn't feel that way about Rafe. Quite simply, she wanted to spend time with him doing one of her favorite things. Based on their discussions, she knew he held the same passion for skiing that she did.

After a hearty breakfast, they were out the door in plenty of time to walk with Kyle to the ski school while Brendan and Chloe headed to the ice skating rink with Madison and Amy. Sam and Jessica decided to stay behind at the condo until it warmed up a little, and Lucia promised that she'd return from skiing early so they could get a couple of runs in.

The morning was one of those gorgeous winter days, with a sky so blue and snow so sparkling white it made Lucia's eyes hurt.

"I'll come ski with you this afternoon after your class," Rafe said to Kyle, "unless you're busy with that pretty girl and you brush me off."

Lucia nudged Kyle with her elbow. "What's this about pretty girls?" she teased. "You're supposed to be learning to ski."

He ducked his head a little, and Rafe said, "Just providing a little incentive, that's all."

"I was studying the trail map last night. Where are you going this morning?" Kyle asked.

"Tiger," Lucia said, naming her favorite ski run and glancing at Rafe. "Or maybe we should warm up on Briar Rose first."

He smiled, revealing his dimple. "You know the mountain better than I do. I'll follow your lead."

Waving goodbye to Kyle at the ski school, Lucia and Rafe got in line for the lift that would take them to the top of Peak 9.

At the top of the first run, they paused a moment as she looked out over the landscape. White snow with a layer of virgin powder, the crystal-blue sky and the dark charcoal-green of the pines were always beautiful to her.

"Every time I get to the top of a mountain, I understand where the phrase *God's country* comes from," Rafe said, leaning on his ski poles with the ease of a man supremely comfortable in the environment. He was dressed all in black, his equipment top of the line and well cared for.

"I know what you mean." Lucia adjusted her mittens and made sure her ski cap was pulled around her ears to keep out the biting cold. "Are you ready?"

"Ladies first."

Lucia pushed off, leaning forward so she was balanced over the center of her skis, enjoying the feel of the snow. A quick glance behind her confirmed Rafe was right with her, the expression on his face a reflection of how she felt. He was enjoying this as much as she was.

Her attention then became totally focused on the run in front of her. Once, she had dreamed of being a downhill skier, which had been met with tremendous resistance by her family, her brothers successful in convincing her parents that of all the winter sports, this was the most dangerous and the one least suitable for her. A small part of her acknowledged that was why she loved it—because it was dangerous, because her brothers told her she shouldn't, couldn't do it. And yet, she never felt more alive than she did right now, the smooth slide of her skis over the snow, the crisp air filling her lungs and the knowledge she was good at this.

The rush was the same one she had felt from Rafe's kiss.

That tiny break in her concentration was all it took to lose her balance as she leaned into a turn. In the next instant, she was sliding down the slope on her back, one of her skis thankfully snapping off her boot. Above her, the sky, clouds and trees swirled into a kaleidoscope of brilliant, changing colors. No longer in control, all she could do was ride out the fall, praying she wouldn't hit a tree.

ELEVEN

Rafe's heart stopped when he saw her go down. Her ski popped off just as it was supposed to do and went careening down the slope. Lucia was sliding on her side, headed toward a copse of trees on the edge of the run. His prayer for her safety was automatic as he raced toward her. By the time he reached her, she had plowed into a bank of snow. He skidded to a halt next to her, terrified that she'd be unconscious, hurt. Or worse.

"Lucia."

She rolled onto her back, her dark eyes dancing, an enormous smile curving her lips. "I love that," she said around a bubbling laugh.

"Falling?" He dug in his downhill ski, unreasonably furious with her. "Scaring ten years off my life?"

"It's as close as you can come to flying," she said.

"Until you kill yourself."

She sat up, her smile fading. "Don't give me a hard time, Rafe. I watched you, and you love this as much as I do."

"I also know my own limits."

"You think I don't?" The last of her smile faded as she planted one of her ski poles and stood, balancing her weight on her remaining ski. "Well, I'll tell you one thing. I don't need one more guy in my life telling me what I can do or what I should do or how I need to be more careful or how—"

"Hold on just a second," he said, reaching an arm toward her.

She gazed up at him, shaking, and he recognized the adrenaline rush that was setting in, even if she didn't.

"My whole life I've had people telling me how careful I'm supposed to be. Careful is boring, careful is—"

"I was out of line saying that you don't know your own limits."

Surprise flared in her eyes.

"But you did scare a year off my life." He reached for her hand. "I didn't intend to yell at you, honest."

"That's a very nice apology, Rafael Wright."

"But?"

"But I really don't want to be coddled."

He drew back a fraction so he could meet her eyes. "Because you're tough."

A reluctant smile curved her lips. "Yeah, something like that."

"You've spent your whole life wanting to be faster and stronger than your brothers, haven't you?"

"You forgot smarter," she added with a full-fledged smile.

"You don't have to prove anything to me, Lucia," he whispered.

Her expression turned solemn. "I have everything to prove to myself." She stared down the slope. "We're not going to get off this mountain by standing here talking, are we?"

With that, she pulled her ski cap more firmly over her ears and adjusted her ski poles. Clearly, she was going to try skiing down the slope on one ski. He'd done it, and he knew just how much pressure doing so put on the skiing leg. After a fall like hers, he admired her for even trying it.

She pushed off, and Rafe stayed right with her. Several

turns later, she came to a stop, putting her ski-less boot down and giving her leg a rest.

"I see your ski," he said, pointing with one of his poles. It was maybe another twenty yards down the slope.

Lucia repeated the process, skiing a couple of turns, then .resting her leg. As soon as she was close to her runaway ski, Rafe retrieved it from the deep powder at the edge of the run.

When Lucia reached him, she once again had a wide smile on her face. "A day skiing, even on one leg, is better than just about any other, don't you think?"

"It's my idea of a perfect day," he said. "I know we're not dating." He paused while she rolled her eyes, her mouth still curved in the smile that lit the inside of his heart. "But if we were, there are two more things I find really attractive in a woman."

"And I suppose you're going to tell me."

"Maybe." He handed her the ski. "Or maybe I should just keep it to myself that…"

She stepped into the binding of her ski, then looked up at him. "That?"

"You don't whine, and you love to ski."

"You could be talking about a hundred women," she said over her shoulder as she headed down the slope, thankfully at something short of her previous breakneck speed.

He caught up with her, and they skied side by side the rest of the way down the mountain, turning in unison, the only sound the slice of their skies through the snow until they were closer to the bottom. In the distance, the village of Brecken-ridge went from dollhouse proportions to full size before it disappeared behind the stands of pine trees.

They ate a nutrition bar during the next lift ride, which took them to the very top of Peak 9. Across the valley to the east, tall peaks shimmered with last night's snowfall. Here, the ski slope was once again marked as a black double diamond—

the designation for the most difficult slopes, runs only for expert skiers. Much as he loved the challenge—and the speed—he hoped Lucia was as unaffected by her earlier fall as she seemed.

"Ready?" she asked him. When he nodded, she added, "I'll follow you this time."

He would have rather followed her so he could keep an eye on her. That would be coddling, though, so he pushed off and immediately gained speed. He understood why Lucia had leaned into her skis like a downhill racer earlier, and he was tempted to do the same thing. Today was about companionship, though, not pushing himself, so he simply let the slope guide him down the run.

When the double diamond run eased into a more gentle one, he slowed until she caught up with him, then they skied side by side as they had before. After two more runs, it was time for Rafe to meet Kyle and for Lucia to head back to the condo.

"How about a movie tonight?" Rafe asked as they took off their skis. When she glanced at him, he grinned. "Not a date movie, just a movie."

As she did every time he put his non-date qualifier on, she rolled her eyes, her teasing expression suggesting that he'd lost his mind. He probably had.

"Of course, if it's not a date," he drawled, "there can't be any good-night kiss."

"Then maybe it should be a date movie," she said.

"That was a good movie," Rafe said that evening after they had come out of the theater in the middle of Breckenridge Village and found a table at a nearby coffee shop.

Lucia supposed that it had been. She had been too aware of Rafe sitting next to her to pay close attention to it. All she knew for sure was that the romantic drama had ended on a bittersweet note, where the hero and heroine hadn't ended up together at the end. Personally, she liked clear-cut happy endings—maybe because of all the trauma her own family had been through over the past long months. Maybe because her brothers had found their own true loves. Maybe because she wanted that for herself. She didn't dare look at Rafe while that thought was in her head.

"Lucia?" he asked.

She met his gaze and smiled. "It was a good movie. It just had me thinking, that's all."

"Thinking?" he teased. "Oh, no."

She laughed.

"Anything you can share?" he asked.

She shook her head. "Nothing that earth-shattering. I've just been thinking about all that has happened to my family over the last couple of years and how going through stuff would be easier if you knew the writer had scripted a happy ending for you."

Rafe reached across the table and took her hand. "The Writer has scripted a happy ending for you." He studied their clasped hands for a moment, then added, "If God is the writer of our lives the way somebody writes a book or a movie, and if God is Love the way the Bible teaches us, then how could there be anything but a happy ending, as you put it, no matter what happens to us along the way?"

The constriction in her chest eased. Rafe was speaking the language that had been part of her family all her life. "Yes," she breathed.

"So you already have that happy ending," he said.

"A reminder that I needed," she whispered.

Without letting go of her hand, he took a sip of the hot chocolate they had ordered a few minutes earlier, his gaze turned inward as though he was weighing what to say. When he looked at her a moment later, his eyes were as warm as the hot chocolate they were drinking.

"There's a verse from one of the Psalms I really like," he said, "that goes something like 'Your word is a lamp for my feet, a light on my path.'"

"I like that."

"Me, too," he said. "I think we sometimes have this idea that having faith means we're walking around on a really bright day where everything is perfect—"

"Like skiing today?"

He grinned and nodded. "But for me, it's often been more like having a night-light. As a kid, I was afraid of the dark, and I really hated going to a new foster home where it would be pitch black and if you woke up in the middle of the night, you were all disoriented. And, I'd be scared, too, because I wouldn't know if they were going to like me or if I was going to like them, you know?"

She nodded, his hand still clasped with hers.

"So I got a night-light and that thing was as precious to me as my mother's Bible. And after I found this verse, I figured faith in God is like a night-light. It doesn't take a real bright light to keep the darkness away. It only has to be enough to find your way."

"That's beautiful," she said softly. "I like the way your mind works."

"As opposed to?" he questioned, raising his eyebrows.

She shrugged. "Being a doubting Thomas, or worse, a cynic."

"What's worse?" he asked. "To be a cynic or a Pollyanna?"

She grinned. "That's easy. A cynic."

"I think so, too."

He thought so, too. Somehow that he did was important.

Pretending to study her cup of hot chocolate, she watched Rafe from the corner of her eye. He talked about God and his faith with the same ease that he skied, as though it was an integral part of him. An odd feeling because, except for the heated debates in college about religion, she didn't remember ever having a talk with anyone outside her family about it. Well, if she didn't count the increasingly contentious conversations she'd had with her ex-fiancé about religion. For him, church was a place to be seen, and he'd told her toward the end that he wasn't a believer and it was unfair of her to expect him to be.

Rafe's views so perfectly expressed what was in her heart that she felt warmed and terrified all at once. It would be an easy thing to fall in love with this man. A daunting prospect because she had promised herself she'd never be that vulnerable again.

With a flash of insight, she realized the only way to fall in love was to be vulnerable.

Their conversation returned to the movie they had just seen as they finished their hot chocolate, then walked hand in hand back to the condo. While they talked, Lucia kept thinking about the verse that Rafe had shared with her. *Your word is a lamp for my feet, a light on my path.* It so perfectly fit where things were in her life right now. It was as though Rafe had some special connection that she was both afraid to acknowledge and afraid to let go of for fear she might never find it again.

They came into the condo, which was a lot quieter than it had been the previous night. The four younger kids were gathered in front of the television, watching the video they had wanted to see last night. Rafe could see that Kyle was also watching, though he was pretending indifference as he doodled on a notebook in his lap. The two couples were gathered around the kitchen table, also subdued compared to last night.

Rafe figured the cause was simply being tired until Lucia asked, "What's going on?"

"Ken was in a plane that was shot down," Brendan said, clamping a hand over Sam's shoulder.

"Our cousin Ken?" Lucia asked, sitting down in a vacant chair.

"Who else would it be?" Sam demanded, his eyes rimmed in red.

Color leached out of her face.

"We don't know all that much yet," Jessica said.

Lucia reached a hand across the table toward her brother. "Is he dead—"

"No," Chloe said. "No. When your brother Peter called a little while ago, he didn't know what Ken's condition was, just that the wreckage had been found and he was rescued."

Lucia bowed her head a moment before looking back at the others. "You said shot down. So he was working?"

Brendan nodded, his jaw tight. "Yeah, he was working."

She reached for Rafe's hand, and an odd sense of relief shuddered through him that she seemed to need him in this moment. He clasped his hand around her fingers, which were cold.

Glancing at him, she said, "Ken is in the air force and his squadron flies reconnaissance missions in Latin America."

Sam slammed a fist against the table. "It's like we're a bunch of puppets and someone else is pulling all the strings."

"Do you think Baltasar Escalante has come back?" Lucia asked, giving voice to a whispered conversation she had overheard among her brothers a couple of weeks ago.

This name—and Alastair Barclay's from last night—was familiar to Rafe only because the news had been saturated with the breakup of a drug cartel and crime syndicate the previous year. Barclay had been caught, made some kind of deal for reduced prison time and had gone to jail. He'd been murdered a few months after sentencing. Escalante had somehow escaped and had been flying back to Latin America when his plane crashed.

"That's what Brendan has been wondering," Chloe said at the same time as Sam said, "There's no way he could have survived the plane crash."

"His body was never found?" Rafe asked.

"No, it never was," Sam said.

"And your cousin flies reconnaissance flights looking for drugs?" When both Brendan and Sam nodded, Rafe added, "I've never believed in coincidence."

"And now someone going by the name The Chief, also known as *El Jefe,* seems to be moving in on Escalante's old network," Sam said.

"This might be a stupid question," Rafe said, "but I thought Alastair Barclay was the head of the crime syndicate. The guy who was murdered in prison."

"He ran it, but Escalante was the real power," Brendan explained. "But you're on to something here." He snagged a sheet of paper off the counter and wrote down Alastair Barclay's and Escalante's names.

"Then there's Harry Redding, who left a suicide note, but appears to have some kind of link to Barclay and Hector Delgato," Sam said.

"And Delgato is?" Rafe asked.

"A foreman on our cousin Michael's ranch," Sam said.

"Who's missing," Lucia said. "He worked for Michael after his other foreman disappeared. Nobody knew what happened to Ben—"

"Until his body was found," Sam finished. "Ben was murdered."

"Is Delgato a suspect?" Rafe asked.

"Let's just say he's a person of interest," Sam said.

"Wait," Rafe said, "there's another murder in addition to your dad being shot? A murder connected to another member of your family?"

Sam nodded, watching as Brendan added that information to his list.

"Don't forget that Redding tried to kill me," Chloe said.

Brendan's eyes glittered as he looked up at his fiancée, his love for her a tangible thing. "I'm not likely to forget that."

"And now Ken's plane was shot down," Jessica said.

Rafe looked around the table. "And you're wondering if someone is out to get you?" He shook his head. "Like I said before, I don't put much stock in coincidence."

"At least the fire at the hospital doesn't appear to be related," Lucia said.

Rafe looked at her, wanting more than anything to confirm that it wasn't. This morning she had announced that careful was boring. Though this was a completely different situation, he was concerned that her safety depended on a healthy dose of caution. "What if it is? What if the arsonist is somehow involved in all the rest of this and *you* were the real target of the fire?"

"Murder by fire?" Sam scoffed. "Nobody would be that dumb."

"Devious," Rafe corrected. "And scheming and smart."

Brendan glanced toward Lucia, his eyes troubled. "Rafe could have a point. Prior to last year's investigation of Escalante, name a single time when so many things have happened." His gaze grew even more somber. "When members of our families have been targets."

"Then it's a good thing you're on light duty, sis," Sam said. "You need to talk to the chief to make sure it stays that way."

"I'm not going to do that," she said. "I want to be back on

active duty. You have no idea what it's like to be in the office with O'Brien gloating over me. At least at the station house, I have Donovan and Jackson to cover my back."

Sam shook his head. "No. You're staying on light duty. You're safer there. I'll go over your head if I have to."

"There you go again, assuming I can't take care of myself and that I need to be wrapped up and put on a shelf somewhere."

"If we're right about all this, you're in the line of fire," Sam said. "Pun intended, sis."

"I can take care of myself."

Sam's scowl grew more fierce. "And the way I heard it, you probably would have died the other day if Rafe hadn't saved your skin."

"That was an accident that could have happened to anybody."

"But it didn't happen to just anybody. It happened to a Vance," Sam retorted. "We care about you! Is that so hard to understand?"

Lucia stood. "And maybe you'd like to continue having this argument in front of everyone." She sucked in a shuddering breath. "Or maybe you'd like to save it for a more private time."

"Lucia," Sam said, standing, as well.

"Not now." She headed for the door. "I'm going for a walk."

Rafe watched her walk out, not at all sure what had happened but certain of one thing. This was simply the latest verse in a long-standing argument between the two.

"About the fire at the hospital," Rafe said, facing Sam and Brendan. "I don't have anything but a hunch and a few details about the other things going on with your family." He waved at the sheet of paper Brendan had been writing on. "But I'm convinced she was the target of the fire, and I think O'Brien is somehow involved."

TWELVE

Rafe headed for the front door, grabbing his leather jacket and going outside to find Lucia. Unlike last night, the sky was clear, and the temperature was bitterly cold, making him put on his knit cap. Overhead, the Milky Way was sprinkled like glistening snowflakes across a pitch-black sky. Zipping up his coat and burying his hands in its pockets, he headed for the parking lot, looking for some sign of Lucia.

A moment later, he saw the beacon of her off-white knit cap. She was walking on the sidewalk that led toward the center of town, and he hurried to catch up with her.

"Lucia, wait!"

She came to a stop, her shoulders slumped.

"Are you all right?" he asked when he came even with her.

She shook her head without looking at him.

"Okay if I walk with you?"

After an imperceptible pause, she nodded. He fell into step beside her, slowing his pace and the length of his strides to match hers, and held out his hand. She took it, her fingers cold against his, so he tucked it into the pocket of his jacket with his own. Without a word, they began walking toward the center of town. While he looked around, liking what he saw of the village, her head was bowed. Figuring the best thing he could do for her was to simply be in the silence with her, he didn't say anything.

Since she was clearly troubled, all he could do at the moment was offer a silent prayer for her that she'd find a way to make up with her brother, that she'd find a sense of peace for the things troubling her.

A block later, she said, "Talk about embarrassing. Just what you needed to hear. A fight between me and my brother."

"It happens. Don't be embarrassed on my account."

"Do you fight with your sisters?" she asked.

"Not much," he said. "They're older by four and seven years. That age difference seemed huge at the time I was first adopted, but it's not so much now. Plus, I wanted them to like me."

"Sam is three years older than me, and my whole life, he's acted as though the age difference gives him the right to tell me what to do." She uttered a soft laugh. "We've been fighting and making up our whole lives. We're close, and I love him, I really do. But he makes me so angry."

Rafe didn't know what to say to that, so he simply remained quiet.

A while later, she said, "I probably overreacted."

He mulled that over, decided there was no right answer, so kept quiet about that, too.

"I want back on full duty," she said. "I'm so sick of the busywork Chief O'Brien has me doing."

"I can understand that." He'd seen the mountain of paperwork that O'Brien had buried her under, and for someone who liked an active job, he could imagine how stifling she found it. "Personally, I hate being in the office."

They walked another block, and then she asked, "Do you agree with Sam? That I should stay on light duty?"

Rafe looked down at her. "I honestly don't know. The part I am sure about is that he's worried and he cares about you."

Inside the pocket of his jacket, her fingers tightened around his. "If I had followed my brothers' advice my whole life, I'd be sitting at home, mastering the finer points of knitting or embroidery."

"A stifling thing for a girl who likes to go fast."

"Yes," she breathed.

"And careful is boring."

"In the way they mean *careful,* yes."

"Maybe there's another way of looking at *careful,*" he said. When she glanced up at him, he added, "Maybe it's going into things with your eyes wide open and being as prepared as you can possibly be."

"I'm not sure what you mean," she said.

"Every summer," he replied, "I travel with a crew of sixteen men and women who put their safety in my hands. Before I take my people into a fire, I want to know everything I can about weather, humidity, tanker support, terrain, fuels for the fire and so on. I want to know about the emotional condition of every person on the crew. I want to know who's not eating enough or drinking enough water. I'm careful."

"Sounds more like prepared to me," Lucia said.

"Tell me the difference."

She was silent as they slowly walked another block down the mostly deserted street, where condos and motels had given way to storefronts that were all buttoned up for the night.

"*Prepared* equals *careful,*" she mused.

"*Careful* equals *prepared,* too."

"When you put it that way…" Her grudging tone gave way to a soft chuckle, and she smacked his shoulder with her free hand. "I see I can expect to lose arguments with you."

"I wasn't trying to win anything. This wasn't—isn't—an argument or a competition." He stopped walking and turned to face her, pressing her hand inside the pocket against his side. When she looked at him, he added, "Not everything is."

"I know."

"I'm not out to win anything." *Except your heart,* came his own silent admonishment. "But I do share one thing in common with Sam."

"What's that?"

He bent a little closer. "I believe you're a woman to be cherished—not put into some confining corner that you label as *careful.* Simply cherished."

Her breath came out on a sigh and all he could do then was kiss her. She leaned into him, kissing him back. Simply standing still without crushing her in his arms required every ounce of discipline. If he could stop time, he thought, this would be the moment. To simply absorb the feel of her against him, of the scent of her warm skin and of the cold winter night.

He was falling in love with her, and it was weeks too soon to tell her so.

"What are you doing here, Vance?" Chief O'Brien demanded a week later when she climbed out of the truck with the other members of her unit. They were all in their turnout gear, responding to a training fire.

"The same as you," she replied. "Training." She had signed up for the cross-training exercise weeks before the fire at the hospital. Today's scenario had a building engulfed by a fast-moving grass fire in this remote corner of Bear Creek Park. The burning building in front of them would be sacrificed for today's training and the site would become the new home for the park administrative offices.

"You're on light duty."

"I know." She met his challenging gaze with one of her

own. "Are you denying me the required training to keep current on my certification?"

"Of course not," he snapped. He stared at her a moment, then strode away.

"I wonder what's got his goat?" Donovan asked, pulling a length of hose off the rack.

"Who cares as long as he goes somewhere else." Lucia grabbed her ax and a coil of hose, then followed her partner toward the building.

There was no such thing as a perfect day for a fire, but if there had been, today would have been it, Lucia thought. The day was a cool March day with high humidity. No rain, no blizzard, no wind.

Fortunately, the day was nothing like the one imagined in their training exercise. According to the script, they were a small cog in a larger, unfolding disaster where a grass fire had grown to inferno proportions within a few minutes, surrounding this building and trapping people inside.

Their first order of business was to get any victims out of the building. Following protocol, Lucia and her partner searched from one room to the next, relaying information back to the incident commander outside.

With other members of the team, she and Luke immediately found two of the dummies—victims—and made note of their injuries, getting both out of the building and passing them off to EMTs, who were also participating in the exercise.

As Lucia worked with her fellow firefighters to extinguish the blaze, she was all too aware of the wildfire units also training. The controlled burn for the long grass eliminated the potential threat of a grass fire that could come within the next few weeks if the usual spring snows failed to materialize. Too vividly she remembered the drought from a couple of years ago that had left the entire state reeling. That year, a hundred-thousand-acre forest fire had burned a scant fifteen miles from town. Since then, no one wanted to take chances with letting Mother Nature run her natural course.

After the fire was out, a search-and-rescue team entered the building, working as methodically as they would have for the real thing.

"That dog of Julianna Red Feather's is good," Donovan said, "but they aren't going to find anyone."

"Let's hope not," Lucia said. Even in a training scenario, the idea they might have left a victim behind who could have been rescued didn't sit well.

While they waited, she watched the wildfire fighters working near the timber, where they were building a fire line. Lucia immediately recognized Rafe's powerful form. Thanks to his extremely busy schedule, she hadn't seen him since they had returned from Breckenridge, but they had talked each evening.

He had told her about his job and the things he was doing to prepare for the fire season that had already begun in southern California. During one of those conversations she had learned that he was one of the planners of the training exercise and that he had chosen to be a participant, leaving the evaluation to his superiors.

He had asked how her father was doing, which was about the same as far as she could tell, though her mother thought he was improving. Lucia had related that she and Sam had made up, though they were still uneasy around each other because they were both entrenched in their respective positions.

He hadn't asked her out, and she couldn't decide what she thought about that. After so adamantly telling the man she didn't date, who could blame him? On the other hand, she had shared more of herself during their telephone conversations than she ever had with her ex-fiancé. Additionally, she liked Rafe's company, liked spending time with him. Maybe he was waiting for her to ask him out, she decided. Maybe, but that would be admitting that she did date.

She gained new appreciation for his definition of *careful* as he had told her about the training regimen hotshots went through. Today's exercise was small potatoes in comparison but one more step toward being prepared.

"Here comes the search-and-rescue team," Donovan said, drawing her attention back to the burned-out building where they emerged.

They carried a body bag with the care and respect they would have given a real person, not a dummy.

"We missed someone?" Lucia questioned. "Dumb thing to ask. Obviously. But how?"

"That's what I want to know," Donovan said as they headed for the search-and-rescue team.

Julianna Red Feather smiled sympathetically when Donovan repeated his demand. "I wouldn't have found this one without my dog, Angel. The identification on the dummy was a child. He'd hidden behind a set of storage shelves in the workroom."

"We should have gotten that," Lucia told her partner. "That's basic 101 stuff."

With the first exercise complete, the incident commander set up another fire inside the building, engaging them in another training exercise. It went like that the rest of the day until so little of the building was left, all they could do was let it burn down and make sure that the fire remained contained.

Lucia caught sight of Rafe every now and then, and she could see his crew was going through a similar process. They'd get the grass fire contained, then another one would be set and they'd do what was required of the new circumstances. Watching him, she kept thinking about his definition of *careful*. That brought her back to the day of the hospital fire, and she wondered again if she had been as thorough— as prepared and as *careful*—as she should have been. She hated that she couldn't precisely remember, and she hated even more that, for once, Chief O'Brien might have had a valid reason to complain.

"Vance," he called.

She looked up to see Chief O'Brien approaching the truck, where she was gathered with other members of her unit.

"A word with you," he said, motioning for her to join him out of earshot.

When she turned around and looked at her fellow firefighters, Gideon Jackson winked at her, mouthing, "We've got your back."

She grinned and turned to face O'Brien.

"Good work out there today, despite not finding the kid," he said.

Praise from Chief O'Brien? That was so out of character she was sure her mouth gaped open.

"You go back to the station house on Monday," he said.

"On full duty?"

His mouth tightened. "What part of 'you go back' don't you understand, Vance? Of course, full duty."

"Why?"

"Because I'm ordering you to." With that, he walked away.

She watched him a long moment, completely floored that she had her job back. And with no apparent reason why.

Slowly, she walked back toward Gideon and Donovan.

"What gives?" Gideon asked.

"I'm back on full duty," she said.

"Well, don't look so glum," Donovan said. "Are you sure that's what he said?"

She nodded. "I just can't figure out why."

"Don't be looking a gift horse in the mouth," he advised. "Do what Jackson here does." Donovan leaned on one hip and made a smooth waving motion with both of his hands in front of him. "Go with the flow."

A couple of hours later, they all gathered under one of the picnic pavilions for the debriefing. Lucia's heart clutched a little when Rafe came to sit next to her, pausing long enough to say hello to several others. His roommate, Malik, was with him, and Lucia admitted that she had forgotten he was also a firefighter. Lucia introduced him to Gideon and Donovan, who were perched on top of a picnic table above her. She scooted down the bench so Rafe could sit down next to her, which earned her a nudge from Donovan.

"You two be good and pay attention to what's going on up there," he said with a grin, nodding toward the group of chiefs huddled in front of them, getting ready to speak to the group.

"I'm nothin' but good," Rafe drawled, which made Donovan laugh.

Rafe winked at her, and her heart did that little lurch thing again, making her feel tongue-tied and about as confident as a fifteen-year-old.

"Did your part of the training go okay?" he asked, setting his hard hat down at his feet. His yellow Nomex shirt was covered in soot, and he had a streak across one cheek.

"We missed a victim." Lucia resisted the urge to smooth her hair, realizing she was undoubtedly as dirty as everyone else around her. That was to be expected, and her sudden notion that she wanted a clean face and brushed hair made her annoyed with herself.

"Ouch." His tone was sympathetic.

"We'll get it right next time," Gideon interjected with his usual philosophical attitude.

"How'd yours go?" Lucia asked.

"Rafe is still trying to kill me," Malik answered cheerfully, leaning around Rafe so he could look at her. "Within five minutes of getting out of the truck, he set his Pulaski down right where he knew I'd trip over it—"

"Grace is obviously his middle name," Rafe said blandly.

"Dangerous is his," Malik returned in the same vein. "Seriously."

Lucia believed Malik and the part about dangerous. Rafe was exactly that to her peace of mind. She didn't get butterflies like this around anyone, but here she sat feeling so fluttery and aware of him that she was sure others had probably noticed.

"I know for a fact that Rafe is tied up this weekend. Something about going to Durango to talk to some guys." Malik winked at her. "Since he's out of town, how about a date Friday night?"

"Are you kidding?" Donovan said. "She doesn't date."

Malik gave Rafe a speculative look. "Really."

"Really," Lucia said, feeling ridiculous. She looked back at Donovan and saw the same considering expression on his face. Since he was the biggest tease in the firehouse, anything he thought he saw between her and Rafe would be fair game for his acerbic and too-often-perceptive comments.

"You know I'm the good-looking one," Malik continued, unfazed. "Plus, you should probably hear about all the broken hearts Rafe has left scattered all over the West."

"Plus, you should shut up," Rafe said, his smile in place, though his tone was firm.

"See what I put up with from my so-called best friend?" Malik said. "Me, I'm the charming one."

Donovan laughed, lightly punching Rafe on the shoulder. "All I can say is, you'd better be good to our girl."

That fast, Lucia's temper surfaced, and she looked up at her partner. "You're not one of my brothers, so stop it. Furthermore, we're not dating. Got it?"

Rafe grinned when he looked from his friend to Donovan. "That's right. You know Lucia. She doesn't date. You said so yourself."

For having the last word, it would have been great if Donovan hadn't roared with laughter and if Lucia hadn't vividly remembered Rafe's kiss the night he comforted her after her argument with her brother. Fortunately, Malik and Donovan were prevented from saying anything further when the debriefing began.

Worse, she was mad that she'd backed herself into a corner where Rafe couldn't ask her out. -

THIRTEEN

"Good morning, Mom," Lucia said the following Tuesday morning as she came into her father's hospital room. As was her custom, she went to her father and kissed his cheek. "Hi, Dad." She perched on the edge of the bed and took his hand. "He looks different today."

"I think so, too. His eyes have opened several times over the last day, but the doctors tell me not to read too much into that. How was your first day back?" Her mom was sitting near the window, reading the morning paper.

Lucia grinned. "Great. The usual twenty-four-hour shift with nothing out of the ordinary."

"Perhaps to you." Her mother inclined her head toward the outside door. "But I hear things, like the car accident you responded to in the middle of the night."

"We did our jobs." Lucia met her mother's gaze, remembering the young woman, barely out of her teens, trapped in her car, which had been struck by a drunk driver. The jaws of life had been used to pry open the crushed vehicle so they could get her out. She had survived the crash, but only barely. She had come through surgery and was now in intensive care.

Her mother replied with one of her noncommittal "hmms,"

a disagreement that pleased Lucia. Since she had always felt ordinary to her parents' and her brothers' extraordinary, the approval meant a lot.

"Sam said you all had a good time skiing last weekend," her mother said. "And that Chloe's kids had a good time, too."

"They did."

"And your friend Rafe. How did he fare with the wild ones?"

"The twins? He did great with them."

"And with your brother?"

Lucia felt her face heat. "Well, you know Sam."

"Overprotective, trying to chase off yet another boyfriend?"

Lucia nodded, realizing too late that she had just agreed Rafe was a boyfriend. She didn't like the term, which sounded too…something, she thought, racking her brain for the right term. Casual or transitory or chic. None of those applied because none of that was how she felt about him. Never mind that she'd set rules that made it impossible for him to ask her out on a date.

"Maybe you should invite him over for Easter."

Lucia glanced down at her father, voicing the first of the two thoughts that surfaced. "You're sure you want to do the whole big family get-together?"

After a moment, her mother nodded, her attention also on Lucia's father. "He would absolutely hate having the family celebration canceled because of his being ill. So the way I see it, this is a way of honoring him."

What remained unspoken was that far too many months had passed since her father had been shot. And they all knew that every day he remained in a coma was another day closer to the probability that he might never wake up.

The second thought that surfaced about Rafe she kept to

herself. Though they often had friends in for the family celebration at Easter, bringing Rafe would be a signal to her family that she was getting serious about him. She didn't want to be serious, though she admitted that she liked spending time with him, that she looked forward to his daily phone calls, that she liked *him.*

Noticing the headline Hospital Fire Still Under Investigation on the newspaper in front of her mother, Lucia picked up the page. The article focused on the ongoing arson investigation and managed to make the connection between Lucia as one of the responders to the fire and her dad's shooting several months earlier, and his continuing to be in a coma. The story included an interview with Chief O'Brien, who was quoted as saying, "Was there arson? Most certainly, and we are vigorously pursuing all avenues the evidence leads toward. Could the fire have been contained sooner with less damage to hospital property? Again, certainly. Were children trapped and put at risk because one of our firefighters didn't follow protocol? Again, certainly, and we are being equally vigorous in that investigation and taking punitive action toward the firefighter involved."

Feeling her lips go numb because *she* was the "firefighter involved," Lucia glanced at her mother. "Did you read this?"

She nodded. "He's blustering. You know that he is. If he'd had anything solid to back up his claim, you wouldn't have been allowed to return to full duty."

"But in the meantime he can trash my reputation and I'm supposed to simply let him?" Lucia clasped her suddenly cold hands together. "I didn't do anything wrong."

"I know that, sweetheart."

"There's something very wrong with this," Lucia said. "And somehow, I'm going to find out what."

"That's probably better left to Sam," her mother said.

Though Lucia understood the context, the idea of once again leaving anything to her brother grated.

"Sam doesn't know everything, and he's not the only capable person in this family."

"I'm not saying that he is. At least be careful," her mother returned.

That word again, *careful*. Instead of her usual knee-jerk response to the word, Lucia heard Rafe's voice in her head about being prepared. So how *did* one prepare for an investigation?

While she and her mother talked about mundane family matters over the next hour, Lucia kept thinking about that. *Prepared* meant getting her facts straight, which meant she needed to write down what she knew so she had a visual reference of how the pieces fit together. *Prepared* meant she needed to find out, if she could, how an open gallon container of lacquer ended up in the storage closet. If she could narrow down the time frame and who had access to the closet, then she might have a better idea of who might have put it there.

As Lucia got ready to leave, her mother asked, "So you'll invite Rafe for Easter?"

"I'll think about it." Lucia wondered if she was ready for the familial speculation that would be rampant if he came. She didn't want that kind of scrutiny, and she was pretty sure that Rafe wouldn't want it, either.

Once more, his advice about being careful…prepared… echoed through her head, this time making her smile. *Careful* was exactly what they needed to be. Nothing would scare a man away faster than the whole family deciding his marriage was on the near horizon. She wasn't serious. She wasn't. But she did want his friendship…and those occasional sweet kisses, too.

Careful was the only way to go. Who would have thought?

* * *

To her surprise, Rafe asked her out when they talked on the phone that evening, adding his usual qualifier, "Just dinner tomorrow night between friends. Not a date. In fact, you can even pay for your own dinner if you want."

"Okay."

"Besides," he added, "I would like to see my friend Lucia before I take off for a few days."

"To Durango," she said, liking that he thought of her as a friend and remembering Malik saying that was where he was going this weekend.

"Yep, a circle trip. I'm hitting the colleges in Alamosa, Durango and Gunnison and finishing up the paperwork so we can get the new members of the crew into training. I leave Thursday."

They talked a while longer, and the call ended with him telling her that he'd pick her up at seven the following evening. No matter what they both called it, she knew it was a date, and she was excited about it.

Mostly to keep her mind off Rafe, she spent the day writing down everything she had learned about the hospital fire on individual sticky notes so she could move the information around as she tried to figure out how the pieces fit together. Arranging them on her kitchen table, she had O'Brien's accusation of her at the center. And none of the pieces supported his accusation. Yet for some reason she couldn't fathom, she was O'Brien's target. Remembering Rafe's speculation that she might have been the target of the fire made chills crawl up her scalp, and she wrote down "Objective of the fire?" on another note and added that to the group.

None of it made any sense, which made her wish she had some of Colleen's journalistic ability to dig up facts to support a story and a healthy dose of Sam's ability to solve a crime out of seemingly unrelated bits of information. Remembering that he had once told her most crimes were committed over money or revenge, she wrote those down, too.

Rafe rang the doorbell promptly at seven.

Wearing another of the outfits that her mother had picked when they had gone shopping together during a trip to Santa Fe, Lucia opened the door.

"Look at you," Rafe said. Instead of the usual leather jacket, he was wearing a navy-blue sports coat, khakis and a cream-colored knit shirt. She thought he looked great.

She glanced down at her black dress dotted in white and accented with a hot-pink belt and matching cardigan. "It's not too much, is it?"

Smiling, he shook his head and came into the house. He took her by the hand and turned her around, making the fabric swirl against her legs. "I'd say it's just about perfect." His glance fell to her stockinged feet. "Though you might want to add shoes. It's not that warm outside."

Lucia returned his smile, deciding then she would put on the hot pink shoes that went with the rest of the outfit rather than the black flats she had originally contemplated. "I'll be right back," she told Rafe as she headed up the stairs.

It was his turn to grin. "You're not going to primp while you're up there, are you? I'm starved."

Primp? Not after she had spent the last hour doing just that.

When she came back downstairs a scant two minutes later, he was staring at the kitchen table that was covered in sticky notes.

"You're still thinking about the hospital fire?" he asked. When she nodded, he pointed toward the note where she had written *My responsibility*. "You have nothing to worry about, Lucia. And if you're referring to that ridiculous quote from O'Brien that was in yesterday's paper, he's way out of line."

"That's almost exactly what my mother told me."

"A wise woman."

Lucia headed for the hall closet, where she retrieved a black wool coat. "All I'm trying to do is look at all the pieces and figure out why O'Brien is so determined to place the blame on me when none of the facts support it. I know he doesn't like me, but this seems pretty extreme, even for him."

Rafe took the coat from her and held it for her to slip into.

"Since you're back on full duty, maybe you should just let it go."

She met his gaze. "I wish I could. It's just that I feel like I'm missing something obvious."

"You look very pretty tonight."

"Thank you." She gave him a mock scowl. "But you're trying to change the subject."

"Whatever works." He took her hand and led her toward the door. "I'm in the mood for that great beef stew served at the Stagecoach Café. Okay if we go there?"

"You know we're bound to run into someone from my family."

He laughed while she pulled the door closed behind her and locked it.

"It's not that funny."

"In case you haven't noticed, you can't walk around this town without stumbling over a Vance. And now that I know the Montgomerys are like family as well, that's doubly true." He tucked her arm next to his as they went down the steps toward his car. "If you don't want to be seen with me, you'd better speak up now."

"Don't be silly. Of course that's okay."

He unlocked the door and opened it. "Then maybe this is a real date."

She looked at him, the car door separating them.

"Since you dressed up for me," he said.

She swallowed that warm, fluttery feeling back. "Kinda like you did for me."

He nodded. "Kinda like that. And I don't care if we run into someone from your family."

She stared at him, lost in the depths of his green eyes. He was, she realized, giving her the choice. She'd dressed up for him, anticipating this time with him, so to call this anything other than what it was would be unreasonable. Absurd even.

Feeling vulnerable and terrified by the idea but wanting to go forward anyway, she took a step closer to him and brushed a soft kiss across his mouth. "I'd like to go on a date with you, Rafe."

His smile melted her a little. "Then maybe you'd like to have the flowers sitting in the front seat."

She turned around and looked down, where a bouquet of mixed flowers was wrapped in cellophane, the colors matching the hot-pink accents on her dress.

"They're gorgeous." She picked them up, slipped into the seat and brought them to her face while Rafe closed the door. "What would you have done if I hadn't agreed this was a date?" she asked when he got into the vehicle.

"Haven't you heard?" he asked with a grin. "I'm the guy who prays and expects to be answered."

"Ah." That teasing statement had a ring of truth beneath his smile. An unexpected lump rose in her throat about that and the flowers. "The flowers are a first."

"What do you mean?" Instead of backing the vehicle out of its space, he looked sharply at her.

"My mother gives me flowers occasionally, but no one else ever has."

"Not even the ex-fiancé?"

She shook her head. "Not even."

"Well, shame on him." Rafe leaned across the console and turned her face toward his. "Here's to the first of the firsts between us."

She smiled. "If you're counting, this wasn't it."

"No?"

"You were the first guy to save my life."

"I don't want to count that," he whispered, then kissed her. "I'm glad you like the flowers, Lucia." One more quick kiss and they were on their way.

For once, the Stagecoach Café wasn't occupied by a single other member of her family when they were seated for dinner, which counted as a blessing. As always, the conversation between them flowed easily. Lucia was sure she would miss him on his trip around the state, a thought that made her stomach tie in knots. If she'd miss him this much during a short trip, how would it be this summer, when he'd likely be gone for months? She knew he enjoyed his job as much as she liked hers, and she'd seen him working, so she knew he was also good at it. Better than good. A skilled expert.

Even so, the idea of him being gone for months and being in danger while he worked... Well, she hated it already.

With that came a flash of insight. This was how her mother had felt when Lucia had become a firefighter. This was how her brothers felt each time she went into a burning building. This was what it was like when you cared about the safety of someone else more than you cared about your own.

"Lucia," Rafe said, reaching across the small table to take her hand. "You look like you've seen a ghost."

She met his eyes and smiled. "I just thought about how much I'm going to miss you when you're gone this summer."

He squeezed her hand, and warmth lit his eyes. "I'm not gone yet."

He ordered dessert after the meal, a big piece of chocolate cake, and though Lucia hadn't wanted dessert, she took a bite of Rafe's every time he held the fork up to share with her. They lingered over coffee, and when they finally left the café, Rafe held her hand as they went through the door and outside into the night.

Striding across the dimly lit parking lot was her cousin Alessandro.

"I'm surprised to see you," Lucia called to him as they approached.

He glanced sharply at them.

"I thought you were still in Europe."

He smiled then. "Ah, Europe. Yes." He made a point of looking around. "As you can see, I am here. I've just returned from Brussels."

"I thought you went to Italy." Maybe his plans had changed, she thought with a pang of disappointment, thinking about the pictures he had promised to take for her.

"Yes, I was there, as well."

Though he normally took her by both hands and kissed each cheek, he didn't come any closer, so she took a couple of steps forward. "I don't think you've met my friend Rafe."

Rafe offered his hand. "Rafael Wright. You're the first relative of hers I've seen today."

"There are so many," her cousin said, "that one can hardly keep them all straight."

Rafe chuckled. "My thoughts exactly."

"Alessandro is a cousin from my mother's side of the family," Lucia said. "There's another huge group of relatives, including Tomas and—"

"Please, no names," Rafe protested. "I'm still having trouble keeping the Vance side of the family straight."

Her cousin's smile flashed in the darkness. "I often have the same problem."

"Alessandro is some kind of international finance expert with the European Union, isn't that right?" She glanced at him. "All very hush-hush and confidential."

"As the saying goes, money makes the world go around." He glanced at his watch. "I have an appointment, and I really must go. It is nice to meet you, Signore Wright."

Lucia closed the distance and kissed him on the cheek, noticing his cologne was different than the one he normally wore. "Don't be such a stranger," she said. As he walked away, she called after him. "Is it okay if I come by tomorrow to get the disk?"

"Disk?" His expression was one of total confusion.

"You know. Of the photos you were going to take for me while you were at home."

"Ah," he said. "That."

"If you forgot, it's okay."

"I didn't forget," he said. "But I really am late." With that, he hurried toward the entry of the café.

"Do people ever call him Al or is it always Alessandro?"

"I've never heard him called anything else. The Donato side is very formal compared to us, especially Alessandro and Tomas, his younger brother. They look so much alike that I can't tell them apart unless they are standing next to each other."

"Your cousin is a little strange."

"That's what my brothers all say. I know he said he didn't forget about the pictures, but he sure sounded like he had." She looked at Rafe. "I told you about the stained glass—"

"Yes."

"And I've been wanting to make something really special for my mother. She talks sometimes about the chapel in the town where she grew up, and when she and I were there, she took me to see it. It's really beautiful, and I want to reproduce one small panel of the window."

"That would be a really special gift."

"She's a special person," Lucia said.

"She's a lucky person," Rafe said, "with an extraordinary daughter."

"Thank you." Of all the things he could have said, those particular words went straight to her heart. She, who considered herself ordinary in the extreme, to be thought of as extraordinary. That was amazing.

"We always have a big get-together at Easter," Lucia said. "Would you like to—"

"Yes," Rafe said, once again taking her hand as they walked.

"What if I was about to say something like 'go skiing instead' or—"

"Yes, I want to spend the day with you," he said. "Skiing would be nice—after attending Easter service. Spending the day with you at your 'big get-together' would be nice, too."

"Good," she said. "It's a date."

At that, Rafe laughed. "At last, the lady says we're on a date."

FOURTEEN

"I won't quote you," Colleen said to Lucia several days later, "but I have an official question for you."

"That sounds pretty ominous."

They were at the home-improvement center, shopping for a wallpaper border and paint for Lucia's guest bathroom. Lucia looked up from the colorful sample of towels billowing on a clothesline to her friend, whose gaze was fixed unseeingly on the display of a pastel row of seashells.

"You have no idea. You've seen the articles I've been doing on drug trafficking?" Colleen said.

Lucia nodded.

"Well, I've been polling each of the firehouses and hospitals. The medical calls you've responded to lately—how many of those are drug related?"

"There are always a few," Lucia said. She mentally went through the cases since she had been back on full duty. "Maybe even a few more than normal."

They moved down the wallpaper display aisle a few more feet, where her gaze skipped over a border of waddling ducks and another of assorted claw-foot bathtubs to a group of flowers in baskets.

"Could you check on how many?" Colleen asked. "I talked

to one of the detectives in vice, and he thinks the drug traffic is as bad now as it was before that cartel was taken down last year."

"Brendan and Sam would be in a better position to tell you about that than I am." Deciding on the border with baskets of flowers, Lucia picked up a couple of rolls. She looked at her friend. "You're not putting yourself in any danger with all this poking around you're doing, are you?"

"Of course not," Colleen said, her gaze still looking around. "Is that Chief O'Brien's wife?" she asked, nodding toward a woman waiting by the paint counter, where a salesperson was adding a custom tint.

"It is," Lucia said.

Just then, Mary O'Brien looked up and noticed them and Lucia waved. She waved back, and Lucia realized the only polite thing to do was to go talk to her.

After they exchanged greetings, Mary pointed to the two rolls of wallpaper border in Lucia's hand and said, "Looks like you're doing a little decorating, too."

"Only a little," Lucia agreed, taking in the pale-yellow paint chip in Mary's hand. "Is the paint for the baby's nursery?"

Mary nodded and patted her belly. "This should have been done months ago, but we still have a bit of time before this little one is due."

"I hope your husband is going to paint," Colleen said, "or that you have someone else lined up. I've heard paint fumes aren't good for either of you."

"Neil is helping," Mary said, then shook her head. "After his last shopping trip for supplies two weeks ago, I decided that I'd better come pick things out so I know everything will be kid-friendly."

"It doesn't take them long to be into everything," Lucia said. "My brother's twins have this idea that everything has to be put in their mouths."

"I've heard about that," Mary said with a smile, "which is why I had to send Neil back to exchange a gallon of lacquer for polyurethane. Can you believe the man wanted to put lacquer on a child's dresser? Not exactly the kid-friendly finish I had in mind."

"When is the baby due?" Colleen asked.

"Eight more weeks."

"It will be here before you know it," Colleen said as the salesclerk set the gallon of freshly mixed paint on the counter.

"I hope so." Mary set the paint in a nearby cart. "I'll probably see you at church. Have a good day."

"You, too," Lucia said, watching Mary walk away.

"She always seems sad to me, but maybe I would be, too, if I were married to someone as overbearing and condescending as Neil O'Brien," Colleen softly said, taking one of the wallpaper rolls from Lucia and heading for the paint display. "What color of paint do you want to go with this?"

"Something neutral, to pick up the straw color in the background, I think," Lucia responded, while the most awful thought lodged in her head.

Lacquer had been the accelerant used in the hospital fire, and Chief O'Brien had purchased a gallon of lacquer. Was he the arsonist? Was that why he was so insistent that she was somehow at fault? To turn attention away from the investigation?

When she got home a couple of hours later, she studied the sticky notes on her kitchen table that she had arranged, then rearranged, then rearranged again. The suspicion that O'Brien was somehow behind the fire was horrible in every way possible, especially when there was nothing even remotely concrete to back it up. A woman's innocent admission that her husband had bought the wrong thing to protect a piece of furniture couldn't be construed as guilt. It couldn't.

Lucia needed a sounding board, someone who was a little

less gung-ho than Colleen would be and someone who would not be looking for concrete evidence like Sam would. So she called Rafe. His answering machine picked up and she left him a message, asking him if he could come over when he got home.

Unable to sit still and do nothing, Lucia taped off the ceiling and the hardware in the guest bath she was getting ready to paint while she waited. Rafe rang her doorbell just as she was finishing.

"Are you okay?" he asked when she opened the door. "You didn't sound like yourself."

"For having knots tying up my stomach, I'm fine."

"What's up?" He came inside, shrugged off his jacket and set it across the back of a chair in her living room.

"This," she said, leading him toward the kitchen table. "On the one hand, I want you to tell me I'm crazy, but if I'm not…" Her voice trailed away as she studied the notes on the table.

Rafe listened intently while Lucia told him about running into Chief O'Brien's wife and the casually related information about the lacquer. He immediately got the connection between that purchase, however innocent it might have been, and the arson investigation.

"Suspecting a fellow firefighter of arson, especially a chief, makes me sick," she said. "But doesn't it strike you as at least a little strange? I might not have thought anything about it, but since he's been so determined to accuse me of some wrongdoing, I keep wondering why."

"It's strange, all right." Rafe looked from Lucia's serious dark eyes to the sticky notes, seeing that she had uncovered all the same things in her informal investigation that he had in his. "The big question, though, is motive."

"Colleen accused him of having a gambling problem," Lucia said. "If he did this, maybe it has something to do with that."

"Follow the money," Rafe said.

She managed a smile. "That's what my brother always says."

Rafe took her hands. "So what was that about you wanting me to tell you that you were crazy?"

"I don't want to have this suspicion. I don't."

"You're simply going where the evidence takes you."

Her eyes became even more troubled as she met his. "I'm not sure if this is evidence or simply a wild leap of my imagination." She squeezed his hands and stepped away. "I keep doubting myself—you know, wondering if I'm so eager to think the worst of him simply because he doesn't like me."

"The fact that you're thinking so is proof that you're not." Rafe looked again at the notes scattered across her kitchen table in a paper mosaic of clues. Every instinct he had made him think she was right. O'Brien was the arsonist, and if not directly, was pulling strings somewhere.

One way or another, Rafe was determined to get to the bottom of this, and the only way he knew how to do that was to get her brother involved. "Why didn't you call Sam?"

She shrugged. "I know he's the logical one to talk to, but I needed someone with a more objective opinion than mine before I made the accusation. If I'm wrong, even voicing this could do a lot of harm. End O'Brien's career, hurt his family. His wife is pregnant with their first child, did you know that?"

Rafe shook his head.

"She is. Colleen said today that she looked sad, and she's right. She does." Lucia wrapped her arms around herself as though she was cold. "I don't want to be responsible for somehow making things worse for her."

"You're not. If O'Brien did anything, the responsibility is his." Rafe took a step toward Lucia and brushed a strand of hair away from her cheek. "You're a remarkable woman, Lucia Vance." When she shook her head, he said, "You are.

O'Brien has a grudge against you, and you have every reason to want to get back at him. Instead, you're thinking about the possible hurt to his wife. That's rare."

"It shouldn't be."

Rafe pointed her toward the door. "Get your coat. Let's go for a walk or get some coffee. Anything to get your mind off this for a while."

He was successful in that, he decided, as he lay in bed hours later still wide awake. At a coffee shop a couple of blocks from her house, they had talked about his trip and the group of seasoned firefighters who would be trying out for the hotshot crew. They had talked about Ramón and Teresa, and Lucia had decided to invite their family to the Easter celebration. They had made plans to attend the sunrise service at the Garden of the Gods on Easter morning. They had shared another of those lingering kisses that threatened his self-discipline and his resolve to take things slow.

The trouble was, he hadn't kept his own mind off the things Lucia had discovered. Her conclusion felt right, and he trusted his instincts about that. Feelings, though, weren't evidence. Evidence or not, he decided that he needed to pass along the suspicions to Lucia's brother. The way Rafe saw it, the worst the man could do was laugh at him. But it could also be enough to tie together some other piece of evidence that the police had access to. Personally, Rafe didn't care if the accusation ruined O'Brien's career. That the man had made it to battalion chief with his level of incompetence was a travesty.

Neil O'Brien was in over his head, and he hated every single thing about the realization. Since that snowy day when he'd first met with her in Bear Creek Park a month ago, everything in his life had turned upside down, and it was all her fault. All of it. Conniving little fortune seeker. How dare she send the copy of the note to his wife. Oh, there was no return address and no message, but Neil knew she was behind it. She had to be.

He could not be blamed that Lucia Vance hadn't died in the fire. So far, Johnson and his team of arson investigators hadn't connected him to the hospital fire, but Neil had the awful feeling that could change at any moment. No matter how careful he had been, he worried that he had overlooked some crucial detail.

The one thing he knew for sure was he needed insurance. He double-checked the small digital recorder to make sure it was working. He had already tested it to make sure that it would clearly pick up a conversation from the pocket of his jacket.

He sat in his car, waiting for the time to finish ticking by for his appointment…if you called being summoned like some low-level lackey an appointment. He knew better than to be late, but being early was no better. He'd been surprised when she had told him to meet at her office. He would have thought she would want a remote location, like she'd insisted on last time. Not that there was much chance he would be seen at this late hour. All the trendy shops had closed up. Lights shone through the second-floor window, where he knew her office was, so he knew she was there.

If he'd had more time to prepare for this meeting, he would have made sure he had a solid alibi and a failproof plan for getting rid of her. Right after she handed over the originals of the promissory notes securing his gambling debt.

Everything about this meeting struck Neil like a scene out of a bad mystery movie—the one where the villain met his doom at the hands of a femme fatale in some dark alley.

He waited until three minutes past the hour before getting

out of his car, locking it and making his way to the door at the side of the building. Inside, there was a short hallway with two additional doors. He knew the one to his left led to the store and the one to the right led to the offices above. The door was unlocked, and the stairwell was brightly lit, which made him inwardly smile in light of his earlier flight of imagination. He pressed the record button on the recorder in his pocket and climbed the stairs.

She must have heard him coming because she appeared in the doorway, her hair swept away from her face in a simple bun at the nape of her slender neck, one of those hairdos that made the rich look even richer.

"It's nice to see you, Neil."

He doubted that but figured playing along was the only thing to do. "You, too."

She closed the door to the expansive office behind him with a soft click. The hardwood floor was covered with a huge Persian rug, and the room held only a couple of pieces of furniture—an ornate, feminine-looking desk and a huge buffet against one wall that looked like it could have come out of a castle.

A lean man stood next to the buffet, watching him with the blackest, coldest eyes Neil had ever seen.

"I don't think we've met," he said, crossing the room and extending his hand.

The other man didn't raise his hand, so Neil dropped his own. Already he was on the defensive, and he ground his teeth against the feeling.

"This is my business associate," she said.

"He knows who I am," the man said. His voice had a husky guttural quality as though his vocal cords had been damaged. His penetrating gaze remained on Neil. "If you think about it a moment, Mr. O'Brien, you'll know exactly who I am."

Neil stared at the man, having no idea who he was—only the certainty that this man was the one who pulled *her* strings.

"Just as you know why you're here," he added.

She came to stand next to the man and Neil admitted they made a striking couple. Something about the man struck a chord. Who *was* he? Neil knew he didn't have the best memory for faces, but he didn't think he'd ever met this man. Something about those sharp eyes set him on edge, and he would have remembered that.

She took a bottle of imported water out of a refrigerator concealed in the buffet, poured it into a glass and took a sip, all without offering Neil anything. A snub, a power play. Effective, too. He'd have to remember this the next time he wanted to put one of his own underlings in his place.

"You're disappointed about the hospital fire," Neil said, hoping he sounded completely unconcerned.

"Disappointed." The man smiled, and there wasn't a single friendly thing about it. The expression was more like a vicious dog baring its teeth. "Such a mild word."

Neil gave a nonchalant shrug, realizing he'd made an admission that could sound like guilt if his recording got into the wrong hands. "There are far more effective ways to achieve your goals."

"Perhaps," the man agreed. "But this will be done as I decide."

He moved to the side then, and Neil's gaze went to a pair of large photographs propped against the back of the buffet. Pictures of Mary. One was of her in profile, her pregnancy clearly evident as she carried a bag of groceries across the parking lot in front of the supermarket. The other was of her in their home, napping in the big chair in their bedroom, her stockinged feet on the ottoman. A red dot had been painted on the center of her head on both, as though a laser scope was aimed at her.

Neil felt his lips go numb, and he clenched his hands into fists. "She has nothing to do with this."

"Ah, but we do understand each other now, don't we?" he said.

Neil stared at the photographs, his thoughts in turmoil. This game couldn't endanger his wife. She'd had faith in him when he'd had none in himself. She was the one good thing in his life. She loved him, despite his considerable shortcomings. After that letter had arrived, he'd had no choice but to confess his gambling, fully expecting that she would walk out the way his mother had when he was eight. Mary hadn't but instead had put her arms around him and told them they would somehow find a way through this.

"There will be another incident," the man said, "at a time and place of my choosing." He inclined his head. "And since it's clear that you cannot be counted on to complete the job as contracted—"

"I want out," Neil said. "My wife already knows about the gambling—"

"Of course she does," the woman said. "I told you that day there would be consequences."

"I want out," he repeated. "Name your price."

"You can't get out," the other man said. "It's one of the rules. The first rule, actually."

"Rule of what?" Neil demanded.

"The Diablo Syndicate. You do remember them, don't you?"

Neil did. The group had been described in the news last year as the most sophisticated organized-crime syndicate that had operated within the state in years. Like a legitimate business, it had diversified to maximize profits. It had been involved in gambling, prostitution and, with a sister organization whose name Neil didn't remember, drugs. The law-enforcement task force that had brought down the syndicate had major connections to the Vance and Montgomery families through both the FBI and the local police force. Last year, the head of the syndicate had publicly vowed revenge on the Vances and Montgomerys before escaping back to his Latin American villa. Only his plane had crashed and his body had never been found.

His body had never been found.

"You're…"

The man cocked an eyebrow.

Neil scowled, trying to remember. The name had something to do with a pair of Spanish priests who had explored the Colorado wilderness, a tale he remembered from a high-school history class. "Dominguez." No, that wasn't right. The other guy. "Escalante."

The man bared his teeth in that semblance of a smile again, his attention fixed on the pictures of Mary. "Indeed, I am. And so, you do understand how very high the stakes are."

Sweat pooled under Neil's arms. The Diablo Syndicate had a reputation for slitting the throats of its enemies and leaving the bodies in highly public places, as though offering a warning to others. Why was the man admitting his identity when no one knew he was back in the area?

This was some elaborate game, Neil decided—part of the revenge he had vowed last year. That didn't explain why he was determined to see Lucia Vance die in a fire, but Neil was sure of one thing now. He had little choice in the matter. Not if he wanted to keep Mary safe. Not if he had a hope of getting out of this alive.

Escalante looked at Neil. "This is how it will be. You will ensure that another fire takes place, and you will ensure that Miss Vance will be there. She will die in that fire, and you,

Mr. O'Brien, will pay a penalty if you fail." He pulled a cell phone from his pocket and flipped it open. Whoever was on the other end must have immediately answered because he said, "I need you."

Less than a second later, the door opened and a burly man came into the room. He was dressed in black pants and a black T-shirt that emphasized a powerful physique.

"Please search our friend and ensure that he didn't bring anything with him that he should not have," Escalante said.

The newcomer approached Neil with a smirk on his face. "Lock your hands behind your head," he ordered.

Neil did so, knowing the recorder would be found. He was more afraid than he had ever been.

The search was quickly, thoroughly performed, and the recorder was pulled from his pocket and handed to Escalante.

He made a tsk-tsk sound. "I thought you were smarter than this, Mr. O'Brien." He studied the recorder a moment, then pocketed it. "You're correct in assuming the information here might be valuable." To the thug who had searched him, Escalante said, "Please take our guest back to his car, and do make sure he understands the gravity of the situation."

FIFTEEN

"Thanks for coming to see me," Rafe said to Sam and his partner, Becca Hilliard, as they came into his apartment.

"What's on your mind?" Sam asked as Rafe led them toward the kitchen table, where his notes on the hospital fire were laid out.

"Did you know Lucia has been investigating the hospital fire on her own?" Rafe asked after he had poured them each a cup of coffee and sat down at the table.

"I told her to leave that to Johnson," Sam said.

Becca said, "That sounds like something she'd do, especially with the accusations that her battalion chief has made."

"I've been looking into it, too, and we've uncovered pretty much the same stuff." Rafe hadn't been able to let go of his hunch that Lucia was right about her suspicion that O'Brien was either directly or indirectly involved in the hospital fire. But he wasn't quite ready to point that finger, especially as doing so meant implicating Lucia. "I keep coming back to that can of lacquer. I assume you've been checking out the surveillance tapes from the hospital's security cameras."

Becca nodded. "That would be reasonable, but we don't normally advertise the direction our investigation is taking."

"That makes sense," Rafe said, "but somebody had to have

brought that in, and you'd think carrying a gallon can would be a little obvious."

"Unless it was concealed," Sam said.

"With all the remodeling and new construction going on, all our arsonist would have to do is walk in like one of the other workmen, acting like he knows what he's doing and has every right to be there."

"Hide in plain sight," Becca said, looking at her partner.

"The only trouble is," Sam said, "we've got three or four weeks' worth of tapes to go through for four cameras. That's hundreds of hours, and the manpower is a little short."

"I can narrow the time for you," Rafe said. "Check the tapes in the final forty-eight hours before the fire, and if you want it tighter than that, check the times just before O'Brien did his inspections."

Sam raised an eyebrow. "That comes pretty close to an accusation."

Rafe nodded. "Yeah. Unfortunately, it does."

"Care to explain why this isn't a wild-goose chase?"

Rafe thought about that for a moment, then decided he didn't have any choice but to tell Sam and Becca about the exchange between Lucia and Mary O'Brien. "Maybe it's nothing," Rafe finished.

"It's a better lead than anything else we've got," Becca said. "Anything else?"

Rafe shook his head. "No. Just this hunch that won't go away."

Sam stood, picking up his cup and his partner's and taking them to the sink. "We'll check into it. And I think it's time to have another talk with my sister and encourage her to leave policework to the police."

"Do that and she'll know I've been talking to you," Rafe said. "And I think she'll take that as a betrayal of her confidence."

"You should have told her to come talk to me."

"I did."

"Give the man a break, Sam," Becca said. "Rafe's in a tough spot."

"I still don't like your interest in Lucia," Sam said.

"You've made that more than clear." Rafe met his gaze head-on. "The last I heard, she's free to choose who she wants to see."

"You'd put her in the position of choosing between you and her family?"

Rafe shifted his gaze to the window while he did a mental count to ten, making sure the first thing out of his mouth didn't make the situation more tense than it already was.

Finally, he looked back at Sam. "Did you know," he asked, "that I was adopted when I was nine? My mother died when I was five, and then I spent the next four years as alone in this world as anyone can be. My point is that I know both sides of that particular coin. What it's like to know right here—" he tapped his chest "—that not a soul in the world really cares what happens to you. I also know what it's like when family comes into your life again. So will I make Lucia choose between me and her family?" He shook his head. "Never. But will you make her choose between being safe from a possible broken heart or having a chance for a love as deep as the one you found with your wife?"

Sam stared back at him, his jaw clenched.

Becca touched his arm. "I think Rafe's had the last word for today. Let's go."

They headed for the door.

"One last thing," Rafe said. When they turned around, he added, "Except for the suppositions about O'Brien that we can't prove, I've sent a letter of complaint about him to the Fire Chief. That man is done bullying your sister."

* * *

"Our sunrise service this morning is not the glorious one where sunlight reminds us of the Resurrection," Pastor Gabriel Dawson began his sermon to the gathered congregation at the Garden of the Gods on Easter morning, "but instead the mist on this gray morning serves to make us imagine what Mary Magdalene must have felt when she came to Jesus's tomb and found it empty. Each of us here knows how she felt because each of us has lost a loved one at some time."

Bundled up in a warm coat on a day that felt more like winter than spring, Lucia sat on a blanket with Rafe and her family members listening to the sermon. All around them, others had come to this service, a huge crowd, despite the cloudy, cold weather. In addition to wearing warm coats, they were bundled in blankets to keep the children warm.

"We can each imagine her despair and her sense of injustice. Not only had Jesus died, but His body was gone. The questions she might have asked herself on that dawn might be ones we ask ourselves from time to time. How can I go on? How can I live with this loss? How can I believe the things the Master Teacher taught me? How can I regain my faith when it is lost?"

The words sank into Lucia because Pastor Dawson was right. She had recently asked herself many of those same questions, but never before had she thought about the Resurrection from this perspective. She had grown up with the sure knowledge that it had happened, not the uncertainty of a future promise. That in turn reminded her of the night Rafe had shared so deeply of his faith and assured her that a happy ending had already been scripted.

He sat next to her with Ramón and Teresa huddled close to him. As if sensing she watched him, he turned his head slightly, his gaze meeting hers. Though his expression didn't change, a warmth lit his dark eyes. Without a word, he took her hand, his attention returning to the sermon.

"The answer to these questions requires that we look at Jesus and the example He set for us. He wasn't a nobleman but rather a man who worked with His hands, as many of you do. He wasn't wealthy, and He spent His time with people the society of His looked down upon. Everything we know about Him suggests that He had a true zest for life while at the same time having an ecstatic relationship with God, who was ever present. He brought a message of hope and love to an oppressed people who had experienced hardship and loss. His ministry was to those who had faced ostracism, violence, hatred and persecution. That ministry is as relevant today as it was then. Each of us can put to work in our own lives the example that He set for us. He lived and died for His teachings so that we could learn to live for love and to die for love.

"One of my daughters recently said to me that love comes first. And so it does. And Easter morning is the time when we most remember that, where the words of the Bible tell us so simply, 'For God so loved the world that He gave His only begotten Son, that whosoever believeth in Him shall not perish, but have everlasting life.'

"'For God so loved the world.' Those are powerful words. Love is the ultimate message of the Resurrection, my friends. Yes, we have the promise of eternal life. But only through the conscious practice of faith can we bring integrity into a world filled with injustice and indifference. Only through putting love first, as Jesus taught us, can we be more fully one with Him, celebrating this day and the ones that follow in greater harmony and fellowship.

"Let us pray."

Lucia bowed her head, the message bringing tears to her eyes. How lucky she was, she thought, to be with so many of her loved ones this morning. Her brothers and their families, her mother. Rafe.

Her breath stilled as she tested that thought. Like a sunrise stretching above the horizon, she felt as if fingers of light poured into her heart. She loved him. She hadn't expected it to happen. Hadn't wanted it to. And yet somehow it had. His hand was clasped firmly around hers, a simple touch but one that made her so aware of him.

Her prayers took flight and she gave thanks for the blessings in her life. She added Rafe to her circle of those to be blessed and kept safe as they moved through each day.

The service ended with a hymn of "Christ Is Risen, Hallelujah." At the end of the service, the conversation around them swelled with wishes of a happy Easter and comments about how it had been warmer at Christmas than it was this morning. As Lucia chattered with her nieces and nephews, who always gathered around her, her own focus was on the realization that she was in love.

All those fluttery feelings she had when she was around Rafe increased a hundredfold, and she kept trying to pinpoint the moment when her appreciation of him as a good-looking man and his friendship had become something more. There had been no single lightning-bolt moment but simply that gradual becoming.

"That was a very nice service," Tricia Vance said, "despite the lack of a real sunrise."

"A good message, too," Travis said next to her as they walked toward the edge of the park like everyone else. Against his chest, their tiny daughter was cocooned against the cold morning. "And to think our daughter slept through it."

Because of the large crowd and the winding roads through

the park, cars weren't allowed in on Easter morning, so they had a long walk back to the vehicles.

Just ahead, Jessica and Sam were with their children, the twins filled with their usual bouncing energy. Peter and his wife Emily walked with their little boy Manuel between them.

As Lucia took in the scene, she realized that she and Rafe looked like a family as well, with Ramón and Teresa between them. At once, that tingle of anticipation was back—the hope and the fear that they would someday have children. That was the one thing they had never talked about—whether he wanted children. She remembered him saying they were a gift, but that didn't necessarily mean he wanted ones of his own.

Rafe kept pace with Lucia and her mother as they made their way out of the park toward the car that was near the park entrance. Theirs and several hundred others, so he knew there was no point in being in a hurry because it would take a while to get out. And he didn't mind because he had Lucia with him. Another first—their first Easter service together.

Every time he caught her eye, she smiled, her color rising slightly. He didn't know what that was all about, but he thought she was beautiful, and looking so much like her mother. Lidia was dressed in a pale-pink wool coat that looked stunning, though she claimed to have had it forever and that it had been the perfect thing to wear on many Easter mornings since they were often as chilly as this morning was. Lucia's coat was the same style, though hers was a deep rose color.

When he and Lucia had picked up Ramón and Teresa earlier, Ramón had declared, *"Señorita Lucia es muy bonita."* Rafe agreed. She was very pretty. The prettiest woman here.

As they walked, many people stopped Lucia and her mother, and both were gracious, responding politely to the things said over and over again; "Mayor Vance is in our prayers" and variations on "Such an awful thing to happen to a good man." This was another aspect to Lucia's family that he'd have to get used to, Rafe thought, if things went forward between them. Her father was a public figure, and as such, that reduced Lucia's privacy, as well. Though it was far from the celebrity status afforded sports figures and entertainers, Rafe was realizing that any time members of the Vance family were in public, they had to expect a certain level of scrutiny. As a member of that family, if it happened, he'd have to anticipate the same.

As they got closer to the car—today they were riding in Lidia's minivan, and she had asked Rafe to drive because, he assumed, each of her sons had driven his own car—he saw Chief O'Brien and his wife. O'Brien looked terrible, his face bruised and a splint across his nose.

"What happened to him, I wonder?" Rafe said to Lucia.

"He came into the station house yesterday morning looking like that. Said he fell off a ladder painting," she said.

Rafe shook his head. "That must have been some fall. Looks more like someone beat the tar out of him."

Their first stop for the morning was Lidia Vance's home, where the family traditionally gathered for brunch. Everyone had their assigned tasks, Rafe soon discovered. The women were bustling around in the kitchen, and it looked as though they were putting enough food together to feed the proverbial army. The men were responsible for putting the additional leaves in the dining room table and adding chairs around it. The kids…they were busy being kids, and Rafe was pleased to see that Ramón and Teresa fit right in, despite the language barrier. They seemed to take a special delight in playing with Peter and Emily's little boy.

To Rafe's surprise, in less than half an hour they were all gathered in the kitchen, where a delicious-looking buffet had been set up along the counter. It was laden with sliced ham, some sort of egg casserole, steaming hash browns, cinnamon rolls and a huge platter of fruit. As Rafe looked around the room, he realized why they needed the extra seating, and despite the overall chaos, he decided that he liked the fact that the dining room and the extended table were big enough to seat everyone together.

By some unspoken signal, they all joined hands, and as Lucia slipped hers into Rafe's, he gave a silent thanks that he was with her this day. Boisterous and noisy as her family was, he liked being here with her, and he liked them.

"Thank you all for being here this morning," Lidia said, looking around the room. Her gaze paused on each of her children—Lucia, Travis, Peter and Sam. Her eyes took on a shimmer when she said, "I know your dad is here with us in spirit, and I know that he'd want us to go through this day with joyful hearts, doing all the things we've always done. Rafe, will you say grace, please?"

Surprised by the request, Rafe bowed his head. *"Heavenly Father, we give thanks for this food in a world where many are hungry, and we offer our prayers for their needs to be met. We give thanks to be in the good company of family and friends, mindful of others who feel alone. Bless all of us here, and especially bless our loved ones wherever they may be. Nourish our bodies with this food and our souls with Your Presence. In Jesus' name. Amen."*

"Nice job," Travis said as he handed his mother a plate. "You first, Mom."

Lidia patted Rafe on the arm. "Yes, that was nice. And I shouldn't have put you on the spot like that. It's just that if I had asked one of my own children I would have been playing favorites."

"No problem," Rafe said.

"Personally, I'm crushed," Peter said, his tone light despite his deadpan expression. "I thought I was your favorite."

Sam handed Rafe a plate. "That blessing was a little long, if you ask me. You could have just said, 'Bless this bunch while we eat our brunch.'"

"It's the same suggestion every year," Lucia said. "Don't pay any attention to him."

The food was delicious, but Rafe was more conscious of the company. Lucia's sisters-in-law were welcoming, and her brothers weren't as off-putting as they had been the first time he had met them, and for that he was glad. He did notice they teased Lucia about how she had dressed up and how they thought she looked better in her usual ponytail. She'd left her hair down today, and the dark strands gleamed. The off-white wool slacks and sweater were classics that managed to look both warm and springlike. Though she ignored her brothers' teasing, Rafe liked the idea that she might have dressed up for him.

The routine after they were finished eating was just as efficient, and by noon they were ready to leave for the Montgomery mansion, where more festivities were in store. Lidia would join them later, but first she wanted to go to the hospital to visit her husband. Lucia and her brothers had all set up times to visit him over the afternoon. Rafe and Lucia were planning their visit in time to see Ramón and Teresa's sister and return them to their parents.

As had happened at the condo, the commotion increased by a factor of ten with the combined extended families and other guests at the Montgomery mansion. An Easter egg hunt was planned, an event which normally took place on the expansive lawn behind the house, but had been moved indoors in deference to the cold weather. There must have been more than thirty children, with an equal number of adults wandering around, all of whom seemed to know each other. Rafe recognized some of the people there—Brendan, with his fiancée and her children, and Pastor Dawson and his family.

Lucia took off her coat and helped Ramón and Teresa with theirs, pointing him in the direction of a room where he was supposed to take them. A portable rack had been brought into the room, and many coats were already hung up.

"Lucia said that you'd be here," Colleen Montgomery said to him when he returned to the huge living room filled with groups of chatting people. "I wasn't sure you'd be brave enough to spend the day around her brothers."

Rafe smiled. "You've heard that old saying—'No pain, no gain.'"

Colleen laughed. "Not in reference to her brothers, but it definitely applies." She lowered her voice. "Now then. Since Lucia won't tell me anything about you two, I'll have to pump you for information."

"You'd better not," Lucia said, suddenly appearing at his side and slipping her arm through his. "C'mon. Time to put you to work. We get to supervise either the spoon walk or the duck walk. Which would you rather do?"

Bemused, he shook his head.

"Hey, I'm not done with him," Colleen complained.

Lucia waved her off. "Yes, you are. Or I'm going to tell him about the time you dyed my hair orange."

Rafe looked at her silky black strands. "Really?"

"Really," she said, threading their way through the groups of people toward another room.

"About this spoon walk and duck walk—I have no idea what you're talking about, so making an informed choice is impossible."

"There's not much choice except to keep the kids busy." She grinned. "But the games really are fun. The older kids have to hold a spoon in their mouth that, in turn, holds an egg, walk through an obstacle course and get a prize on the other end."

"I see," Rafe said. "And why do I have the idea that everyone walks away with a prize?"

"Sooner or later, they all do, but we're very competitive. I won a purple hippopotamus one year, and it was a prized possession."

With that, Rafe realized this was a tradition that had been going on since Lucia had been a child. Once more, his impressions of what a shared life with her would be like changed, this time including this other big clan. Since Brendan's brother and Colleen's brothers were all welcoming to Rafe when Brendan introduced him, that prospect wasn't quite so daunting. Once again, he was reminded of the camaraderie that he deliberately fostered with the hotshot crew.

The games got underway, and Lucia was right. From the toddlers to the older children, the kids were having fun. Ramón and Teresa got right into the spirit of things, and Rafe was pleased they were having a good time. His prayer was that by next year, their sister would be well enough to come, too. And with that, Rafe admitted that he kept seeing himself in Lucia's life and wanted her to be in his.

Over the course of the afternoon, Lucia introduced him to other friends, her arm casually through his as they talked.

Some of his feelings for Lucia must have shown because, during a lull between games, Colleen said, "I'm glad to see someone finally recognizes what a special woman she is."

Rafe didn't even pretend to not know who she referred to. "How could they not?"

"Exactly."

"When did you become good friends?"

Colleen laughed. "I can't remember a time when we weren't. Holly—that's her over there in the blue dress standing next to my cousin Jake—has two older brothers, I have two older brothers, and Lucia has three. We were hopelessly outnumbered, and being the youngest plus the only girls—"

"You were all spoiled rotten," Rafe couldn't help but tease.

"Hey, be nice. I'm trying to tell a story here."

"Undoubtedly about the awful big brothers," Travis interjected, coming to stand next to Colleen. "We called Holly, Colleen and Lucia the triple threat because, trust me, there's nothing they couldn't do when the three of them got together."

"That's right," Lucia agreed, appearing at Rafe's side. "Girls rock."

A while later, after they had all gathered next to the dining room where another huge meal was laid out in a buffet and Pastor Dawson had said grace, Jake Montgomery said he had an announcement. Pulling his wife, Holly, to his side, he said, "My family and Holly's have been friends for years. We became family when Holly and I got married. So we figured sharing our news that we're expecting a baby when the whole family is together was only fair."

"Congratulations" were called out while the women, all chattering at once, surged toward Holly and the men gave hearty slaps on the back to Jake.

As he went through the buffet with Lucia, Rafe asked about the man with professional-looking equipment shooting a lot of pictures.

"The editor of the *Sentinel* has been pestering Mom for months about doing a feature on the family. She finally agreed, but she didn't want any private pictures taken, so today's event was a compromise." Lucia met Rafe's gaze. "One of these days, when Dad retires from public life, all this will change."

As if recognizing what she had just said, her eyes took on a sudden shimmer.

"He'd be angry if he knew he was missing this," she softly said, her voice choked. "My dad is the best at this sort of thing. By now, he would have talked to everyone here. He has the most amazing memory for the little details of a person's life, and he really cares what happens to them. You'd like him."

"I'm sure I would," Rafe said, then added, "and I'm sure I'm going to get the chance."

The party began to wind down soon after the meal. Lucia and Rafe gathered up Ramón and Teresa, who were bubbling over with excitement from the day—and possibly the sugar they had consumed. They each carried Easter baskets filled with colored eggs, brightly wrapped candies and little treasures.

As they said their goodbyes, Colleen's mother gave Lucia another basket, with a "For their sister." She gave Rafe a hug, whispering in his ear, "You've been good for our Lucia. Welcome to the family."

SIXTEEN

Before Rafe could respond to Colleen's mother, she was gone.

As they headed for the hospital, where they were to meet Ramón and Teresa's parents before visiting Lucia's father, Rafe kept thinking about that statement of "Welcome to the family."

He'd be lying to himself if he said he hadn't thought about the possibility...a lot. He had. He simply hadn't realized his feelings for Lucia could be that transparent to anyone else.

"It's been a really good day," Lucia said from the passenger side of the car.

"The best part has been being with you." Rafe reached for her hand.

When she placed hers in his, he gave it a squeeze.

"You're not going to get all mushy on me, are you? Today is not a date."

"Really?" He sent a teasing glance in her direction. "Guess I'll have to adopt my non-date behavior for the rest of the day."

She glanced at the backseat, where Ramón and Teresa were chattering with each other in Spanish. "Since we have chaperones, that's probably smart."

At the hospital, they visited with the kids' parents for a few minutes, Rafe translating for Lucia and the kids talking a mile a minute about everything that had happened over the day. Little Ana was feeling well enough to be out of bed, which seemed to ease some of the worry in her parents' eyes.

When they were finished with their visit, they headed to the wing where Lucia's father was. As she had done the other time Rafe had been with her when she visited, she kissed her dad's cheek.

"I'm here with my friend Rafe," she told him, taking his hand. "You missed a good party today, Dad." Then she launched into a narrative of all that had happened over the day, her smile too bright.

Rafe got up from the chair and came to stand next to where she was sitting. "What do you normally do during your visits?"

She glanced at a stack of books next to the window. "Sometimes I read to him. He's a big Zane Grey fan, so I read those." She looked from Rafe to her father. "*Wild Horse Mesa* is your favorite, right, Dad?"

He didn't answer, of course.

Rafe watched the exchange, which made his heart hurt for Lucia. *Give this man his full healing,* Rafe silently prayed. *Provide relief and comfort for his family.*

They stayed until Travis and his family arrived, and they had just stepped outside the hospital doors when Lucia stopped suddenly and turned into his arms, hers tightly around his neck.

Surprised, Rafe held her, feeling her slender form shake. "What is it?"

"I hate these visits," she whispered against his neck. "Talking to him and never being sure if he's hearing a single thing we say, even though the doctors tell us that talking to him is important. I hate every single thing about it."

"I can understand that," he returned softly, holding her— just holding her—because that was all he knew to do.

"And that makes me feel guilty and ungrateful."

"I can understand that, too."

She leaned back a little to look at him. "You do, huh?" The tone was teasing, but the question wasn't.

Soberly, he nodded. "When my mom was sick, I was only five, but I knew she was dying, and it was the scariest thing you can imagine. I hated watching her slip away, and I remember being angry about that."

She touched his cheek with a cool hand. "I wish you hadn't had to go through that."

"No amount of wishing can change it."

Her smile quivered a little. "I pray for my dad every day, but I'm never sure whether I'm wishing or praying." She sighed. "I do wish he'd wake up. I'd like for him to know you."

"I'd like that, too," Rafe returned.

He kept thinking about that through the rest of the evening after he had taken Lucia home. There, they sat and talked for a while. He had the strongest urge to tell her that he loved her, but he didn't. Even though he had every indication she had deep feelings for him, he knew how badly she had been hurt by her ex-fiancé.

Plus, today's activities had given him a lot to think about. Her large, boisterous family was so different than the one he'd grown up in. He wasn't sure he'd ever fit in. And before this went a bit further, he had to decide if he wanted to fit in.

When he left Lucia's house a little before eleven, he found himself heading back to the hospital, where he climbed the stairs to the second floor and the wing where Lucia's father was. As usual, there was security stationed outside his door. Since he had been there a few hours earlier, the guard recognized him and merely nodded when Rafe went into the darkened hospital room.

Now that he was here, he questioned the instinct that had brought him. The room was quieter than it had been while other visitors were here. No conversation, no mindless noise from the television.

Rafe pulled a chair close to the bed and sat down, bowing his head and praying for the right words to talk to Lucia's father.

Finally, Rafe said, "You probably already know, sir, but I've fallen in love with your daughter." The sound of his own voice in the quiet room made him pause, made him feel afraid that he was being a fool to talk to a man in a coma. Remembering how Lucia had spoken with her father as though she was confident he heard her, Rafe cleared his throat and continued. "And I guess I should introduce myself. I'm Rafael Wright. I grew up in Montana, and now I'm a superintendent with the Sangre de Cristo hotshot crew. You might be thinking that isn't exactly the profession you'd like for a man in love with Lucia."

Rafe paused, staring at the man's peaceful face, thinking about what he had just confessed. This was the first time he'd said the words aloud, and he wanted to tell Lucia how he felt in the worst way. Except he was completely convinced that she wasn't ready to hear him. Not yet. Soon, maybe, but not yet.

Picking up the thread of what he wanted to say to Lucia's father, Rafe continued. "As for being a hotshot... it's been a good career, sir. I like the work, and I'm good at it. I can tell you, though, lately I've been feeling old. I now have people on my crew who were preschoolers when I started fighting fires. Though I've been thinking about making a change, I'd still like to do it for a couple more years. I'm finishing up my master's degree in fire science, so I have options that I didn't a few years ago. And I guess that would be important for you to know. Your daughter is an independent woman, and I like that about her. But if there comes a time when she wants to make a change, to have a family with me, I can take care of her."

Rafe paused again, staring a long moment at his hands clasped together, his elbows resting on his knees. "Today was an interesting day, sir. I got to spend it with your family and your good friends, the Montgomerys. And I can see how much you all mean to one another. I'm a stranger to most of them, but they welcomed me as a friend, and that meant a lot.

"So you may be wondering what I'm doing here, and to tell you the truth, I'm not too sure myself. Under other circumstances, I'd be asking for your blessing when I ask your daughter to marry me. I'm hoping you'll come out of this coma soon so I can do that."

Rafe fell silent as he looked at the man's face, which was all in shadows in the darkened room.

"He'd like you," said a male voice from the doorway.

Rafe turned around and watched Sam Vance enter the room. When Rafe started to stand, Sam pressed a hand against his shoulder.

"I've been out there listening." When Rafe looked up at him, he grinned. "You've just told me everything I need to know about the kind of man you are…if there had been any doubt after you came to see me the other day with the info about O'Brien." He paused, his glance shifting to the sleeping man in the hospital bed. "I'm pretty sure my dad would say something to you along the lines of 'Be good to my daughter, and you'll have no argument from me.'"

"I hope so," Rafe said, standing.

Sam extended his hand. "The same goes for me. Be good to my sister and you'll have no argument from me."

* * *

"I am so ready for spring," Lucia told Rafe while they were having lunch at the Stagecoach Café a couple of days after Easter. She glanced outside at the snow falling in huge wet flakes. Her day off, and it was snowing. Granted, she hadn't had anything planned for outside since she was finishing up the job of painting and wallpapering her bathroom. Still, it would have been nice to have a springlike day.

"Personally I'm glad to see all this moisture. It should knock down the fire danger, at least for a while." Rafe broke open a package of crackers and picked up his spoon for the bowl of thick chicken-noodle soup that had just been set on the table. "I saw your cousin in front of that new art museum over on Fourth Street. Did you ever get the disk of photos from him?"

"No, the dog," she replied, smiling so Rafe would know she was teasing. "Since I'm nearly finished with hanging the wallpaper in my bathroom, I'm almost ready to start the next project, and I'd like to get the window started so I can have it finished by my mother's birthday." She shook her head, thinking about that last conversation she'd had with him. "He's usually very conscientious about that kind of thing, too."

The front door of the café jangled, and she looked up. To her surprise, her mother and Colleen came in, laughing about something. For as long as Lucia could remember, there had been a special bond between the two—one that she sometimes envied. Like now, when they were talking so intently with each other that neither one noticed her as the hostess led them toward a table in her direction.

"Hi," Lucia said as the hostess brought them past the booth where she and Rafe were sitting.

"Honey, I almost didn't see you," her mom said, looking from her to Rafe as a smile lit her face.

"I noticed," Lucia replied. "You'd think you two were

cooking up something. Want to join us?" she asked, scooting over in the booth. "Or is this a supersecret meeting?"

"Just girls having lunch," her mother assured her, waving off the hostess with a thank-you and sitting down next to Lucia. "I received the flowers you sent, Rafe. Very thoughtful. Thank you."

He ducked his head a little as though he'd been caught with his hand in the cookie jar. "The thanks is all mine. I had a good time with your family."

Lucia hadn't known he had sent flowers and decided this was one more thing she liked about the man. He did kind things without expecting any notice.

"You don't mind us joining you?" Colleen asked, her attention mostly on Rafe.

He shook his head and like Lucia, moved closer to the window, making room for them.

They ordered lunch, and while they were waiting for it to come, Sam came through the door, immediately noticed them and headed in their direction. Predictably, he wanted to be with them, so they squeezed in a little more. After he placed his order for lunch, the conversation once again moved to the weather, the predicted cold snap and how tired they all were of winter. Except for Rafe.

"All this snow means skiing at A-Basin until June," he said with a grin. "Not that I'm likely to enjoy it. We might be having a lot of moisture, but the northwest is still in a drought, and the fire danger is so high that we could find ourselves headed there at any time."

Though Lucia knew his busy season was coming and that he liked his job as much as she liked hers, she was dreading seeing him go. She'd miss him. He'd told her that he'd been gone for ninety-three days one summer, although the usual was about sixty. Even that sounded too long.

To get her mind on something else, she asked her mother, "Have you talked to Alessandro since he got back?"

"Mr. Tall, Dark and Mysterious?" Colleen caught her glance. "Not to mention handsome."

"He's still in Italy," Lucia's mother said. "I talked to him on Easter."

"Well, he's back," Lucia said. "Rafe and I saw him last week, coming into the café, and Rafe saw him—"

"This morning," Rafe filled in.

"I'm sure he's still in Italy," her mother said, her brow crinkling a little. "He was at his mother's house, and I spoke with the whole family."

"Relative or not, he's a good one for you to stay away from," Sam said, pointing a finger at Colleen. "That tall, dark and mysterious baloney just means he's a slick guy that no one can get a handle on."

"Are you casting stones, Sam?" Lucia's mother asked.

He immediately nodded. "In his case, yes. You know, if it looks like a duck and walks like a duck, blah, blah, blah."

The waitress interrupted by bringing the other three meals, which was just as well, Lucia thought. The dissent between Sam and her mother over Alessandro wouldn't find a solution today, and maybe never.

"Speaking of 'walks like a duck,'" Sam said after he had eaten most of his lunch, "the security tape at the hospital confirmed your hunch, Rafe. We haven't been able to identify the guy, but we know the exact date and time when someone brought a gallon paint bucket into the hospital and headed for the children's wing. It was only five hours before the call came in."

"You guys have been talking about the hospital fire?" Lucia asked, her gaze on Rafe. "And you didn't tell me?"

While he nodded, Sam said, "Thanks to a couple of angles

he had on the case, we uncovered some evidence we might not have." Sam looked at Lucia. "And if he's right, sis, you should be back on light duty, not in the line of fire."

"We've had this discussion already," she said, "and the answer is still the same. No."

Sam waved a hand. "Maybe you can talk some sense into her, Rafe. She won't listen to me."

"Maybe," Rafe said blandly.

As always happened when challenged by her brothers, Lucia felt her temper slip. "Just try it, buddy."

She intended the words to come out as teasing but realized they didn't when Rafe looked sharply at her.

Since that she had finished her lunch and realized that she was on the verge of yet another blowup with her brother, Lucia said, "I've got to go. I'm in the middle of hanging wallpaper and…" Boy, did that sound lame. "I really do have to go."

Her mother got up so Lucia could slip out of the booth. She dropped a kiss on her mother's cheek. "I'll call you later."

"Okay, honey."

"I'm ready to go, too," Rafe said.

"You don't have to leave on my account," Lucia said. "You could stay and *talk* to my brother."

She headed for the cashier at the front of the café and had already gotten her money out to pay for lunch when Rafe caught up with her.

"I can get it," he said. "I invited you, after all."

"I can pay for my own lunch." Once more, the words came out sharper than she intended.

Rafe could see that she was upset but wasn't sure why. Arguing with her about something as stupid as paying for lunch didn't make sense. After she paid, she hurried outside, and by the time he had left the money for his own lunch, she was at her car.

"Hey, Lucia, wait," he called to her.

She paused in the act of unlocking her car.

"Are you mad at me, too?" he asked when he caught up with her, giving her a smile.

"No," she said, then, "Yes."

"Why?"

"Because you've been talking to Sam about the fire and because you agree with him."

"Okay," Rafe said. "We did talk, and I'm sure I do agree with him about some things, but maybe you'd like to be a little more specific."

"Go use that calm tone on somebody else," she said, pulling her keys out of her purse. "Exactly what did you tell him about the hospital fire?"

"I told him about O'Brien and the lacquer purchase because I think you're on to something, Lucia. It's no big secret that I've been looking into this, too. O'Brien came across as a lowlife that very first day, and I don't like the way he's treated you."

"He thinks I got my job because I'm my father's daughter," Lucia said. "He's been riding me like this since he became the commander of my firehouse."

"I think there's more to it than that. For him to be accusing you of making the fire worse when there isn't a shred of evidence to back it up worries me. I hate to admit it, Lucia, but your brother might be right. Until things cool off a little and he finishes his criminal investigation and Johnson finishes his arson investigation, maybe you should be on light duty."

"Not you, too." She opened her car door. "I am so sick of being coddled like I'm some little incompetent—"

"I don't think that. You know I don't."

"But you talked to my brother and you left me out of the conversations—"

"Because there was nothing too concrete that I could tell you." He came a step closer. "I didn't want to worry you with my suspicions."

She looked at him, her mouth set in an angry line. "It's the same old thing, then. 'Let's keep things from Lucia because she can't handle them' has been the way I've been treated by my brothers and my father my whole life." She sucked in a shuddering breath. "Did you know that my dad and I argued about this very thing the day he was shot? I wanted something different, something more from you." Her voice trailed away, and she looked at him with tears shimmering in her eyes. "I had hoped you were different."

"I am different," he said, his own temper rising. It was on the tip of his tongue to tell her, *I'm the guy who's in love with you, the guy who can't imagine his life without you in it.* Telling her that in the middle of an argument didn't meet a single romantic image he had of the moment, so he added, "I'm concerned that if O'Brien is involved in the fire, you're somehow a target."

"That's just another way of telling me to go to my protected little corner and do something safe like knit a sweater. And I won't."

SEVENTEEN

With that, Lucia climbed into her vehicle and started the engine. Rafe watched her go, those unshed tears twisting his gut. He wasn't exactly sure what had happened, but he did know that he'd hurt her. And at the moment, he wasn't sure how to make things better between them.

The more he thought about their exchange, the more sure he was that her hurt had more to do with that argument between her and her father than anything he'd done. Except that wasn't anything he could tell her, but rather a realization she had to come to on her own. All he knew with any certainty was that he wanted to take away her hurt, which would also put him in the no-win situation of sheltering her—something she obviously didn't want.

Snow fell the rest of the afternoon, and the temperature dropped. Rafe's drive home from work that evening was miserable, making his surly mood even worse. His thoughts circled around the argument he'd had with Lucia, and he admitted to himself that he was no closer to understanding what had caused it than he had been at the time.

After he reached the apartment, he parked his car and made his way through the deep slush that would be ice by morning. Lucia was right. It was time for spring weather.

She was also right that he hadn't been as sensitive toward her feelings about light duty and her pride in doing her job well as he might have. And since medical calls made up nearly eighty percent of the emergencies they responded to, the chances of her being involved in another arson like the one at the hospital were remote. Unless…and it was that elusive *unless* that kept bothering him. He did owe her an apology, and the sooner he took care of that, the better.

His head down as he walked through the snow that had become fine, biting sleet over the last hour, he bumped into someone coming down the outside stairwell.

Instantly, he reached out to steady the person as he looked up. Mary O'Brien's startled gaze met his. Or at least he thought she was Mary O'Brien since he'd never seen her up close before.

"I'm sorry," he said. "I should have been paying more attention to where I was going. Are you okay?"

She nodded, but she didn't look okay. In fact, she looked as though she might burst into tears at any moment.

"You're Mrs. O'Brien, right?"

Again, she nodded. "Mary. And you're that guy who saved those two children that day at the hospital. I've seen you with Lucia—"

"Are you sure you're all right?" Rafe asked, his hand still gently holding her arm.

"I was looking for Brendan Montgomery," she said, gazing around the building, which looked exactly like the seven others in the complex. "I'm not even sure I have the right building."

"You do," Rafe said. "Would you like me to walk with you?"

She gazed at him a moment as if weighing some internal struggle. Finally, she nodded, her brown eyes troubled. "I probably should have gone to his office but…" Her voice trailed away, and once again, unshed tears made her eyes shimmer.

Rafe lightly touched her elbow as they climbed the stairs to the second floor where he lived—his apartment at one end of the hall and Brendan's at the other. At the top of the stairwell, he opened the door, the inside hallway feeling much warmer than the chilly temperature and sleet outside.

"Brendan's apartment is right here," Rafe said, "and I live at the other end of the hall."

"Thanks for your help," she said, then knocked on the door that Rafe had indicated.

"If there's anything else I can do…" he added, heading toward his own door.

Now that he'd met O'Brien's wife, Rafe understood why Lucia had expressed so much concern for her. The woman looked fragile. Granted, he hadn't been around that many pregnant women, but he remembered his sister when she'd been expecting. She had glowed. Mary didn't.

Casting a final glance down the hallway where Mary O'Brien stood, he unlocked the door. When she glanced up, he waved, then went into his apartment.

"Hey, bro," Malik called from the kitchen over the sound of his favorite jazz album on the stereo. "Hope you're in the mood for chili."

"What are my choices if I'm not?" Chili sounded good, Rafe thought, despite teasing Malik about it. Rafe took off his jacket and hung it in the closet next to the front door, knowing the chili would taste as good as it smelled.

"Eye of gnat, flank of flea," Malik immediately responded.

Rafe came into the kitchen. "You put only a half bottle of hot sauce in it this time, right?"

"In deference to your tender palate, I did." Malik grinned. "I aced the chemistry exam that I took the other day, which means the final exam will be extra credit instead of trying to bring up my grade."

"All that worry for nothing," Rafe said, taking a glass out of the cupboard and filling it from the pitcher of sweet tea in the refrigerator.

"Your sister called and said to tell you that she has good news," Malik said, adjusting the temperature on the burner where the chili sat. "Maybe that means things are going to be okay with her marriage?"

"Let's hope," Rafe agreed as someone knocked on the door. "That would be good news."

When he opened it, Mary O'Brien stood on the other side, an uncertain smile on her face.

"Brendan isn't home," she said. "And I wondered… It's so far from home, would you mind if I waited here for a little while?"

"I wouldn't mind at all," Rafe said, motioning for her to come in. "If you'd like, I can call him. Maybe we could find out how long he'll be."

"Oh, would you?" She moved timidly into the room, holding her purse in front of her like a shield. "That would be nice, thank you."

"No problem." When Malik came into view, Rafe said, "This is my roommate, Malik Williams."

"Hi," he said.

Rafe told her to have a seat while he went to the cabinet next to the phone to find Brendan's phone number. The man had given him a card with his business cell phone number on it, so Rafe figured that was the number to give Mary. And he admitted that he was a lot curious to know why she wanted to see him. Was it as a friend? Or in his role as an FBI agent?

While he was doing that, Malik was chatting with her about the awful weather, encouraging her to sit down and offering her something to drink.

Rummaging through the stack of cards, Rafe soon found

the one he wanted, and he brought it and the cordless phone to Mary.

She took the receiver and the business card from him, then dialed the number. She must have reached an answering machine because her face fell, and she looked uncertainly at Rafe. "What's your number here?"

He told her, and she repeated the number into the phone, which Rafe also found very, very odd. Why hadn't she given her own telephone number?

As soon as she disconnected, she handed the receiver back to him. "The message said he should call me back within half an hour. Would you mind if I waited?"

More curious by the second, Rafe shook his head. "Now maybe you'd like something to drink. It's cold outside, and you look a little chilled." So far, she'd made no move to take off her coat.

"Well, yes. If it's not too much trouble."

"We have coffee or I can nuke some water for hot chocolate," Malik said, his bland expression giving away none of his thoughts. Rafe suspected he was just as curious. "We might even have some herbal caffeine-free tea left over from when Rafe's sister visited a few months back."

"Herbal tea, please," Mary said, her gaze fastening on Rafe. "You have a sister?"

"Two of them," he said, going into the kitchen and getting out the box of tea while Malik put a mug of water into the microwave oven.

Still wearing her coat, Mary followed them into the kitchen, and for the first time since arriving, gave a genuine smile. "It smelled so good when I came in that I had to come peek to see if you make as big a mess as Neil does when he cooks. This kitchen is way too clean for guys."

Rafe glanced around, imagining the counters from her

perspective. Since he was often called away with no notice, he'd figured out early in his career that it was just as easy to keep things neat so he didn't have to come home to a mess. Fortunately, Malik had the same habits, which had made being roommates easy.

Malik winked at her. "If that's a compliment, ma'am, I'm taking it."

Her smile faltered once more, and Rafe pulled out a chair from the table.

"Are you sure you're okay?" he asked.

"I was just thinking of Neil." She shook her head slightly as if clearing her thoughts, then gave them a murmured thanks when they set the hot water and tea in front of her.

While they waited for Brendan to call, Rafe sat down with her. "I imagine you're looking forward to the baby's arrival," he said. "I remember how excited my sister was."

Mary nodded. "We're both nervous, too. We've been married a long time, so it's a big change." Her gaze turned inward once more. "He was reprimanded at work this week, and he's taking it really hard."

Rafe felt a pang, since he had a hunch that the letter he sent to the fire chief would have been the reason for the reprimand. At the time, he'd had only one thought—make sure O'Brien was accountable for his actions. He hadn't once thought about any possible fallout to anyone else. Rafe stared at his hands, knowing he had done the right thing by complaining to O'Brien's superiors about his treatment of Lucia. Even so, he felt bad that his actions had caused this woman problems.

Mary slipped off her coat and picked up her cup of tea for another sip. "Is that chili on the stove?"

"Yes, ma'am," Malik said.

"Tell me about your recipe," she said. It was the beginning of a more relaxed conversation that filled the next half hour.

Through it, Rafe kept thinking about Lucia's comment the other day that she hadn't wanted to hurt this woman with any accusations. Now that he had met her, he understood that. To all appearances, she was a gentle person—not the kind of woman Rafe had imagined O'Brien being married to.

A little while later, there was a knock on the door, which Malik answered. When he came back to the kitchen, Brendan was with him.

"Hey, Mary," he said, dropping to his haunches next to the chair where she sat. "I sure was surprised to hear from you."

"I've been thinking about this for days," she said, "and I simply don't know what to do." She reached for her coat pocket, pulled out an envelope and handed it to him. "I am sure this is illegal, but it wasn't the kind of thing I could take to the police. Since you're an FBI agent and all, I was hoping maybe you could help with this." She tapped the envelope with a finger. "I'm sure there must be a law or something."

Brendan looked from the envelope to Rafe and Malik, then back to Mary. "Why don't we go someplace where we can talk?"

She glanced at Rafe, then stood up with her coat in her hands. He took it from her and held it so she could put it on.

"You've been very kind," she said. "Thank you for everything."

"It was nothing," he said.

Brendan guided her out the door with an absent wave in their direction.

"Weird," Malik said when the door closed behind them.

"Yeah," Rafe agreed, wondering what was in the envelope. He suspected it had something to do with O'Brien's possible involvement in the hospital fire. "I forgot to pick up the mail when I came in," he said, heading for the door. "Be back in a minute."

"Well, hurry," Malik said. "Soup's on."

Rafe went outside to go downstairs to the front of the building, where the bank of mailboxes was. He was sure that it was even colder than it had been when he'd come in a few minutes earlier—a really miserable night to be out. He got the mail and climbed the stairs two at a time, glad he didn't have to drive anywhere and hoping that Mary O'Brien was composed enough to make it home safely.

When he got back to the apartment, Brendan was there, which surprised Rafe. The talk with Mary had been an extremely short one.

"Do you know if Lucia is working tonight?" Brendan asked.

"It's her day off," Rafe said, the hairs on the back of his neck rising. "Why?"

Frowning, Brendan headed for the door. "You didn't hear a thing from me, but I worry when I see firm evidence that a man has a definite, serious gambling problem. You know all those suspicions we talked about the weekend we went skiing?"

Rafe nodded.

"When that same man is overheard saying a certain firefighter is toast—and those were the exact words, no name mentioned—I worry even more. The only problem is," he continued, "I don't have a single solid piece of evidence that would allow me to go forward or turn anything over to the local police."

"It could be another idle threat," Rafe felt compelled to point out, though the words bothered him. "I sent a letter to his superiors, identifying all the reasons why his investigation of Lucia was a witch hunt that had no basis in fact. The comment could be referring to that."

"Do you believe it? I mean, really believe it in your gut?" Brendan asked.

Rafe shook his head. "I had lunch with Lucia today and the whole business of these threats came up. She had a fit when Sam suggested that she go back on light duty."

Brendan opened the door to head toward his apartment. "That's a tough situation. I understand Sam's concern, but I can't blame her any for wanting to do her job. She wouldn't be the Lucia we all know and love if she were any other way." He went into the hall with a wave. "See you later."

The Lucia we all know and love. Rafe's gut twisted once more with worry, especially now that he was part of the circle of those who loved her.

Rafe went to the phone and dialed Lucia's number. There was no response on the other end until her answering machine clicked on. He left a message, telling her that he was sorry he had upset her when they'd had lunch and asking her to give him a call. When he glanced at the clock on the kitchen stove, the time was not yet seven. She could be anywhere, and to expect her to be safely at home was ridiculous and put her into the safe cocoon she hated.

Rafe and Malik took their chili to the living room to eat in front of the television. After they finished eating and put their bowls into the dishwasher, Rafe restlessly prowled the apartment, the sitcoms on TV failing to hold his attention. He kept thinking about the conversations this evening with Mary and Brendan and about the argument with Lucia and the fact that she hadn't called him back. Waiting was his least favorite thing, and his first, strongest urge was to go see her. Remembering how skittish she had been when they first began "dating" was the only thing that kept him from calling her again or going to her house.

By the time the late news came on, Rafe wished he'd gone to see Lucia instead of calling her. This was the first time since they had met that the day had ended with them being at odds with each other. He didn't like it, and he vowed it would be the last.

"I'm going to bed," he told Malik.

"Me, too, as soon as I watch the news."

Rafe was brushing his teeth when Malik rapped on the bathroom door and said, "You've gotta come see this."

Rafe opened the door and followed his friend to the living room, where the picture on the television showed a reporter standing in front of a blazing fire.

"This is one of three fires that apparently broke out at the same time this evening," a young reporter, bundled up against the cold, was saying, "and in a bizarre twist, they all have connections to the Montgomery and Vance families. In addition to this fire at Montgomery Construction, which is a long way from being contained, there have also been fires at the office of AdVance Investigations and the Double V Ranch near Cripple Creek."

Behind the reporter, another fire truck rolled up, the insignia on the side of the vehicle reading Engine #22, which Rafe knew was Lucia's unit. He scanned the firefighters coming off the vehicle, frustrated because the camera was too far away to identify any of them and relieved to know that Lucia was off today.

Still, without conscious thought, he picked up the phone and called her once more. Once more, her answering machine picked up. His attention went back to the television news, which had moved on to another story. "Lucia, it's Rafe," he said. "I know it's late, but please call me when you get in."

Just then, his pager went off, and a second later, Malik's did, as well. When Rafe checked the display, the number was from the volunteer wildland fire unit.

"Wright here," he said when he called in. The dispatcher told him that the Colorado Springs volunteer wildfire units were being asked to respond to the fire at Montgomery Construction. Rafe said he and Malik were on their way. That could only mean that, in spite of the freezing temperatures and icy conditions, the blaze was threatening nearby property.

A certain firefighter is toast. The words shivered through Rafe as he quickly changed into the heavier clothes needed to protect against tonight's freezing weather. Surely she was safely at home, with her mother or somewhere else since this was her day off, he thought, adding a prayer for her safety. When he came out of his room, Malik had also changed his clothes, his Pulaski in one hand and his hard hat in the other.

When they came out of the apartment, it was snowing again, fine, biting flakes. They arrived on scene following their equipment truck for the last half mile. A police car, its emergency lights flashing, was parked across the street, blocking access. Rafe showed his volunteer ID, and the cop waved them through. The flashing emergency lights and glow of the fire lit the sky, and through the dark in front of them was the controlled chaos of the responding emergency units.

Rafe parked his pickup and he and Malik grabbed their gear and ran to catch up with the truck. They came through the open gate, the compound bigger than it looked from the street. Various vehicles belonging to the construction company were parked on one side of the facility; a large, old-fashioned wood and brick warehouse dating from the early twentieth century was on the opposite side; and in between was a historic barn that was a well-known landmark and one of the oldest buildings in the city. In front of the warehouse was a smaller building, the words Montgomery Fine Cabinetry in huge raised letters visible above the door and a bank of windows.

Three engines had responded in addition to the wildland

fire fighting unit Rafe and Malik were assigned to. An EMT bus rolled to a stop a short distance from the other trucks.

Battalion Chief O'Brien was talking to the driver when they caught up, and his glanced skipped over Rafe.

"The wildfire crews are assigned to protecting the barn," he said, waving in that direction. "Find Barney Fields—he's directing that action."

"You're the incident commander?" Rafe asked.

"That's right," O'Brien said. "Now get going."

"This night is getting stranger by the minute," Malik said to Rafe. "First his wife coming to the apartment, and now this."

"No doubt," Rafe agreed, taking in everything around them. The blanket of smoke generated by the fire hung close to the ground, the acrid smell making their eyes burn and the heat of it turning the falling snow to mist. The wind couldn't have been worse for protecting the buildings, as it was blowing in the direction of the only access to the facility.

Rafe lifted his fisted glove toward his friend, who lifted his own fist. They knocked together and Rafe said, "Be safe," as he always did.

They found Barney Fields, the crew boss for their assignment.

"Your task is simple," he told them. "Protect the barn. If the cabinet shop at the front of the warehouse goes like it might, it will burn mighty hot."

Rafe could imagine that too well. With the high volatility of varnishes, lacquers and other finishing materials, it would be a raging fire that could only be contained, not put out. Beyond him, Rafe could see that the back of the warehouse was engulfed in flames. With all the dried lumber and other building supplies inside, there was plenty of fuel for the fire.

Like the well-oiled team they were, Rafe and Malik worked with the other volunteer members of the crew, running the hose and wetting down the roof and side of the barn that faced the worst part of the fire.

The unit stood as a barrier between the warehouse and the barn. Individually, their attention was on the sparks continually blown across the roof of the barn from the burning warehouse, the streams of water attacking each one.

Rafe remembered Lucia telling him that it was often used for various social functions for their two families, and she had related stories about coming here as a small child.

Icicles formed on the eaves of the barn, an odd contrast to the roiling warehouse fire that burned hot enough Rafe could feel its heat through his turnout coat. Sparks continued to rain down on the barn roof, instantly turned into harmless soot by the water their unit sprayed onto the structure.

While keeping an eye on their own task, Rafe was very aware of all the efforts going on around him, especially as the fire seemed to be gaining the upper hand and the call was put out for additional engines to respond.

A group of firefighters suddenly came past their position toward the part of the warehouse that housed the cabinet shop and finishing center. Rafe recognized Luke Donovan—and an instant later, saw Lucia.

EIGHTEEN

Lucia.

No, Rafe thought in stunned disbelief. He didn't want her to be here.

Except she was and, as was usual for her, she was in the thick of things. She didn't notice him, and Rafe didn't expect that she would have since her focus was correctly on her assignment.

Some of the crews, like Rafe's, were involved in the defensive protection of the structure—to keep the fire from taking hold, as with the barn. In the case of the warehouse, to keep it from spreading. That meant pouring water into the fire, eventually putting a damper on its sources of fuel.

The spray back from the nozzle was bitterly cold, with frost forming on the brass fittings. An enveloping cold vapor created by the snow and water fogged the compound, reducing visibility and giving the emergency lights a halo. A sheen of frost began to cover everything—the ground, the hoses, the various apparatus.

Fire and ice. As the fire grew worse, so did the danger from the ice.

Offensive operations were also underway, a more effective and more dangerous assignment for those firefighters inside the building fighting the fire at a closer range.

The crew Lucia was with disappeared into the warehouse. Rafe hated every single thing about her being inside the building, even though he knew it was her job, knew she was capable and that her partner had her back and vice versa. Her accusation that he'd prefer she be in a protected corner doing something safe like knitting burned because it was true. However capable he knew her to be, he would have much rather had her anywhere else than this too-dangerous fire tonight.

Too many things about this reminded him of the fire at the hospital, especially since O'Brien was once again the incident commander. That fire had been contained in short order, but it could have too easily become the kind of inferno taking down the warehouse. All the suspicions Rafe had from the earlier fire churned inside him. *A certain firefighter is toast.*

Was it the threat of a disgruntled chief, a mere turn of phrase reflecting his frame of mind at the moment? Or was it more sinister? Rafe hated thinking anyone he knew personally could be that evil.

At odds with the rational knowledge that Lucia was a professional doing her job was his continued worry about her because of all the unknowns. He wondered if she knew that fires had also broken out at her cousin's ranch and at her brother's investigative agency. Better for her concentration, he decided, if she didn't know.

Once more, he was struck with the irony of the thought. She would undoubtedly interpret his not wanting her to know just how extensive the problem was as shielding her. He decided they were going to have a serious talk about this, since his very nature was to protect her, to shield her from hurt and danger.

Over the next little while, the fire grew more intense, and as it did, the weather grew steadily worse, the snow falling harder. Slush formed on the ground, making it difficult to move around easily.

Sometime later, a crew of firefighters ran from the warehouse. Seconds later, there was a huge groaning, crackling sound from the warehouse as the roof collapsed. An instant of utter blackness followed from the smoke rushing out in all directions. In the next second, the fire flared again, this time inside the cabinet shop in the adjoining building. Rafe could see that despite all the precautions, not enough water had been put on the structure to keep it from going up.

O'Brien came by, speaking into his radio. "Donovan, get your team inside and get water on that finishing room."

Rafe heard the words through a surreal haze as he recalled the day of the hospital fire, when Lucia had been sent into the heart of the fire with similar instructions. Only now she was being sent into a room where the danger was far greater. O'Brien should have been ordering his people to get out of there, not in. *A certain firefighter is toast.*

Every single instinct Rafe had said this was a trap.

With all the experience of eighteen years of fire fighting, he looked at the barn and instantly decided there were enough people left to make sure their assignment was safely fulfilled.

"I'm going after Lucia," he told Malik.

"I'm your partner, and you're not going alone," he said back, handing off his hose to one of the other volunteers standing next to him.

Just that fast, they headed across the open space between the barn and the cabinet shop. Fire flickered through the glass windows like the gleaming eyes of a monster. And the name of the monster was flashover, which could happen at any second. The single biggest killer of firefighters was flashover, and in this case, it was a danger that O'Brien should have seen coming.

Rafe knew the vapors from any leaking finishing compounds were as likely to be hugging the floor as rising to the ceiling, creating a situation that firefighters should never have been put in. O'Brien had to know that. He had to.

Rafe ran toward the building with Malik hot on his heels. Through the open door, Rafe could see the four firefighters inside, wielding the hoses in place and pouring water on the blaze. Flames were roiling across the ceiling. Mixed with the hot smell of the fire were the odors of the chemicals and solvents used in the finishing of cabinets.

"Get out!" he shouted, tapping the first of the fire fighters on the shoulder. "Get out now!" He pushed the firefighter in the direction of the exit.

Ahead of him, he saw Donovan's burly form and a slighter one next to him that could only be Lucia.

"Donovan," Rafe shouted.

The man didn't hear him, so Rafe grabbed the hose. "C'mon."

Lucia turned then, and she saw him. Rafe, and dressed in his turnout gear! He was frantically gesturing to them to leave the building.

His sense of urgency warred with her astonishment of seeing him here.

"Get out," he was shouting over and over. He pointed toward the floor. "The vapors are about to ignite!"

She tapped Donovan's arm, who nodded his understanding.

In the next instant, the joists above them groaned, and the ceiling began to cave in. One beam at the back of the room collapsed, then the others fell one by one like dominoes.

"Let's go," Donovan yelled.

They weren't fast enough to keep ahead of them. The next one slammed down in front of them, cracking as it hit a work-table and a group of cabinets that had been lined up. Debris splattered everywhere. The broken end of the beam hit Rafe on the head, knocking his helmet off and sending him to the floor.

Lucia ran toward him.

Donovan and Malik were ahead of her, pushing away the debris from around him. The raging fire behind them cast flickering shadows.

She knelt next to him, her paramedic and firefighting training kicking in, overriding her fear. She pulled off a glove and placed her fingers on the pulse at his neck. To her relief, it beat strongly. A gash above his eyebrow was pulsing blood.

Donovan went to the end of the heavy beam, "You pull him out," he ordered her and Malik, "when I say 'go.'"

He braced his shoulder under the beam and lifted. It groaned and moved a fraction but not enough to pull Rafe out. Malik rushed to him, and together they pushed, then shoved some more. Finally, the beam lifted mere inches, then, with a screech, lifted a few more.

"Now!" Donovan yelled.

Lucia grabbed Rafe beneath his arms and pulled with all her might. He was heavy, far heavier than she had imagined. She pulled again, the effort sinking her to the floor. At last, he slid free of the beam and Donovan and Malik let it drop.

Together, they picked up Rafe, and Malik pulled him across his shoulders in a classic fireman's carry. Behind them, the tone of the burning fire changed, and they raced toward the exit.

They burst from the building an instant before the fire flashed over, breaking out the windows, the blossoms of flame reaching toward them. A thunderous whooshing roar assaulted them as they ran away from the building.

"Get the EMTs," Donovan yelled into his radio, "right now."

Lucia ran through the water and icy slush to keep up with

Malik, who carried his friend as though he weighed nothing. Questions crowded her mind, keeping pace with her fervent prayer that Rafe be safe. Where had Rafe and Malik come from? What were they doing here?

Behind them, an explosion thundered, the concussion of it pushing them forward. A huge ball of flame rose into the sky, shimmering through the falling snow in a mad orange balloon of color that lit the area like slow lightning before disappearing into the clouds.

At last, they met up with the EMT bus. Only then did Malik set down his friend, laying him gently on the gurney.

"What's this big guy's name?" one of the EMTs asked as she raised the head of the gurney slightly.

"Rafael Wright," Lucia and Malik said at the same time.

He was holding on tight to one of Rafe's hands, concern bracketing his mouth in harsh lines.

Over the next few minutes, it was all a matter of doing the routine she had been through hundreds of times. A routine different this time because she had never before been so frightened for another person. Not simply another person, but Rafe. Her Rafe, who had become more important to her than she had ever imagined possible.

He had been there to warn them of the impending disaster and get them out. How? How was that possible?

Her throat choked as she thought of him paying the price for his warning. *Take care of him, Lord* was her fierce prayer.

She helped the EMT put a pressure bandage on the gash above his eyebrow. Though Lucia had checked his pulse earlier, she did so again, needing the reassurance of the strong beat beneath her fingertips. The EMT pulled open one eye, then the other, flicking a light across them.

"Responsive pupils," she said.

"Good," Lucia breathed, looking once more at Malik,

whose chin quivered with suppressed emotion. She grabbed his free hand. "He's going to be okay."

Malik nodded and managed a smile, one that fell far short of his usual huge one. "He'd better be."

Minutes later, they helped load him into the back of the ambulance, which then threaded its way through all the emergency equipment and headed toward the street.

The usual routine was to go back to the task at hand as soon as the patient was evacuated to the hospital. Except there was nothing usual about this situation. Lucia gazed around at the controlled chaos all around them, memories of all the times she had been here crowding out the activity to put out the fire.

Except she didn't see any of it, lost in that moment of stunned recognition that Rafe had been here and that he had come to get them at great risk to his own safety. She knew just how dangerous the chemicals used to finish furniture were, and yet she had ignored her instincts and training when they had gone into the building. All because she hadn't wanted to make waves with her battalion chief.

She began to shake. She owed her teammates more than that, and if she couldn't put her own good judgment first, she had no business being here. That idea shook her to her core.

On top of that came the memory of the argument she'd had with Rafe just this afternoon. Had it been only this afternoon? Her accusations had been unfair, borne out of frustration that she had taken out on him. The idea that he could have died a few minutes ago filled her with such a sense of loss that it felt like the night her father had been shot. She had argued with them both, and she'd left things unsaid and unsettled. Her dad had deserved more from her. Rafe deserved more from her.

She looked around the compound, the physical loss mirroring what she felt in her heart. She had so many good memories of being here, and even though the barn had been saved, it would never, ever be the same. Still, the memories poured through her.

The day she had come here with her mother to pick out the wood and the finish for the new cabinets to go in her townhome. The barbeques and parties that had been held in the old barn. The generations-long tie between the Montgomery family and her own.

With that came the memory of the night at the condo in Breckenridge, where they had discussed all the things that had happened to their families in recent months. And now this fire.

"You haven't heard a word I've said," Donovan complained.

Lucia looked at him, realizing that he had been talking all this time and that she hadn't heard him at all. "I'm sorry. What?"

"O'Brien has lost his mind. And I wasn't paying close enough attention," Donovan said. "I smelled fumes the instant we went into the building and knew we had no business being in there. Everything about that went against the standard protocol." He pointed a finger at her. "I know you're toeing the line because of all the problems with him, Lucia, but you knew it, too."

She nodded. She had. But her first thought at the time was to follow orders and not give O'Brien a single reason to come down on her.

"We've got to have each other's backs, partner. Are you with me on this—filing a complaint?"

"Yes," she said.

"Did you hear?" Malik asked. "About the fire at Advance?"

"What fire?" Lucia felt the blood drain from her face. AdVance Investigations belonged to her brothers Peter and Travis, and they often worked at night, depending on the type of caseload they had.

"It was on the news just before we were called out to this fire," he explained. "A fire broke out there at the same time this one started."

Donovan fished his cell phone out of a deep pocket in his coat and handed it to Lucia. "Call," he urged.

With shaking fingers, she dialed Peter's cell phone. When there was no answer, she dialed Travis's. When his voice answered, Lucia began to shake. "I just heard about the fire. Are you okay? Is Peter?"

"We're fine," Travis said. "Everybody got out. Sam needs a little first aid for a cut from flying glass, but it's nothing serious."

"All three of you were there?" she asked.

"Yep," Travis said. "And Brendan Montgomery, too."

"Why?" Lucia wanted to know. What were the odds that they'd all be at the same place at the same time and have a fire start?

"You don't sound so good," Travis said instead of answering her question. "Are you okay?"

Lucia wanted to rail at her oldest brother. "Don't try to change the subject, Travis. Tell me why you were all there."

"Sis, this isn't the time—"

"I'm not twelve anymore, big brother," she ground out. "And since Sam and Brendan were with you, it has something to do with Dad's shooting. Tell me I'm wrong."

His heavy sigh came over the phone. "No, you're not wrong. We had a lead on Baltasar Escalante."

The name made her shiver. The man whose drug cartel had been taken down last year. The man who had publicly vowed revenge on those involved before he escaped last year. The man who should have died in a plane crash but whose body was never found.

"Thank you for telling me," she said. "Travis, how bad was it?"

Such a long moment of silence followed that Lucia imagined the worst. That something had happened to Peter, Sam or Brendan that he wasn't telling her about. Lucia looked frantically around at the damage caused by the fire here, wondering if it had been this bad at AdVance, unfamiliar panic rising from her stomach and suffocating her.

"It could have been bad, but we are all okay."

As if sensing she was about to fall down, Donovan's strong arm suddenly hoisted her up, and he took the phone from her.

"She's going to call you back," he said, then ended the connection. Leaning closer and peering into her eyes, he said, "Talk to me, partner. What's going on?"

She shook her head against the thought that had taken root. Lifting her gaze to Donovan's, she whispered, "I think somebody intended for my brothers and me to die tonight."

NINETEEN

Lucia's eyes burned as she fought the realization that some unknown enemy wanted her dead. Not just her but her brothers, too. The same one who had come after her father, possibly the same one who had murdered her cousin's ranch foreman, whose body had been found a mere month ago.

Once more, she relived the stunned feeling she'd had when she realized Rafe was in the inferno of the burning cabinet shop with them. She couldn't have borne it had he died tonight.

"Lucia, talk to me," Donovan said, shaking her arm a little.

"I shouldn't have been here tonight, and neither should you. But we both got called in to work when two other guys called in sick."

He nodded, his attention intently on her. "So far, I'm following you."

"The reason they were all at AdVance tonight was because of a lead." She broke off, realizing that anything she told Donovan could jeopardize the investigation. That had certainly been drilled into her all her life.

"A setup?" Donovan asked.

"I don't know."

"A bizarre coincidence," he said.

From next to them, Malik said, "Rafe doesn't believe in coincidence."

"I know," Lucia whispered.

Barney Fields, another battalion chief, came up to them, his attention on Malik. "That was good work, getting the crew out of the cabinet shop."

"I just followed Rafe," Malik said.

"And got him out when he was injured," Fields said. "I saw who was carrying him. I imagine you want to get to the hospital as soon as you're wrapped up here."

"Yes, sir." With that, Malik walked toward the unit of volunteer firefighters whose turnout gear matched his. Lucia watched, realizing they must have been assigned to protect the barn and once again wondering how Rafe and Malik had come to be in the cabinet shop.

"What in the world was your crew doing in the cabinet shop?" Fields wanted to know.

"O'Brien ordered us in," Donovan said flatly.

"You're sure about that?" Fields asked.

"One hundred percent," Lucia said. "You can ask the other two guys with us. They'll tell you the same thing." She looked around the compound for Chief O'Brien and didn't see him anywhere.

Fields didn't say anything else, his attention on what was left of the building. It was nothing more than a shell, the roof caved in and the supply warehouse behind it completely demolished. The west wall was the only part of the building left standing, and she was sure it would have to be razed.

Once more, she looked all around trying to catch some glimpse of Chief O'Brien, even asked several other firefighters if they had seen him. No one had. Since Battalion Chief Fields was left on site, it wasn't that odd that O'Brien had left, but Lucia still wondered about it. There could be a dozen reasonable explanations for why he was no longer here, but instead, she kept thinking about her earlier suspicion that he had been involved in the hospital fire. Was he somehow involved in this, too?

As the implications of that sank in, her shakes were back. Three other firefighters had been sent into that building with her. If the intent had been to kill her, whoever was responsible didn't care who else got hurt. And that made her furious. Donovan, the father of three with another one on the way, not to mention her partner and good friend. Andy Smith, the new guy at the station house, whose sly wit eased even the most tense situation. Brad Mason, their favorite cook.

Mopping up after the fire was out took most of the rest of the night, and because of the cold temperatures and the snow that continued to fall, the job was miserable. There was no rolling up and stowing the hoses because they had turned to ice, spread across the compound like the carcasses of giant snakes. They would have to be left behind until they thawed out.

When everything was tallied up, two other firefighters besides Rafe had also been injured, and four others were taken to the hospital to be treated for smoke inhalation. Chief O'Brien was nowhere to be seen, and someone thought he had gone home because his wife was in labor.

Lucia hoped the rumor was right because it would mean all her suspicions were groundless. She hoped the rumor was wrong because it would mean their baby was arriving eight weeks too early.

Donovan worked side by side with her, his usual sarcastic wit in place. Never had she been more grateful for it, since he kept her from dwelling on Rafe's condition and on the near-miss they'd had tonight. Twice, Lucia called the hospital to see how Rafe was doing. Since she wasn't a relative, the only thing the nurse in the emergency room would tell her was that he was stable. She hated the term because it didn't tell her anything useful.

Whistling under his breath, Baltasar Escalante retrieved the morning newspaper from the hallway of the upscale hotel he was staying at and brought it back into the sitting room of the suite. He glanced at the headline, hoping he'd see the bold, black words announcing the tragedy that had befallen the Vance and Montgomery families last night. Instead, the headline read Fuel Prices Rising. That was hardly a headline since it was almost always true.

He frowned, annoyed there wasn't the least mention of anything to do with last night's fires on the first, second or third page of the paper.

The door to the bedroom opened, and his lover came toward him, wrapping a bronze silk robe around her slim waist. He was surprised that she was up.

"Good morning," she murmured, heading for the coffee cart and rolls that room service had delivered a few minutes earlier.

"The papers have no mention of last night's tragedy," he said.

She finished pouring her coffee, then turned to face him. "Last night's tragedy may have happened too late to make the deadline before the paper was sent to print."

Hers was an excellent, though annoying, point. He should have thought of that. He should have arranged for the fires to break out earlier so everyone could read about his brilliantly conceived plan in the morning paper. At the time of the planning, though, there was something poetic about having his enemies die at the eleventh hour. And so, he had arranged that they would be eliminated at just that moment. An effective, if subtle, message. A minor thing that he had not counted on missing the deadline. The news would be in tomorrow's newspaper. In fact, he thought, that would even be better since reporters would have the whole day to scurry around and find every little tidbit of the tragedy that their small minds could find.

"The news you want is undoubtedly on the television." She picked up the remote off the end table next to the couch and pressed the power button.

"One can hope." He felt better now. His plan was flawless.

She flipped through the channels, stopping on the local station. And there it was, the smoldering remains of Montgomery Construction. Ah, yes.

His sense of anticipation increased, and he sat down on the sofa beside her while she turned up the volume.

A young reporter, dressed for the cold, was facing the wreckage and saying, "Firefighters had their hands full last night as they battled this blaze. Not only did it cause extensive damage to this business owned by the prominent Montgomery family, it threatened to get out of control, and a few homes close to the facility were evacuated during the night as a precaution. Several firefighters suffered injuries."

Escalante took the remote from her and turned up the sound even more. Injuries couldn't be right. He had to mean deaths. The plan had been perfect. Maxwell Vance's children were all to have been killed last night.

The reporter turned slightly to face the camera. "A hospital spokesman said the most serious of those was one firefighter, yet unidentified, who suffered a concussion. Four others were treated for smoke inhalation and two others had minor injuries. This was an unusual night for the fire department, which had one other serious fire they responded to at almost the same time. The second was at AdVance Investigations, and it was quickly put out."

"Are these fires related?" asked the news anchor, dressed in a suit and looking warm compared to the field reporter who was wearing a heavy parka.

"Of course they are related," Escalante said to the television.

"Officials will not comment on that," the reporter said, "until the investigation on both fires is completed, but there is speculation they are connected and that both were caused by arson."

Escalante stared in disbelief at the screen. No one died last night? Not a single person? Fury simmered through his veins, that anger building until he sprang from the couch and paced to the window, then back again. They had stolen everything from him. They were the ones responsible for every loss that had befallen him over the last year. His business, his empire, his home. And they still were untouched?

"Idiots," Escalante muttered. He glanced at her. "I am surrounded by idiots."

She took a sip of her coffee. "Surely, you don't want me to remind you of that old saying, 'If you want it done right, do it yourself.'"

He leveled her a glare. "And you, *querida,* don't want that to apply to you."

She gave a negligent shrug. "When have I not done your bidding, *El Jefe?*"

She had done exactly as he had asked, but he was never quite sure whether it was for his purposes or some unknown one of her own.

Unlike O'Brien, who had not managed to do anything right. Arson was a simple crime, and O'Brien had botched the job, not once, but twice. The useless, bumbling idiot. Useless, and now a liability that Escalante could not afford. He hadn't decided what to do about that, but he would. Soon.

And it couldn't be an apparent suicide. Not since Harry Redding's death was still under investigation.

Another imbecile who was deservedly dead. Harry Redding had failed at his assignment of killing Mayor Maxwell Vance. Security was so tight around him now it would take a bomb to get close to him.

A bomb. Now that was something to consider.

Vance's sons, his daughter and that meddling FBI agent should all have been dead this morning. But they weren't. Denied that, more drastic measures were called for.

A bomb. Yes. Orchestrate the time when they would all be together. Yes.

And since he was able to move about the city without being recognized, he would be able to plan the exact time and place. Satisfied he once again had the upper hand, he sat back down.

"Look at this," his lover said, handing him the middle of the newspaper, the boring, too-sweet section that focused on lifestyles. The headline read Vance Family Lives in Hope. The human-interest story was from Easter Sunday, focusing on the family's faith in God. They knew the healing of the family patriarch, Mayor Maxwell Vance, was in the Lord's hands. In the meantime, they were determined to live life as normally as possible. The article went on to extol the virtues of the family members, who were involved in various charitable and civic causes.

And then Escalante looked at the color picture of a small boy with dark, soulful eyes. He knew those eyes, and he began to shake as he read the caption. "Manuel DeSantis Vance, son of Peter and Emily Vance."

DeSantis? Rosalina had been pregnant when he'd cast her aside? Escalante knew his former mistress was dead—reports of her death had been passed along to him, but no one had mentioned a child. Perhaps her brother, the trusted assistant he'd known as Snake, had given the baby to Peter Vance and the lady doctor, Emily, when Peter infiltrated his compound as Pietro Presti. They were all traitors, and they needed to be destroyed. He had not yet found Snake's hiding place, but he would…

Escalante blinked to clear the red haze. He had a son… who was being raised by an enemy.

Once more, Escalante's thoughts turned back to the idea of a bomb. "An eye for an eye," he whispered. Before the month was out, he would destroy the Vances and the Montgomerys and have his son back.

All the misery his enemies had heaped upon him, he would return in a measure so great they would not be able to calculate the loss.

TWENTY

When Rafe came to in the hospital emergency room, it was to find his best friend, Malik, sitting by his side, his expression worried. Rafe closed his eyes against the throbbing pain in his head. And then, it all came back. The cabinet shop totally engulfed, the fumes, the falling beams.

He opened his eyes, this time his gaze going to the three men standing behind Malik, their expressions just as grim. Lucia's brothers. Oh, God, the only possible reason they could be here was that Lucia hadn't made it out of the burning building.

Rafe's heart gave an awful lurch, and he lifted a hand to wave them away. "Please, God, no," he whispered, closing his eyes. "Lucia—"

"Is fine," Sam said, coming to stand next to the bed.

Rafe opened his eyes.

"She's fine," he repeated, pressing a firm hand against his shoulder. "I should have figured you'd think the worst."

Rafe's glance shifted to his best friend, who nodded, his worried expression easing into a grin. "The man's telling you the truth. She helped me put you on the ambulance, and she was all in one piece. Personally, I can't figure out what you see in her. Now that pretty nurse who works upstairs, that's another story."

Rafe's throat felt raw, and he'd had smoke inhalation enough times to know that was the reason. His head pounded as well, an uneven rhythm of a bass drum.

"Everybody else?" he said, his voice a hoarse croak.

"Everybody made it out, thanks to your quick thinking," said Travis.

"And thanks to your investigative work," Peter said, "we've been able to connect the dots and pass a whole lot of information on to the FBI."

Rafe shifted his gaze to Lucia's middle brother.

"We now know that Baltasar Escalante was behind our dad's shooting. We know the direction the investigation needs to go to find him."

Rafe stared from one man to the other, trying to make sense of what they were telling him. He wasn't at all sure what possible clue he could have had to the whole mess.

"As soon as I find Neil O'Brien," Sam said, "we should be able to get this case solved."

"He's missing? He was there," Rafe croaked. "He was the incident commander."

"We know that," Sam said.

"Can you prove he was involved in the arson?" Rafe asked.

"No proof we can take to court," Sam replied. "But yeah, you can take that to the bank."

"That's a shame." Rafe shook his head slightly—a mistake that hurt. What a terrible thing for O'Brien's wife.

"One more thing before you fall back asleep," Travis said.

Rafe opened his eyes, focusing on Lucia's brothers, who were once again standing together in a united front the way they had been that very first night he had met them at the prayer service for Lucia's father.

"Are you in love with Lucia?" Peter bluntly asked.

"I am," Rafe said, looking from one man to the next, hating

that he was laying here on his back instead of on his feet facing them man to man.

"The way we see it is like this," Travis said. "A man willing to risk his own life for hers is okay in our book."

"More than okay," Sam interjected.

"We figure our dad would give you his blessing," Peter said.

"And so you have ours," Travis finished.

Rafe stared at them, pretty sure he was having some sort of vivid hallucination. His gaze shifted to Malik, who was grinning from ear to ear.

"I'm still unconscious, right?"

Malik shook his head. "No, buddy, you're wide awake."

The pounding of his head grabbed his concentration, and sometime in the middle of that, Lucia's brothers disappeared, convincing him that they hadn't really been here. They were giving him their blessing? That didn't seem right, so he closed his eyes, the bustling sounds of the emergency room fading.

When he awoke a little while later, Malik was still sitting next to him.

"Lucia?"

"She's fine," Malik said.

"How long have we been here?"

"Four hours maybe," Malik said. "The doc says if you can stay awake they might even let you come home instead of keeping you overnight. Obviously, I'm a better nursemaid than you were, since I had the same kind of injury and they kept me here overnight."

"My head is harder," Rafe said.

Malik laughed. "I knew that about you. Rafe, the hardhead."

It evidently wasn't that hard because try as he might, he couldn't keep his eyes open.

* * *

When Engine #22 got back to the firehouse shortly after dawn, Lucia's three brothers were waiting for her. One by one they hugged her, despite the fact that she was filthy.

"We'll wait while you clean up," Sam said as he released her. "We've been to the hospital and Rafe is going to be fine. But we figured you should have some company when you go."

"How did you know?" she asked.

Travis glanced in Donovan's direction. "Let's just say that we have a very good source and we know that you guys came out of this okay because Rafe came after you."

"We're pretty sure he'll like seeing you a whole lot more than he liked seeing us," Peter said.

She narrowed her eyes. "What did you guys say to him?"

"Nothing," Sam said, a little too innocently. "Trust us, we just went to check on him, that's all. Go take your shower so we can get to the hospital."

Lucia stared at him. Of all her brothers, he had been the most critical of Rafe, despite the weekend they had spent together in Breckenridge.

"What?" he asked, swiping a hand over his face. "I've got dirt on my nose? I can't be any worse than you."

"You went to check on him?"

He nodded, looking as though he was trying to hide a grin. "The guy kinda grows on you."

She took the three steps it took to close the distance and throw her arms around him.

He hugged her hard, then pushed her away from him. "Get going, slowpoke. We're not going to wait all day."

Then she hugged Donovan, even though she knew he'd hate it. "I'm mad at you," she told him. "No more calling my brothers."

"If this is you when you're mad, partner, I think I'm pretty safe."

When they got to the hospital an hour later, Rafe was in the emergency room, still being assessed as to whether he would be admitted for observation. Lucia found Malik sitting next to Rafe inside the partially closed curtain of an emergency-room cubicle.

"How is he?" she asked.

"Beginning to show signs of coming out of it," Malik said, his usual flirting smile back in place. "Here I'm his best friend, and he keeps asking for you right before he dozes off again." His glance shifted to her brothers. "You guys are back."

"We keep turning up, just like old pennies. Have you had breakfast yet?" Peter asked Malik, who stood as they gathered inside the curtain.

"No."

"Why don't you join us while Lucia keeps watch over Rafe?"

Malik's glance fell to Lucia, his usual easy smile nowhere to be seen. "There's never a good time to say the hard things, but sometimes they have to be said." He glanced back at Rafe. "He's my best friend, and though we give each other our space, we both take that pretty seriously."

"That's the impression he's given me, too," Lucia said softly.

"I was nothing more than a punk when we first met ten years ago. The man I am today…he's responsible for that." Malik brushed her shoulder and headed toward the curtain surrounding the cubicle. "He plays things pretty close to the vest. But don't let that fool you. Are you getting what I mean?"

Tears welled in her eyes as she thought of their argument

yesterday and the fact that he had once again been there at the time he'd most been needed. "I think so, yes."

"We'll be back in a while," Travis said, slapping Malik on the back in one of those male gestures of support. "C'mon, I'm starved."

Lucia took off her coat and set it across her lap when she sat down on a chair next to Rafe's bed. His eyes were closed, and he had been cleaned up and put into a hospital gown. He had always seemed big to her, dressed in his leather jacket or ski gear, or that one night when they had dressed up for a date. In the white hospital gown, he somehow looked even bigger, the·muscles of his chest and arms well defined.

The field bandage over his eyebrow had been replaced with clean gauze that was stark against his tanned skin and dark hair. She stared at him, taking in each feature of his dear face and remembering how moved she had been when he had told her about his mother's death when he was a small boy. How she had sensed a small measure of the happiness he had felt when he'd been adopted. How she admired the faith he had somehow maintained throughout his life.

"Hi," came a soft voice from the edge of the curtain.

Lucia looked up to see Chloe Tanner come in, dressed in her nurse's uniform. "I heard you were down here." She gave Lucia a hug. "I just checked with his nurse. She said he's doing okay. A concussion and some smoke inhalation."

Lucia shuddered, remembering the moment the beam hit him. "It could have been a lot worse."

"That's what Brendan told me when he called. What a night it was."

Lucia shook her head just then, remembering that her brothers and Brendan had all been at AdVance when a fire had broken out there. "Do they know yet what caused the fire at AdVance?"

"Not definitively. I heard Brendan and Travis talking though, and it had something to do with a gas line. When the furnace came on, it ignited the leaking gas. Thanks to the new sprinkler system they recently installed, the fire didn't spread."

Once more, all the possible loss swept through Lucia, making her shiver.

"Have you talked to Michael yet?" Chloe asked.

Lucia stared at her. "My cousin Michael?"

Chloe nodded. "The fire at the ranch didn't do much damage, either. Just—"

"Wait. There was a fire at his ranch last night?"

"I thought you knew." Chloe reached a hand toward Lucia. "Boy, I don't mean to be the bearer of all this bad news."

"What about the ranch?"

"It took down a hay barn, but because of all the falling snow—they got nearly a foot last night—the fire never really took hold and they had it mostly out by the time the volunteer firefighters got there. It could have been a whole different story if it hadn't been snowing so hard."

"I'll have to call him later," Lucia said, thinking about all the trauma he had been through last month when his foreman's murdered body had been discovered and his cows had been poisoned. In the middle of all the problems, though, he had fallen in love. Just as she had, Lucia thought, looking back at Rafe. "We have a lot to be thankful for."

"God is good," Chloe said. "I've got to get back to work. You call me if there's anything you need."

Lucia nodded, her attention once more returning to Rafe. She took his hand and bowed her head in a silent prayer, thankful that he hadn't been more seriously injured than he was, thankful that in all the fires last night—all of them directed toward her family somehow—only property, not life, had been lost, asking for all of them to be kept safe through the obvious war that had been declared on them by an unknown enemy.

As she remembered the times she and Rafe had talked about faith, her prayer went from being a silent one to a whispered one. *"This man is part of the One Life that is so good in all ways. Thank You for bringing him into my life, for showing me how to once again open my heart to love. Thank You for sending him last night in my hour of need. From the bottom of my heart, thank You."* She paused for a moment, the first verses from the Bible she had been taught as a small child coming to her. *"The Lord bless thee and keep thee. The Lord make His face to shine upon thee and be gracious unto thee. The Lord lift up His countenance upon thee, and give thee peace. Amen."*

Rafe clasped her hand as tightly as she was clasping his, and his whispered voice joined hers in the last words of the prayer. She opened her eyes to look at him.

He was staring back at her, his dark eyes clear and bright.

"Hi," she whispered.

"I love you," he said.

A huge lump filled her throat as one tear, then another, welled and slid down her cheek.

"Don't cry," he whispered. "I'm sorry—"

She pressed a finger against his lips. "Don't you dare tell me you're sorry."

"I don't want you to cry."

She brushed at the tears with her free hand, fine lot of good it did since more fell. "I love you right back." What a relief it was to say the words, as much of a relief to know that he loved her. The feeling expanded in her chest, making her smile and cup his cheek with her hand.

He reached for her and she stood, bending over the hospital bed so she could hug him.

"Please don't tell me you're sorry for telling me that you love—"

"I'm sorry for the argument yesterday," he said, his cheek against hers. "I'm not going to give up wanting you to be safe, so we're going to have to figure out some middle ground."

"I can live with that." She pressed a kiss against his cheek. "Especially since I can see that sometimes I have to keep you safe, too."

"Ah, Lucia." His arms tightened around her. "My love, you are everything I never knew I wanted." He let go of her, and she lifted herself up far enough to see his face. He brushed one of the tendrils that had come loose from her ponytail away from her cheek. "You know what I thought the very first day we met?"

She shook her head, remembering that day vividly. Of having the breath knocked out of her by the explosion and then finding she had no breath at all because the best-looking man she had ever met had rescued her. She'd known he was something special, but at the time she hadn't understood *how* special.

"I kept seeing the face of my children in you," he said.

"I wondered if you wanted children," she whispered.

"I want yours. However many we are blessed with."

She grinned. "Is that a proposal, Rafael Wright?"

A smile lit his face. "Maybe we should try dating first."

"I'm thinking that head injury has addled your memory. We've been dating since the night you gave me flowers."

He sat up, too fast for a man with a concussion but steady as a rock. He reached for her hand. "In that case… Lucia, will you marry me? I know it has to be a nice long engagement while I win over your brothers, but will you?"

She put her arms around him. "Yes. Anywhere, anytime."

TWENTY-ONE

That following Saturday afternoon, Rafe came up the walk with Malik to the front of the Vance family home. It was a Queen Anne Victorian house framed by beds of blooming tulips and daffodils surrounding the front porch. Finally spring had arrived with a burst of color. The lawn was dotted with the pale pink blossoms of crocus, something Rafe knew only because he had helped his parents plant them a few weeks after he had been adopted all those years ago.

He had been a small boy, all alone then, who had been worried about being accepted by his new family.

"Nervous?" Malik asked.

"A little." He was no longer a small boy, but he was just as nervous about being accepted by this family. Though the engagement party was being thrown by Lucia's brothers, Rafe was still half-convinced he'd walk through the door and find he was the object of some nightmarish practical joke.

"What's to be nervous about? Lucia has only three brothers." Malik knocked his sports-coat-clad shoulder against Rafe's. "There's two of us. We can take them on."

"Let's hope it doesn't come to that," Rafe drily replied, thinking of the day he had promised Sam he wouldn't make

Lucia choose between her family and him. Though he had meant every word, his first impulse was more of the caveman variety, claiming her as his own by fair means or foul.

Today, he had an engagement ring in his pocket. She had told him she didn't want or need an engagement ring. A plain gold wedding band was enough. It might have been enough for her, but it wasn't for him. He'd spent hours looking for the right ring, and he'd finally found it last night. It felt heavy in his pocket, and he worried whether she'd like it.

Sam must have seen them coming because he was at the door, opening it before Rafe could ring the bell.

"You're late," he said, a good-natured grin on his face. "Is this going to be a habit with you?"

"If it is, you'll straighten me out?"

"That's right. Glad you recognize it." Sam slapped him on the back. "Come on in, Malik."

"Is Lucia here yet?" Rafe asked. He had wanted to pick her up and come to this party with her, but Colleen had insisted she and Lucia would come together.

"Oh, don't you look nice," Lidia said, carrying a tray of hors d'oeuvres from the kitchen.

Rafe glanced down at the tan microsuede sports coat layered over a mock-turtleneck sweater, then back at Malik, who grinned. Rafe had let his friend dress him, admitting that Malik's sense of style was a thousand times better than his own.

"Told you," Malik said, taking the tray from Lucia's mother. "Tell me where you want this."

"In there," Lidia said, pointing toward the family room, then guiding Rafe in the opposite direction toward the dining room, where the table was set for a buffet. She turned and held out her hands to him. "It's going to be crazy in there with the whole clan here, so before everything gets too…" She took a breath and squeezed his hands, her dark brown eyes as luminous as Lucia's often were. "You're part of this family now, and I know that wasn't something you may have bargained for."

"Now that I know almost everyone by name, it's not so bad."

Lidia laughed. "Not so bad, huh?"

"That didn't come out quite right," he said, wishing he didn't feel quite so tongue-tied.

"Your parents and I talked this morning."

"I'm glad." Both of them had been happy for him when he had called them a couple of days ago. They were thrilled with the news and looking forward to meeting Lucia. "You love her," his mother had said. "I know we'll love her." She had added that maybe now she could count on him to provide her with more grandchildren while she was still young enough to enjoy them.

The other piece of good news that had come this week was that his sister and her husband had reconciled. When Rafe had called her, she had sounded happy. Content. Another prayer answered.

"I'm glad you chose my daughter," Lidia said.

"She chose me," he said. "That's the amazing thing."

"My only regret is that Max isn't here today." She squared her shoulders and stepped away. "Now then, I wonder what is keeping Lucia and Colleen?"

Rafe wondered the same thing as Lidia took him by the arm and guided him toward the large family room at the back of the house, where everyone, if you didn't count Lucia, was already gathered. Most of them were already clustered in small groups, eating from the trays of canapés scattered throughout the room.

"There's one more member of the family to introduce you

to," Lidia said. She led Rafe toward a powerfully built man standing next to Holly and Jake Montgomery. "Rafe, this is Captain Kenneth Vance," she said. "My nephew and Holly's twin."

"Nice to meet you," Rafe said. The last time he had heard any news about this man, he was still in a military hospital recovering from the plane crash that had happened the weekend he had gone with Lucia to Breckenridge. "I'm sure everyone is relieved to have you home in one piece."

"That's what they tell me," Kenneth said. "And under the circumstances, I guess I'm glad to be here. You must have impressed my cousins some for them to be throwing this party for you."

Rafe glanced across the room at his future brothers-in-law, remembering the day they had come to his hospital room. They had been as united then as they had been the night he had first met them at the prayer service for their father. Only this time, it was to tell him they were speaking on behalf of Lucia's father to let him know he had their blessing.

There was a stir at the wide archway coming into the room, but all Rafe could see was Colleen, wearing a vibrant coral dress and a wide smile lighting her face.

"Here she is," Colleen announced from the doorway of the family room, stepping aside to reveal Lucia standing behind her.

She looked beautiful and even more nervous than he felt. A shimmering pale-pink dress swirled around her legs, the color making her skin glow. Her eyes lit when they met his, and then she smiled, the one that always melted his heart.

He was drawn across the room to her as surely as a bee was drawn to nectar.

Too aware that all eyes were on them, he dropped a casual

kiss on her cheek. He looked down at her. "Got a minute before we talk to all of them?"

"For you, maybe even a little more than a minute."

Feeling more nervous than he ever had in his life, he took her hand and she led him toward a small sitting room near the front door. Rafe guided her to the small couch near the window, then sat down beside her, fishing the small velvet box out of his pocket.

Swallowing, he met her gaze. "An engagement party deserves a woman wearing an engagement ring." He glanced down at the box. "I know you told me you didn't want one."

"And you believed me?" she teased.

He looked back at her, and her smile was radiant.

"Are you going to open that box, or do I have to rip it out of your hands?"

He held it out and opened it. Nestled inside the royal blue velvet was the biggest pink sapphire he could afford, the pale color a match for her dress. The stone was surrounded with diamonds and white gold in a feminine filigree design. The matching wedding band had even more diamonds.

Her breath caught and she pressed a hand against her throat. "This is how you see me?" she breathed. "This feminine, this—"

"You're beautiful," he said softly to her, "whether you're all dressed up like you are now or headed off to work in your usual ponytail and jeans."

"Thank you for that. The truth is, I love dressing up for you, but I never know if I've gone over the top."

He grinned. "Kinda like I felt with this ring." He took the engagement ring out of the box and slipped it onto her finger. A perfect fit.

She glanced at her finger, then looked at him. "I love you."

He kissed her then, rubbing his hand across the top of the ring on her finger, a prayer taking flight in his heart. *Thank You, Lord,* he thought, *for all the blessings this day and for all the days going forward.*

She was smiling once more when they stood. "Are you ready for this?"

"With your brothers, I'm never too sure," Rafe said. "But as long as we're in this together, I can face anything."

"With God's help and guidance," she said.

"If there's anything I'm sure of, it's that." He took both of her hands in his. "Remember? I'm the guy who prays—"

"With the expectation of being heard," she finished.

He nodded. "The Lord answered my every prayer when He brought you into my life."

"Mine, too," she said, touching his cheek, then kissing him.

He folded his hand around hers, and they returned to the family room, where spontaneous applause broke out.

Sam crossed the room toward them, a big smile on his face. He kissed Lucia's cheek, shook Rafe's hand and turned to face the room with them. The buzzing conversation faded, and he said, "It's no real secret why we're all here today." He lifted his glass in a toast. "To Lucia and Rafe." He paused and grinned at Rafe. "And to a very long engagement."

"Not that long," Rafe warned, then whispered to her, "I'm thinking a Thanksgiving wedding. What do you think?"

"Sounds good," she whispered back.

Rafe added another prayer, this one a request that Lucia's father be awake and well and able to walk her down the aisle at their wedding.

"And to Kenneth's safe return home," Sam added.

"Hear, hear," came the murmured response.

"And to my new family," Rafe added, catching the glances

of each of Lucia's three brothers, her mother and finally her. He was a lucky man, he thought, as he drew Lucia close to his side. As his father had said a long time ago, Wright place, Wright time.

* * * * *

Dear Reader,

I suspect I'm not the first author to write to you that
writing a novel is easier than writing a letter to you.
Letters should be personal, and since we haven't met,
this one cannot be as personal as I would like. Even so,
thank you for choosing this book where you'll spend a
few hours escaping into a world where hope prevails.

That sense of hope…of faith, even…is my favorite
thing about romance novels. Whatever challenges
characters face within the pages, they move forward in
faith, hoping things will work out. That moving forward
in faith is the reason why I chose the particular Biblical
quote that I did. "As thou hast believed, so be it done
unto thee." *Matthew* 8:13.

For any of us embarking on a new endeavor or going
through a difficult time, it may be hard to predict a
successful outcome. If you're at all like me, you'd love
the certainty of a happy ending. For me, that's where
faith steps in, where I do my best to move forward
as though the thing is already done. It's the same for
Lucia Vance and Rafael Wright in *Through the Fire*.
They can't be certain the challenges they face will
be successfully overcome—all they can do is move
forward in faith.

Again, thanks for choosing this book.

Blessings to you and yours, always,

Canine search-and-rescue expert Julianna Red Feather must team up with Air Force pilot Kenneth Vance, home on medical leave after being shot down, as they try to protect Montgomery Construction—and Vance Memorial Hospital—from whoever is out to destroy both families in Marta Perry's IN THE ENEMY'S SIGHTS.
And now, turn the page for a sneak preview of
IN THE ENEMY'S SIGHTS,
the fourth installment of FAITH AT THE CROSSROADS.
On sale in April 2006 from Steeple Hill Books.

Maybe a good long run would tire her out enough to sleep tonight without dreams. One thing about having Angel along—Julianna could run any time of the day or night without fearing for her safety. Nobody messed with a woman accompanied by a German shepherd.

The office was dark and quiet. She picked up the basket she'd left on the counter next to the coffeemaker. No one would appreciate coming in to leftover gnocchi congealing in the casserole dish. Good as it had been, she hadn't been able to finish it. She'd intended to have the rest for supper, but had gotten busy and forgotten to take it home.

Well, everything seemed quiet enough tonight. She went out, Angel at her heels, and locked the door behind her. As she set the basket on the backseat of the car, Angel woofed softly. She glanced at her.

The dog stared into the shadowy yard, her ears pricked up, tail waving.

"What is it, girl?" She closed the car door, looking across the yard, her eyes adjusting to the dimness. "Do you see someone?"

No. Angel had heard something, and now she heard it, too—a soft footfall, somewhere beyond the circle of light cast by the fixture over the office door.

A frisson of apprehension slid across her skin. It was probably nothing—just the night watchman on his rounds. But with everything that had happened lately, she couldn't ignore it.

Making a swift decision, she took the flashlight from the glove compartment, stepped outside of the car and locked the door. She dropped the key into the pocket of her jean jacket and turned toward the yard.

Angel was with her. She didn't have to fear any intruder— one snarl from the dog would probably be enough to send anyone running.

She started toward what she thought was the source of the sound, moving quietly, Angel close against her side. She strained her ears for any noise, even though she knew Angel would hear anything first.

Pallets of lumber arranged in rows, innocent enough in the daylight, loomed over her like pallid giants waiting to pounce. There were too many hiding places in the dark. She sent the beam of her flashlight probing along the row, lighting up the dark corners.

Nothing. Maybe she'd imagined the sound. Or it was the night watchman, moving along on his lawful rounds.

But that rational explanation didn't erase the apprehension that skittered along her skin, making the hair stand up on her arms.

Angel's hair stood up, too, making a ruff around her neck. Because the dog picked up on her nervousness, or because Angel sensed something wrong, too? Impossible to tell, but dog or human, the response was the same.

They reached the end of the row of pallets, where an open space ran like an alley between the rows for access. She stopped, hand on Angel's head, and aimed the light down the alleyway between the pallets. Lumber gleamed palely in the light, and down toward the far end, something moved.

For an instant the breath caught in her throat. Then she recognized that erect military posture, the set of the strong shoulders. It was Ken. He'd said he and Quinn were taking turns to patrol.

She could slip quietly away. He need never know that she'd been here.

But even as she started to turn, Angel began to bark. Not a soft woof—a full-throated alarm. She felt the dog's muscles bunch under her hand.

Ken whirled toward them at the sound. She had a glimpse of the pale shirt front under his dark jacket. Angel strained against her hand, barking furiously.

"Angel—"

But the rebuke died on her lips. The stack of lumber that loomed over Ken—ten or twelve feet high at least—seemed to shudder. For an instant she thought it was an optical illusion. Then she saw that the whole stack was moving, gaining momentum as it went.

Her cry was lost in Angel's fierce barking. The stack of heavy lumber toppled toward Ken. She saw his startled face, saw his arm flung up to protect his head.

And then the lumber fell, crashing to the ground with a roar that reverberated, shattering the night air with a million echoes.

She couldn't see Ken any longer, just a cloud of dust that billowed into the air like a dense, malignant fog.

SUSPENSE

RIVETING INSPIRATIONAL ROMANCE

The Texas Gatekeepers:

Protecting the border...and the women they love.

Atoning for her sordid teen years, Bernadette Malone
had spent her life in service to God. When her past
caught up with her, she turned to border patrol
agent Owen Carmichael. Even so, would her
powerful enemy kill to prevent the revelation
of his scandalous actions?

On sale April 2006
Available at your favorite retail outlet.

www.SteepleHill.com

LIWOD

Steeple
Hill®

Love Inspired®

APRIL IN BLOOM

BY

ANNIE JONES

Sheriff Kurt Muldoon was only being neighborly when he let Miss Cora and April Shelnutt into his home after the elderly woman injured herself. Letting April into his heart wasn't going to happen. Yet God had other plans for Kurt and April!

On sale April 2006

Available at your favorite retail outlet.

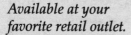

www.SteepleHill.com

Steeple Hill®

LIAIB

A LEAP OF FAITH

BY LENORA WORTH

Texas Hearts

Sometimes big love happens in small towns…

Coming home to care for her ailing father, Autumn Clancy didn't expect someone else would be running the family's firm. Campbell Dupree, her new boss, sensed the headstrong Autumn was one special lady. Would the good Lord deem him worthy enough to win her heart?

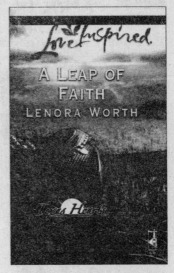

On sale April 2006

Available at your favorite retail outlet.

Steeple Hill®

www.SteepleHill.com

LIALOF

2 Love Inspired novels and a mystery gift... Absolutely FREE!

Visit
www.LoveInspiredBooks.com
for your two FREE books, sent directly to you!

BONUS: Choose between regular print or our NEW larger print format!

There's no catch! You're under no obligation to buy anything. We charge nothing—ZERO—for your first shipment. And you don't have to make any minimum number of purchases.

You'll like the convenience of home delivery at our special discount prices, and you'll love your free subscription to Steeple Hill News, our members-only newsletter.

We hope that after receiving your free books, you'll want to remain a subscriber. But the choice is yours— to continue or cancel, anytime at all! So why not take us up on our invitation, with no risk of any kind!

Love Inspired®

LIGEN05

Love Inspired

SUSPENSE
RIVETING INSPIRATIONAL ROMANCE

faith at the crossroads

*Can faith and love sustain two families
against a diabolical enemy?*

Recuperating air force pilot Kenneth Vance was
temporarily working for Montgomery Construction,
where Julianna Red Feather was training canine search-
and-rescue teams. The two paired up to discover who
was targeting the Vance and Montgomery families...
while fighting their growing feelings.

On sale April 2006
Available at your favorite retail outlet.

Steeple
Hill®

www.SteepleHill.com

LIIES